The
FROG
PRINCE

⭐

The FROG PRINCE

JANE PORTER

WARNER BOOKS

NEW YORK   BOSTON

Warner Books

Time Warner Book Group
1271 Avenue of the Americas, New York, NY 10020
Visit our Web site at www.twbookmark.com

Printed in the United States of America

First edition: May 2005
10 9 8 7 6 5 4 3 2

Library of Congress Cataloging-in-Publication Data
Porter, Jane
    The frog prince / Jane Porter.—1st ed.
        p. cm.
    Summary: "The story of a woman who must start a new life as an event planner in San Francisco after her fairy tale marriage falls apart"—Provided by the publisher.
    ISBN 0-446-69449-5
    1. Divorced women—Fiction. 2. San Francisco (Calif.)—Fiction.
3. Special events—Planning—Fiction. I. Title.
    PS3616.O78F76 2005
    813'.6—dc22
                                                            2004027777

Cover design by Brigid Pearson
Cover photo: Xavier Bonghi/Getty Images
Book design and text composition by Nancy Singer Olaguera/ISPN

For my father, S. Thomas Porter

(1934–1979)

I will miss you forever.

Acknowledgments

This book was a joy and an adventure, and I wouldn't have taken the journey if it weren't for a handful of really good people. First, thanks to Susanna Carr for her early encouragement. She read the first fifty pages and loved it, and her enthusiasm was contagious. Karen Solem, my really wonderful agent, read a longer version of the partial and asked for more. Her insights and support made all the difference in the world. Thanks, too, to Karen Kosztolnyik and Michele Bidelspach at Warner for liking *The Frog Prince* when it landed on their desks. Holly Bishop needed a good, loving home and Warner Books gave it to her. Thank you. And to Barb, Carla, and Sinclair, thanks for reading the manuscript and giving me feedback during the writing process, as well as Samantha Nuxoll, an amazing Cheshire girl who knows her chick-lit and is always sharing great books with me.

And one last heartfelt thanks—to my family and everyone in Visalia, California. I love being your small-town girl.

The FROG PRINCE

Here comes the bride, all dressed in white. There goes the groom, running from the room . . .

And there's my single mom, spending the next twenty years paying for a lavish wedding for a marriage that didn't even last a year.

Frick.

What happens now? What happens when you've had the fairy tale?

When you've done the big wedding? The dream honeymoon? What happens *after* the fantasy's over?

You file for divorce. Di-vorce. Such a big concept for what amounts to a little word.

I still can't quite say it, can't feel anything when I think it, can't imagine that we're now talking about me.

But I was the one in the wedding gown, and then I was the one talking to a lawyer, and I was the one who had to ask my brother and my girlfriends and their boyfriends to help me pack so the movers could move me.

I've recently changed cities. Jobs. Lives. I'm starting all over again. But of course, it's not the same. It'll never be the same. Because I've done it. I've been married and divorced, and I'm not even twenty-six.

Long and short of it? He was perfect. I was raised in the country; he was French; together that made us French country. Perfect. The house was perfect; the car, a smoky-gray Citroën, was perfect; the clothes and restaurant and champagne . . . perfect, perfect, perfect!

Not perfect.

Hindsight's amazing. I can see now there were problems in our relationship—huge problems, like trust, respect, and sexual compatibility. I should have known Jean-Marc wasn't attracted to me. I should have known he was avoiding physical intimacy. But I didn't. I blamed it on the wedding, new financial commitments, the stress of my moving into his house.

Maybe if I'd dated more . . .

Maybe if I'd had more realistic expectations . . .

Maybe if I hadn't read fairy tales and then later all those romance novels I bought at the used-book store . . .

But back to reality, and I've got more than enough to deal with in reality, what with my new job, in my new apartment, in my new city, with my new boss who doesn't seem to approve of anything I do.

In fact, right now my new boss, Olivia Dempsey, is

standing next to my desk at City Events here in San Francisco, and she isn't happy. She's currently conveying her unhappiness in a very loud, crisp voice.

"I thought we talked about this," Olivia says, fashionably slim, toned arms crossed. "You *have* to take charge of your life, Holly. You're dying on the vine, girl."

I don't look up, because I don't want to hear this, at least not again, not so soon this week. Didn't I just get the need-to-get-out-more pep talk on Monday?

"You were crying in the bathroom again, weren't you?"

I open my mouth to deny it, but she holds up a finger and wags it in front of my face. "Oh, no, no lying. No denying. And you weren't just crying; you were sobbing."

"I wasn't sobbing." I shoot her a disgusted look because even the word "sobbing" is irritating, but I know my eyes are red.

Olivia leans down, puts her face in mine. "Sara heard you." Sara being another member of Olivia's team.

I'm beginning to think I'm not ever going to warm up to Sara. She tries too hard to get Olivia to like her.

"I'm over it," I say, forcing a toothy grin and feeling absurdly like the wolf from "Little Red Riding Hood." "See?"

"*Hmmph*" is all Olivia gives me, but Olivia has no idea how hard all this is for me. No one knows how hard this has been.

There are days I still don't know how I manage to climb from the bed and stagger into the shower, days when I still cry as I make coffee and try to apply mascara and eyeliner between mopping up tears. It's just that I'd barely gotten used to the idea of being a bride, and now I'm a . . . divorcée?

"You need to start getting out," Olivia adds firmly, her tone no-nonsense. "It's time for you to be proactive, not reactive."

Of course she'd think like this. She grew up immersed in the world of professional sports, and everything to Olivia is about offense and defense. If Olivia were an athlete, she'd be a quarterback and a pitcher rolled up into one.

"I'm getting out," I say, shifting uneasily, knowing that Olivia's voice carries and not being particularly eager to have the rest of the staff hear my shortcomings. Again. "I'm here, aren't I?"

It was supposed to be a joke, but she doesn't laugh. "This is *work*, Holly."

"Exactly."

Olivia rolls her eyes. She's beautiful. Even when she rolls her eyes, she looks sleek. Sexy. With the ultimate in DNA—Olivia's mother is a former model, the blonde, glossy type that graced the pages of *Sports Illustrated*, while her father dominated the Oakland Raiders' offense, a star wide receiver still talked about in hushed voices twenty years later. Olivia is perfection. She modeled for two years in Paris but *hated* it, apparently modeling wasn't *challenging*, as it did nothing for her *mind*.

"This is no social life," she says, leaning against the edge of my desk, her long legs even longer in snug, low-waisted trousers, her black cashmere turtleneck sweater cropped short enough to reveal two inches of flat, toned midriff.

I feel like a slice of Wonder bread. "I don't need one."

Her gray-green eyes narrow, squint. She looks at me hard, the same up-and-down sweep she gives decorated ballrooms before handing responsibility over to an underling. "You need something bad, girl."

Yes. I need my bed with my duvet pulled up over my head, but it's only Wednesday, and I have two more days before I get to dive back between my covers and stay there for the rest of the weekend. "Am I not performing?" I ask, trying to shift the focus from personal back to professional. Olivia was the one who hired me three months ago. She'd be the one who'd fire me.

Another narrowed-gaze inspection. "You've lost your . . . edge."

Edge? I don't remember having an edge. I was desperate when I interviewed for the job, but there never really was an edge. I mentally add "Get edge" to my increasingly lengthy to-do list.

"You need attitude," she continues. "Presence."

I say nothing because, quite frankly, I do have an attitude, and I suspect it's not the one she wants.

"What do you do when you go home, Holly?" Olivia's fine arched brows beetle. "Sit down in front of the TV—"

"No . . ."

"Eat your way through a bag of chips? A carton of Ben and Jerry's Chunky Monkey?"

"I don't even *like* Chunky Monkey."

Olivia is gaining momentum. Her purple-black polished nails tap-tap the laminate on my desk. Her stellar eyebrows flatten. "You're getting fat."

The word "fat" hangs there a moment between us, pointed, sharp. *Ugly.* This is a full-scale assault.

For a moment nothing comes to mind, and I inhale hard, topple forward in my chair, feet clattering to stop my fall.

I check to see if anyone else has heard. This is about as low as anyone could go. She knows it. I know it. "I'm not fat."

Surreptitiously I glance down at my lap, homing in on my thighs. They do look rather big, but that's because I'm wearing speckled wool pants, and the fuzzy spotted texture isn't exactly slimming. "My clothes fit fine."

Olivia shrugs. Says nothing.

I feel all hot on the inside, hot and prickly and a little bit queasy. I move my right thigh, check the shape. It does look rather spread out on the chair. "I need to work out," I add awkwardly. "I haven't joined a gym since moving here."

She shrugs again, and I look down, see my lunch still sitting on my desk: a half-eaten burrito, guacamole and sour cream oozing, obscuring the chicken and black beans.

I can picture my leg naked. Or what it must look like naked if I ever looked at myself in a full-length mirror anymore, because I avoid mirrors, especially full-length mirrors. I haven't taken a look at myself naked in, oh, three months—ever since I moved to San Francisco and realized I couldn't bear to look me in the eye, couldn't bear to see what I, once so pathetically hopeful, had become.

But beyond the burrito and the mirror, it's not all bad. I still drink Diet Coke. I've always drunk Diet Coke. There are limits to indulgence, and I know mine.

"The point is," Olivia says more delicately, "you go straight home after work. You sit on your couch. Veg in front of the TV. That's no life, and you know it."

For a moment I say nothing, because I'm not even thinking about my new apartment in San Francisco, but about the house I left in Fresno, where until recently I'd been a brand-spanking-new wife.

The house in Old Fig Garden was originally Jean-Marc's, a 1950s ranch that looked cozy and cottage-y with a split-rail fence and hardy yellow summer roses. After we married, I couldn't wait to make the house mine, too, and I loved personalizing it, adding festive, feminine touches like the new cherry-sprigged dish towels from my bridal shower, hanging on towel bars in the kitchen, or the sparkly crystal vase with zinnias and yellow roses displayed on Jean-Marc's dining table. We had new 300-thread-count sheets on the king-size bed and fluffy white-and-blue towels in the bathroom, and it was like a dollhouse. Charming. Warm. Storybook.

Turns out I wasn't the storybook wife.

"*Holly.*"

Olivia's impatience cuts, and I look up quickly, so quickly I have to bite my lip to keep the rush of emotion away.

"You moved here to start fresh." Olivia taps her nail on my desk. "So do it."

Olivia's right. I'm lonely as hell, but I've hit the place where it's not just a little lonely but *really* lonely. The lonely where you slide below the radar screen, lonely where you've become pathetic, lonely where it's better just to stay inside, hidden from civilization.

I don't belong in civilization. I'm a misfit. A blight.

Well, maybe not a blight. But I definitely feel like a pimple on a chin. As you know, *not* a good way to feel.

Cautiously I shift my left leg, checking to see if the left thigh spreads as much as the right. It does. I suppress the rising panic. I'm in trouble, aren't I?

I look up, meet Olivia's eyes. "I am a little . . . big . . . ger."

The light of battle shines in Olivia's eyes. "It's not the end of the world. *Yet.*" She sounds crisp now, decisive, as if we've settled on a plan, and she leans forward, urgency in her voice. "The key is to get a grip. Face whatever it is you're avoiding." She pauses, considers me. "Are you still in love with him?"

Him? Him, who? And then I realize she's talking about Jean-Marc. "Y—no. No!" I repeat more forcefully, because I'm not. How could I still be in love with a man who essentially rejected me on our honeymoon?

But Olivia isn't convinced. "Do you need professional help? There's no shame—"

"No." God, this is so humiliating. Olivia could be my mother. My mother would handle a conversation this way. "I'm fine. I'm . . . better. Getting better." And bigger, according to Olivia. I squeeze out a smile. "But you're right. I need to take charge. Join a gym. Take better care of myself."

"What else?"

What else? I thought that was really good stuff.

Olivia rises, and her stomach goes concave, making her trousers hit even lower on her magnificent hip bones. "You need friends."

"I have friends."

"Where?" I open my mouth, but she holds up a slender honey-cocoa finger. "Don't say 'here.' Work isn't your social circle. If you got fired—"

"Am I getting fired?" Olivia doesn't own the company, but as a director she's high up in management, knows everything, has a say in everything. It doesn't hurt that Olivia has that enviable trait called star quality. People want to be around Olivia. Customers flock to City Events to work with Olivia. Olivia makes things happen.

"No." Olivia glances at my half-eaten burrito in the

foil wrapper, the crumpled napkin on my desk, the Diet Coke with the smudge of lipstick on the rim, and the files spread open in front of me. "You work hard; you're conscientious, detail oriented."

But?

"But what happens here, at your desk, is only part of the job," she adds. "We're all responsible for bringing in new accounts, for promoting City Events, and one of the best ways to sell City Events is by selling *you*." And she smiles, a dazzling smile of lovely straight white teeth—her own, not veneers. "But you know that, Holly, and that's why I hired you."

I like her, I really do, and yet right now I'm wanting to crawl under my desk and stay there forever.

More pathetic internal monologue: if Jean-Marc had loved me, I wouldn't be here, in San Francisco, in a strange, cold apartment, at a strange, confusing job, trying to figure out where I got it wrong, how I failed in love, why I'm the first of my friends to marry, as well as the first to divorce.

Rationally, I know that Olivia is trying to help me. It's her job to give me feedback and direction, but honestly, her cool, crisp analysis cuts, wounding my already bruised self-esteem. I know we're not supposed to rely on others for our self-worth. I know we're supposed to look inside for validation, but how are you supposed to like yourself, much less love yourself, when the person you trust most asks you just to go away?

"Two words," Olivia says, holding up two fingers and looking down her long, elegant nose at me.

"Zone diet?"

"Image. Success."

I can feel my thighs sprawl on the chair, the weight of my limp ponytail on my neck. How can it be only Wednesday? I need Friday. I *really* need Friday.

"You've got to take charge, Holly. I know you said in the interview you've just been through a rough patch— divorce, you said—but it's time to return to the land of the living. Get back in the ring. Make something happen."

"Right." And she is right. More or less.

"We're going out for drinks after work. Join us. You already know some of my friends, and you'll meet some new people. It'll be good for you."

"Right." Her friends are gorgeous. And manically extroverted. A thought comes to me. "But cocktails have calories."

"A *lot* less than a pint of Ben and Jerry's."

Enough said.

Olivia walks away. I stare at my desk.

So that's where we are. I'm Holly Bishop, living the suddenly single girl life in San Francisco, which is also the turtleneck capital of the United States. Everyone here wears turtlenecks, lots and lots of black and gray turtle- necks with the inevitable leather coat, barn coat, barn leather coat. It might be the City by the Bay, but it's also the City of Cold Hands, Neck, and Feet.

Despite the need for sweaters even in July, I'm told that San Francisco is a great city to live in. You don't have to drive to get around; there's decent public transportation, but I don't know anyone who actually takes the public transportation. We *drive* on the West Coast.

And drive.

And drive.

We also pay huge sums to park. We pay for parking at work. We pay for parking at home. We pay for parking each time we head out to shop or see a flick or do anything remotely fun. (This is new to me. I was raised in a small town where you got free angle parking on Main Street.)

But I'm not in Kansas anymore, or in California's Central Valley, for that matter. I live in Cow Hollow, a great neighborhood not far from San Francisco's Marina district, and work South of Market, which used to be cagey but now is cool, at City Events, which, as you can tell, is far hipper than I am.

Olivia hired me because I had the good sense to talk sports during the interview (thank God for a sports-loving brother) and because I pretended my limited PR skills from Fresno translated into something bigger than they did. Olivia, showing rare sensitivity during the second interview, didn't call me on the fact that a Fresno golf tournament isn't exactly on the same swish scale as San Francisco's annual Leather & Lace Fund-Raiser Ball, and hired me despite my profound lack of interesting experience.

For three months she's let me work at my own pace, but clearly she's ready for change. She wants something more from me. And she's not the only one. I'd love more, too.

But what?

And how?

I eye my cold burrito in the creased foil wrapper. I should throw out the rest of it. Get started on my new life plan now. But I don't have a new life plan yet. I don't know what to do . . .

Correction. I don't know what to *feel*.

This is the part I can't talk about, because it's been so long since I felt anything, much less anything good, that I just don't know what's normal anymore. But I *am* trying.

I left Fresno, a huge step for me since I knew next to no one in San Francisco, but I did it. I found an apartment on my own. Searched the want ads and applied for jobs. I interviewed, even though most of the time I had no idea where I was going, and once I was hired by City Events, I put on my happy face and went to work. Every day. On time.

Despite the fact there's this ridiculously gaping hole in my heart.

And people who say there's no such thing as a broken heart, or pontificate on the physiological impossibility of a heart actually breaking, these people don't know hurt. Because the day Jean-Marc finally said, "I don't love you, and I will never love you that way," my heart just stopped.

It *stopped*. It stopped because everything inside me was squeezing so hard and tight and kept squeezing until there was nothing left of me, at least not in the middle of my chest where my heart used to be.

So here I am in San Francisco, trying to start over as well as figure out what to do with the rest of my life.

And that's where it gets murky because, honestly, what am I supposed to do with the rest of my life? I'm a disappointment to my mother (I hate that she'll be paying for my wedding forever). I've lost my new in-laws, although they do live in France and only met me once. And even my oldest friends have gone strangely silent.

So *what* do I do now?

I eat what's left of my cold burrito.

Five thirty arrives, and Olivia appears at my desk with her coat and purse slung over her shoulder. I save the document I'm typing up and look at her.

"Ready?" she says, and I'm momentarily perplexed.

Ready? Ready for what?

"The others are waiting at reception." Olivia taps her watch. "Drinks. Remember?"

No. I've obviously forgotten, and I open my mouth to beg off, but Olivia shakes her head. "I'm not letting you out of this. The city will never feel like home if you don't give it a chance."

She does have a point, and I could use a new home. I can't remember the last time I really felt as if I belonged somewhere. "Give me just a second," I say, pushing away from my desk and heading for the ladies' room, where I do a painful inspection.

Pale. Lumpy. Frumpy. My God, I look tired.

I rummage in my purse, search for something to help revive the face, and find an old lipstick—a brownish shade that does nothing for me—and apply some. Hmmm. Brown lipstick, a black turtleneck, lavender circles beneath the eyes. Not exactly a come-hither look.

Maybe some hair would help, so I lift my limp brown ponytail, pull on the elastic, freeing hair that becomes limp brown hair with a slight kink in it from the hair elastic. I fluff the hair. Comb the fingers through it. The ends stick out. Doris Day crossed with Chewbacca.

Irritably I pull the hair back into a ponytail again before wiping off the brown lipstick. *Just get the hell out of here*, I think, particularly since I don't even know why I'm doing this. I'm not in the same league with Olivia. Olivia's friends are all city girls. Sophisticated, urban, glam. I'm one step removed from country, and it shows. I wasn't raised on a farm, but I know my farm smells. They call Highway 99 the scratch-and-sniff drive because it's all sulfur, dairy, and manure. But the 99 leads home. Or to what used to be home.

Olivia's waiting at the front door with Sara and a couple of other girls who work in various City Events departments. "You look great," Sara says with a big smile.

We both know she's lying, but that's how we women are. Practical and impractical. Helpful and cruel.

We leave our loft office, take the elevator down, and exit from the building, and Olivia's cell phone rings before we've even crossed the street.

"The Barrio," she says into the phone, "and if we're not there, then try Lucille's."

The phone rings three more times during our five-minute walk. She gives the same info each time. Try the Barrio, and if not the Barrio, then Lucille's. Olivia always makes the decisions, but then, she is the queen, and everyone wants to know the queen and they want to keep the queen happy.

We reach the Barrio. "How many people are coming?" I ask, as the club's salsa vibe pulses out the windows and the Laffy Taffy purple front door.

"Five, ten, fifteen." Olivia shrugs. "Who knows?"

And twenty minutes later I wish again I'd just gone home. I feel huge. Plain. Horrendously fuddy-duddy. The salsa music is hot, sultry, sexy, and Olivia and her circle feel it, slim shoulders shaking, amazing toned bodies in the groove.

I stand at the tall red-and-stainless counter holding my drink, feeling like a Popsicle stick. I don't really know what to do with salsa music. Or reggae. Or rap. Where I come from, it's country or hard rock. Jocks and goat ropers. In Visalia I was exotic, but here I'm just white and self-conscious and uncoordinated.

Olivia laughs and I glance her way. She's sparkling, and her laugh still hangs in the air. Despite the loud music, the raised voices, the speakers thumping, Olivia commands attention, and her dramatic coloring just plays off the crimson-and-ocher-painted walls. Here at the Barrio she looks tall and thin, and as she leans back against the bar stool, even more of her stomach shows.

I hate her.

No. I hate me.

Olivia was right. I am fat. Whenever I stop tucking my shirt in, that means I'm fat. And I've given up belts. Another sign of fat. The long, loose skirts—fat.

Fat, fat, fat.

Rejected, dejected. I'm beginning to scare even me.

This has got to stop.

I need my old jeans back. I need the old me. The one who was fun. The one who laughed and didn't take herself so damn seriously. The one who didn't spend an entire Saturday in bed reading Oprah Winfrey's Book Club novels in which every child either drowns or gets abducted, which I read crying and sniffling into my pillow because, while I haven't drowned or been abducted, I do feel lost. Really lost, and I'm not sure how to find where it is I'm supposed to go.

How pathetic does that sound? *Snap out of it, Holly,* I say, taking another sip from my icy salt-rimmed margarita. *You're not Hansel or Gretel. Not Snow White, or Belle from* Beauty and the Beast. *You can't be lost. You're an adult. Twenty-five. College educated. There's a way out of this, and you're going to find it.*

The thing to do is keep it simple. Take it a step at a time. Maybe Olivia is right. Start a diet. Then join a gym. Then get the legs waxed and, you know, reclaim the self.

I take a bigger sip from my hand-blown margarita glass, thinking it wasn't so long ago that I had a decent body. Eighteen months ago I was that wide-eyed bride, and I'd worked hard to look magnificent for the wedding. Slim, toned, fit. Ready for my close-up, Mr. DeMille.

The wedding photos never made it into an album. I still have the photos, though, in a big brown mailing envelope, a stack of glossy photos that will never get looked at, a stack of photos of a bride and groom laughing, smiling, photos that should have been cherished but won't be.

I wish I'd known then that it wasn't going to last. I wish I'd known what he was thinking. Feeling.

Funny, when I look at the photos now, especially the one where we're dancing—our first dance—Jean-Marc's unhappiness is so obvious. If you look at his face, you can see it there in his eyes. If you know Jean-Marc, you can see the emptiness behind the smile, the distance there. He's not actually smiling. He's already detached himself.

He's already divorcing me.

"Another drink?" Aimee, Olivia's friend, director of fund-raising for the Met Museum, is gesturing to me and my now nearly empty glass.

I look up at her, but I don't see Aimee; I see Jean-Marc, and we're on our honeymoon in the South of France.

We're doing everything big, everything splashy, and I'm standing in the doorway of our suite's living room, wearing a Victoria's Secret pink lace teddy and not much else (but the hair's done, lots of sexy tousled curls, and flawless makeup). I'm smiling at him even as I try not to cry.

You don't like this?

It's fine.

You don't want this?

You look great.

But you don't want me.

I'm just not in the mood.

It's our honeymoon, Jean-Marc.

Holly, I can't.

Why not?

He says nothing. *Why not?* I shout.

Because I don't love you that way.

I drain the rest of my hand-shaken fresh-fruit-juice margarita. Tequila's good. It works. "One more," I say to Aimee, blinking hard, refusing to cry, refusing to think about the disaster honeymoon, refusing to think about the pile of sexy lingerie that never got worn, refusing to accept that I own more Rosenthal than common sense.

That way? What the hell does *that way* mean?

Touching my tongue to the edge of the salt-rimmed glass, I'm suddenly hugely grateful for tequila and lime juice and mariachi bands. California would be nothing without Mexico.

★ . 2 ★

Two strong margaritas and three hours later, I don't think I can drive home, even if it's only fifteen minutes across town. I have this thing about driving in San Francisco as it is (scary steep hills, runaway cable cars, foreign tourists snapping photos, unaware that I'm behind the wheel), and I take a cab home instead of my own car.

The cab drops me off in front of my building, the sun having disappeared sometime when I was in the bar, leaving my street of Victorians dark. I check the mail. Nothing good.

I head on up the front steps to the house, needing to enter the front door to reach my door. The owner of the house, Cindy Lee, rented me the apartment after the most exhausting background check ever. But then, as she explained to me later, she lives above me, so she has to be careful. She needs a good, quiet tenant because she often works at home, and fortunately my background check said

I was good and quiet, so I got the apartment. Even if I'm not exactly financially solvent.

But who is solvent these days? Economics are brutal. Everyone's trying to keep ahead of the tax man and MasterCard.

At least I have a job. And an apartment (for now). Which makes me better off than 99.99 percent of the people in the world, and right now strong fresh-fruit-juice margaritas are creating a nice little buzz in my head.

Unlocking my apartment door, I hear footsteps descend the staircase above my head, and I try to shove myself into my apartment before I'm seen.

"Holly."

I stop shoving myself. I turn, watch hiking boots appear. Jeans. A man's muscled thighs. Hips. Chest. Indecently broad shoulders. It's Drew, Cindy's significant other, and he's carrying a bike on his shoulder. The guy's a sports freak. And so good-looking it makes my eyes hurt.

"Hi, Drew." I wish I'd escaped. Cindy's not tall, but she's lean, mean, looks killer even in padded biking shorts, and I look nothing like Cindy. Besides, Cindy's a savvy decision maker. She's aggressive. She plays to win. I don't know that game.

"How are you settling in?"

"Fine." Drew and I have bumped into each other only a couple of times, but he's always really nice, very friendly—not that Cindy appreciates the friendliness. She's never rude to me, but she doesn't invite conversation. She doesn't want conversation. She's made it clear on several occasions (like when two weeks after I first moved in, when I asked if I could borrow an egg since I'd dropped one) that I'm her tenant. I'm just business. Nothing more.

I look at the bike on his shoulder. "Going for a ride?"

"I did earlier. Heading home now." He smiles, great smile, great teeth, little creases at his eyes from all the sun exposure. "The offer still stands. If you ever want to join me—"

"Right." *Right.* Like I need to get evicted. "Thanks." I tense, hearing footsteps on the stairs again. Cindy's on her way down. I'm not in the mood to deal with her tonight. "Good night."

"Night."

I disappear into my apartment, shut the door, lock it. Cindy's shadow passes by outside the frosted glass. "Who were you talking to?" Cindy asks, and I hesitate inside my door before turning on my hall light.

"Holly."

"*Why?*"

I move away from the door. I don't need to hear more. My apartment's got a great big bay window with lovely crown molding, but it's also got Cindy, and I don't like living beneath her apartment. It's okay if I can hear her music, but she doesn't want to hear mine. She can have guests, a wild party, but I have to get permission before I have anyone stay overnight (like who would be overnighting?). She gets three parking spots, and I get the street. I know it's her building, but maybe that's the problem—it's *her* building. It's her everything. I'm paying a fortune, and yet I don't even feel as if I belong here.

In my kitchen with the cute little table in front of the window, I stand there and look around. The kitchen's fine, everything's fine, and yet I don't know what I'm doing in San Francisco. I'm not a city person. I'm a small-town, angle-parking, everybody-knows-me kind of person.

I grew up riding my Schwinn bike with the plastic floral basket on the handlebar down Main Street, waving to everybody I knew, and I knew a lot of people. We bought our cakes at Bothof's Bakery, medicine at Main Drug, shoes at Dick Parker's, stationery at Togni Branch. It was a one-horse town, and I loved it. People knew me.

And then, when my dramatic whirlwind marriage to the handsome foreign husband fell apart, people knew. *Too* many people knew. Which is what drove me out of the valley and into the city. Too many people knew me, and every one of them had an opinion.

No one thought I'd get married and divorced in less than ten months. No one thought I'd be the one unable to honor a commitment.

Least of all me.

I strip off my clothes in my bedroom, and just when I'm naked, the doorbell rings.

With a robe wrapped around me, I answer the door. Cindy.

I open the door, smile my tired, tight smile that I only know how to smile anymore. "Hi."

"Holly."

Is she mad at me? I open the door wider, when I want to shut it in her face. "Want to come in?"

"No."

We look at each other for a long minute. Cindy's five years older than me. She went to Stanford. She's a successful money manager. In fact, she makes a lot of money. She's attractive in a serious, hard-ass kind of way, and she's got Drew, Mr. Fit, and I don't know why she doesn't like me better. Maybe it's because I didn't go to as prestigious a college as she did; maybe it's because I studied English, not finance and international economics; maybe it's because she's very thin and doesn't overeat and it's obvious from my pants size that discipline isn't my forte.

"I'm going away this weekend," she says, and her gaze stays fixed on a point behind my shoulder. She's checking out the fireplace. "Make sure you keep the front door locked at all times."

We share a common entrance and front door. "I will."

"And please don't let your guests park in the driveway."

What guests? "I won't."

Her forehead creases. She stares harder at the fireplace. For a moment she says nothing, and then, "Is there a crack in the surround?"

I turn around, look at the fireplace and the pink marble surround that's original to the place. The apartment looked so much fresher and prettier in the sunshine that very first day I saw it, three months ago, than it does now. But three months ago I was desperate for a place of my own, and right now all I want to do is close the door and be alone. "There's always been a crack."

"There was never a crack."

The good margarita fizz is wearing away, leaving the bad margarita fuzz. "The marble's been cracked since I moved in."

"No."

I don't want to do this anymore. Any of this. I've had it with people I don't like, people I don't know. I want the Marshes back, who ran Main Drug and let us charge everything to our account—Band-Aids, toothbrushes, grape sodas, Jean Naté perfume sold in sets. I want Mr. Parker, who always gave us balloons when we bought our shoes. I want the short, stocky lady at Togni Branch, who could get any filler for any academic planner, you just watch. I want my brother and sister and the sprinkler in the front yard, and most of all I want my dad back with my mom and to have him happy that we're his family again.

"I'll pay for it," I say, hating Cindy, hating Jean-Marc, hating growing up and what it did to me and my heart. I used to like me. I used to believe in me. I used to believe in happy endings. What the hell happened?

Where did Holly go?

What happened to my future?

Why isn't life more like fairy tales?

I was never going to live in San Francisco. I was never going to wear turtlenecks seven months a year. I was never going to be ruthless and severe.

I was supposed to be charming and fun, lively, entertaining, a cherished wife who'd wait a year or two and then have adorable children.

"You said it was already cracked." Cindy's voice snaps.

I take a quick breath and look away to stare down the dim hall that seems to wind forever to the back, where the bedroom and kitchen are. "It was," and my patheticness just grows. I'm drowning here, I think, and I used to be a good swimmer. I was the strongest swimmer I knew.

"Then forget it." She turns, walks out, her tiny heinie marching toward the stairs, leaving the door wide open.

I hear her climb the steps back to her apartment, the two-story apartment that dominates mine.

Shit.

Shit, shit, shit.

I let the door shut, harder than I'm supposed to, and in my bedroom I throw myself face-first onto my queen-size bed with the girlish headboard. I bought the bedroom set when I left college, when I got my own first apartment and thought it was pretty and grown up, and it wasn't until I was divorced and forced to use it again that I realized the furniture set was never grown up. It's a princess wannabe set, with a pale pink princess headboard, the kind of headboard I never had as a kid.

So I bought it as an adult.

For the adult I wanted to be, the adult I was trying to be. Oh, God. I've spent my whole life kidding myself.

I thought if I just played my cards right, if I did what I was supposed to do, I'd end up like one of the heroines from the stories my mother read to me as a little girl—beautiful, clever, happy.

Happy.

And it hits me, harder than ever before, that I've screwed up, that I'm just possibly the most screwed-up woman on the face of the planet (North American continent, anyway) and that those fairy tales my mother read me (she loved them) and the lessons I take away from them (I loved them) were simply fiction.

I've based the most important decisions in my life on fiction. So not-good.

I pick up the phone, dial a number with a never-forgotten area code.

He answers on the third ring. There's music playing in the background. Voices laughing. "Jean-Marc?" I say, and my voice, which is never particularly strong, wobbles.

"Holly?"

"Hey."

"I can hardly hear you."

It's your music, I want to tell him. But I don't, because I can see his rambling storybook ranch house, with the set of French doors that are open onto the trellis-covered patio, where guests must be lounging in comfy chairs near the pool. It's summer in the valley, which means hot. And moonlit. And scented with the unforgettably sweet fragrance of orange blossoms.

I should be there. I *would* be there. If he had let me.

I close my eyes. Why am I calling? Why am I doing this? I must like torturing myself. "Do you have a second?"

"Sure. Let me go into the house."

So he was outside. A rock falls from my throat to my stomach and lands hard.

I can hear him talking to others, his voice muffled as if he's put the phone to his chest, and then I hear footsteps, a door closes, and a moment of silence. "Holly?"

"Hi." Be calm, be calm, be calm.

"Something wrong?"

God damn it, *yes*.

You once said you loved me. And you married me. In front of God and my family and everybody.

I see us at my family's old-fashioned church in Visalia with the marvelous stained-glass windows, the same church I attended every single Sunday from birth until I went away to college. I see us in St. Tropez in lounge chairs on the pier, sunlight glinting madly off the perfect turquoise water, me obsessed with Jean-Marc's indifference while Jean-Marc is obsessed with Rimbaud's poetry. I see us stiff and silent, signing the divorce papers at the ugly Fresno courthouse, the building more suitable for a prison than for an office building.

"No." But I'm going to cry; I'm going to break open fast. Jesus. How can it be so easy for him? How can it—

we—have been nothing at all? "What happened?" I ask, and I know I'm a fool, know that this is ground that's been covered a thousand times without any insight gleaned, but I still need answers, something definitive, something to save me. Make me human again. The truth is, I have to understand how his feelings changed. I need to know what makes love fade, or if it was something I did.

"Oh, Holly." He sighs. "Are you having a bad day?"

Stupid tears sting my eyes. *No, Jean-Marc,* I want to scream, *not a bad day, just a bad life. I thought you were my Prince Charming, and instead you were a toad.* I sniff unattractively, and somehow, thinking of him as a toad, a really awful warty, stinky toad, makes me feel marginally better. "Are you having a party?"

"Just a few friends over."

I say nothing. What can I say? I was the one who filed for divorce. I was the one who played bad cop to Jean-Marc's good cop. I was the one who moved. He got to stay behind. He got to keep the friends. Even better, he got the great Waterford glasses—a complete set, minus the eight white wine I have, which he doesn't miss since he has twelve red—so he ought to be having parties.

"It takes time to settle into a new place," he says, his accent suddenly becoming thicker, more Gallic. The guy knows when to play his French-foreign-hero card. "You have to be patient. Give it time."

"Yeah."

"Starting over is never easy."

I nod, not that he can see, and scrub my face dry.

"It was the same for me," he adds. "When I left Paris, came here, everything was so different. I felt like a fish out of water."

Oh, shut up.

Jean-Marc's a professor of French literature at Fresno State, the local university. When we met at the Daily Planet in Fresno's Tower district, I fell for him hard and fast. I loved everything about him: his Frenchness, his style, his incredible accent. He was so different from anyone I'd ever met, so interesting, so romantic. Our dates were like something out of a romance novel—champagne (*French* champagne, not Napa Valley sparkling wine), intimate little restaurants (Continental cuisine, of course), expert seduction with real French-kissing.

"What went wrong?" I repeat, growing angry all over again. *Why did you stop loving me?*

He sighs, a heavy Gallic sigh. "I don't know, Holly. These things happen."

Do they? Why? *How?*

I used to phone him more often, a call every two or three weeks under the auspices of checking in, and every call is like this. We have conversations of nothing. I ask hopeless questions, and he has no answer; he gives me no help. I'm desperate. And he's a stranger.

It wasn't supposed to turn out this way. I'm still shocked. Mortified. I was always the good girl. I was the one who worked so hard not to make mistakes. I was the one who made sure everyone else was happy first. But here I am in a drafty apartment in a city that feels strange, trying not to fall apart.

No one told me this part. No one talked about what happens after the happily-ever-after. Fairy tales usually conclude with "The End," but in my case, there was another page that said, "The Beginning Again, Part II."

Part II.

How awful.

I know Olivia says I must get out, meet people, start dating, but dating again scares me to death. What do I tell people? What do I tell them about myself?

A Cancer, born in the year of the rat, I like sushi, Italian food, movies, travel, and hiking. Oh, and I'm divorced. Yeah. We lasted just under a year. But hey, that's life; it's cool.

No.

You can't tell people that. You can't just spill stuff like that. I know. I've tried. And people freak. First they say, "You're so young!" and when I don't elaborate (how can I?), they get that frosty look, all frozen and cold, and I feel more alone than before.

So now I don't say anything about the divorce to anyone, and I just smile. Even though on the inside my eyes are stinging and my jaw aches because, honest to God, I don't want my own apartment. I had a house—a *home*—with Jean-Marc. I had a squashy down-filled sofa and bookcases filled with books, yellow climbing roses on the trellis, flagstone pavers from the patio to the pool, and a perfect little gated side yard with lush green grass that would have been perfect for a child's swing set.

I thought I had a future, a husband, a life. I wasn't prepared to be starting over. Wasn't prepared at all.

"Jean-Marc," I croak because I'm thinking of the lawn where I'd pictured the swing set and the little guest room off the master bedroom, where there'd be a bassinet and a changing table. Baby clothes are so small and sweet, and babies after a bath smell so good, and I really wanted the whole thing—the family. The love. The happiness. *"Please."*

"Give it time, Holly. You've only been in San Francisco a couple months."

I don't want to give it time. I want him to say he's sorry, that he's made the worst mistake. I want him to say he's lonely and his bed feels empty and that no one makes him laugh like I do, and no one is as fun, and no one looks as cute eating an orange as me, because those were the things he used to say to me. Those were the things that made me feel beautiful and special.

But he's never once said he wants me back, not even when he admitted—very quietly a couple of months ago—that he never meant to hurt me. Apparently things just got carried away. He should have put a stop to the wedding plans before they got out of hand. Sadly, he didn't. He couldn't.

"Cherie, forgive me," he says now, "but I've got to get back. They're calling me."

He's sorry. But for all the wrong reasons. He's sorry because he's going to hang up on me.

Why did he let this get out of hand in the first place? He didn't need a green card. He didn't need money (not that I have any). He didn't need a social life.

What was I?

But he can't tell me that, or won't tell me that, and I'm left tangled up in knots, knuckles white from gripping the phone so hard.

"Don't go, Jean-Marc—"

"It's going to be okay, Holly."

It hurts so bad; his words hurt endlessly. It's like when my dad left my mom, but it's worse because this is Jean-Marc leaving me.

"Holly."

But I don't speak. I can't. My chest burns. My heart, even with the hole, aches, and I screw my eyes closed even tighter. I feel like shit, like the worst person alive. I did love him. I really believed in him.

I believed in *us*.

"Take care of yourself," he says, and then he's gone.

Gone.

For thirty seconds I think I'm going to be sick. For thirty seconds I want to rip my heart out and throw it in the street and hope some goddamn cable car runs over it, but that's really dramatic, a little too *Gladiator*, not to mention Lorena Bobbit.

Before Jean-Marc, I was the most romantic person I knew. I was going to be the one who never got divorced. I was going to be the one who did it right. I grew up on Barbara Cartland romances (with some Erica Jong and Xaviera Hollander thrown in for good measure), and I believe in soul mates. Marriage. Commitment.

Being good doesn't really pay off.

And I didn't know it until now. My mother (God forgive me) not only read me the wrong books, but told me a pack of lies. Everything she passed on to me had to do with being good. And there were so many goods I can't remember them all, but in short, these were some of the biggies by academic year:

Kindergarten:	Good girls don't show boys their underpants.
Second grade:	Good girls eat their lunch quietly.
Fourth grade:	Good girls go to church on Sundays.
Sixth grade:	Good girls don't backtalk their parents.
Seventh grade:	Good girls sit with their knees together.
Eighth grade:	Good girls do all their homework.
Tenth grade:	Good girls don't kiss on a first date.
Eleventh grade:	Good girls don't go past second base.
Twelfth grade:	Good girls don't get reputations.

And I did it all. I was the ultimate good girl. I followed the rules, made my mother, my teachers, my high school guidance counselor happy. I wasn't a problem. I didn't need attention. I didn't require energy. I took care of myself. I managed my needs. I was so damn good.

And it was a mistake. I shouldn't ever have been good. I should have been bad. I should have broken every rule and made up my own rules and experimented like crazy and spent the summer between high school and college on my back . . .

Well, not really. But close. I should have at least messed around. Being a good girl screwed me over.

To hell with the good girl. I hate her/me right now. I hate reality. I would prefer to return to fantasy.

I need some fantasy because I can't be divorced. I can't be the person who is sending out little apology notes so soon after the wedding thank-yous. I can't be the person who is stopped on the street by the second cousin of the soon-to-be ex-husband, who says, "We're just so surprised, Holly. It doesn't seem like you. You were the last person we ever thought would do this."

And, of course, I just stand there with my stupid tight little smile, trying not to cry, trying not to shout, *Do you really think you're helping things? Do you think I like being me right now?*

Finally my survival instinct kicks in, and I can breathe again. I exhale and inhale while I'm trying to get a grip.

Why do I call him? Do I like pain? Do I need pain? Is there any reason to continue torturing myself like this?

I might as well take a whip and beat myself. I'd probably get as much enjoyment. There's an idea. *Holly Bishop's Guide to Self-Flagellation.*

Suddenly I have to know how bad it is. Not just the relationship with Jean-Marc, but everything, all of it. My body. My life.

I strip off my robe, stand stark naked in front of the mirror, and look. And look. And what I see isn't exactly pretty. There's a lot more of hips and thighs than I remember, and I've grown a stomach where there never was one. Happily the breasts are bigger, but so is the roll on my ribs where my bra strap would hit.

The knees still look good. The shins and calves are reasonably shapely. Shoulders are fine. Upper arms rather heavy, but the forearms are presentable. I need some work, but the body is salvageable.

(There's no point in being too hard on me. It's going to take time to get in shape—can't hate myself forever.)

Resolution: Stop eating so much crap.

Resolution #2: Start getting more exercise.

In fact, why not start getting more exercise right now?

Push-ups. Right here. Right now. I drop to the floor. Let's do ten.

I manage two.

That's okay. Let's finish them off girl-style. By seven I think my arms are going to fall off. I roll over onto my back, start my crunches. I heard somewhere that basketball great Karl Malone does a thousand crunches every day—surely I can do fifty.

Or forty.

By twelve my abs are burning. By sixteen I know I'm

scaling back my goal. Forty was a little ambitious. I'm just starting out. I have to be practical.

I die at twenty.

Reaching for my robe; I cover up, enthusiasm waning a little. It wasn't a great start for the rest-of-my-life fitness program, but it's a start.

And that's the key thing.

I shower, dry off, avoid the mirror. Diet plans always say to avoid the scale and mirror in the early weeks of any new program (I'm sure they said the mirror, too), and in my favorite ratty winter pajamas—we wear the flannel winter stuff year-round in the city—I head to the kitchen, open the freezer, look at the carton of Dreyer's Rocky Road Light (*not* Chunky Monkey, Olivia). I know I shouldn't have ice cream. Even the light stuff isn't on the diet plan. But ice cream isn't really crap food. It's dairy. Calcium. Protein. Strong bones. Helps with sleep.

I eat right out of the carton. Three bites. Four. I should stop. I really only need a taste. Anything more than a taste is just empty calories, and the experts say it's the sensory we're wanting when we eat anyway. The texture. The flavor. The oral need. One bite and we should have met that need.

But I don't seem to have met the need yet.

Just a couple more bites. Let me just get a couple of extra marshmallows (I love marshmallows), and with my mouth full of nuts and ice cream and sticky marshmallows I see myself the way others would see me: wet-haired

Holly standing at the fridge with the freezer door still open, ice-cream carton clutched to her flannel-covered breast, right knuckles smeared with melted ice cream, cheeks packed, stretched, eyes glazed. And I'm appalled.

I'm no better than an animal. It's disgusting. I have two sets of dishes—everyday Mikasa and my gorgeous Rosenthal—and I still can't use a bowl?

I take one more bite and hurriedly put the ice-cream carton away. Feeling very guilty at the moment. All those good intentions are already out the window.

No. It's okay. You've had a momentary lapse, a stumble, but not a big fall. I'm back on the diet plan. I'm serious about losing weight.

In fact, I'm going to do three more push-ups right now.

On the kitchen floor I squeeze them out: one . . . twoooooo . . . thhhhhrree.

Back on my feet, I dust off my hands because the floor is surprisingly dirty, and glance around the kitchen.

It crosses my mind that I really need a roommate. I don't know what the hell I'm doing push-ups for. I'm so lonely I've become my own source of entertainment.

Holly beats herself.

Holly needs a life.

At least Jean-Marc was company. One of the advantages of sticking together almost a year despite knowing he didn't want me anymore (besides being able to keep the wedding stuff) was not being alone. But now I am alone. In the kitchen.

I'm suddenly so tired.

My kitchen is so quiet. The street noise doesn't reach the back of the apartment, and I can't even hear Cindy's music tonight. It's just me. Me alone with my thoughts.

How did I get here? Moving truck, yes. But how did I get to be twenty-five and divorced? I don't even remember ever dating.

Slowly I put the tea kettle on the stove, grab a box of herbal mint tea from the cupboard, and sit down at the cute table by the window to wait for the kettle to boil.

The panes of glass are cold, and all the warmth in the kitchen rises to the ten-foot ceiling. I hunch over the table, stare at the green tea box with the picture of a bear in a nightcap. I like the idea of a sleepy bear, and when the kettle finally boils, I fill a big mug with hot water, drop in my tea bag, turn off the kitchen light, and head back to my room.

I sit in the middle of my princess bed, hold my big mug, and think of Goldilocks. I think of all the different bowls of porridge she tried, all the different beds she lay down in before she got it right.

Maybe I need to take a page from Goldilocks's book and get out more.

Maybe one bowl, one bed, isn't enough. Maybe you have to try lots of porridges and lots of chairs and lots of beds before anything feels right. I never really sampled different chairs and beds.

Was that the mistake? Was that where I got it all wrong?

I think more on Goldilocks, think about how angry the bears were when they returned and discovered the little human-being girl asleep in Baby Bear's bed. I don't remember Papa or Mama Bear saying, "Oh, how sweet, let's keep her." If I remember right, they chased Goldilocks away, threatening to eat her.

What a bad story to read to little girls. Talk about passing on erroneous information.

I need better info.

I also need a life. As Olivia pointed out none too gently, I need to start meeting people, making friends, settling down into my single life in the city. I suppose that means I'll even have to test the dating scene—not that I know where I'll meet single guys.

Oh, God. A spike of panic. Am I really going to put myself on the market again?

Yes.

I take a deep breath, hold a mental picture: Holly smiling, Holly laughing, Holly looking killer in tight brown suede pants and spike-heel boots.

Maybe tight jeans and spike-heel boots.

Maybe comfortable Levi's and medium-heel boots in case the Bears come home and get pissed and threaten to eat me, and it becomes a Nike ad—you know, *Just do it.*

Anyway. The visual isn't about wardrobe. Or bears. It's about taking risks. Going for it. Putting myself out there.

I've been legally separated for six months, but I've been alone far longer than that. Jean-Marc and I slept in separate bedrooms since returning from St. Tropez. For ten months we tried to play the part; for ten months we kept the pretense going, but I'm done. Can't pretend anymore.

The marriage is over. There's no going back. The divorce isn't final yet, but you could call me Holly Available.

*L*ess than twelve hours later, I'm at my desk at City Events, preparing to work through my lunch hour because I always feel as though I'm a day late and a dollar short in the team meetings, when Aimee phones and then Olivia suddenly appears and is hovering over me.

"I thought you were going to the gym," Olivia says, hands on hips. She's wearing a silk turtleneck the same misty gray as her eyes, a minuscule black pleated skirt, dark hose, and high heels with pointy toes. They're probably very fashionable and very expensive, but I couldn't tell you what they are, because I buy most of my shoes at the Nordstrom Rack.

"It doesn't look like I'm going to be able to break free after all," I say, sitting back in my chair and running a hand through my hair. At least it's clean today, not quite so flat. "There's so much I need to do."

"But the front desk has a guest pass waiting for you."

"I'll try to go after work." I smile with more confidence than I feel. I don't really care about going to the gym. I can always do push-ups and crunches in the privacy of my own home.

"We talked about this," Olivia persists, and it's true. We did discuss my going to the gym earlier this morning, and I'd agreed to try Olivia's state-of-the-art fitness facility, but I don't remember committing to a lunchtime workout.

"I'm still trying to get through to the appropriate writer at the *Examiner* and *Chronicle*."

"Good luck. You'll be trying all day."

"Why?"

"The feature writers aren't going to give you what you want. They're not interested." Olivia says it kindly, though. "You'll discover soon enough that newspapers have their own agenda. And they always will."

"But you were the one that wanted me to get the write-up in the first place for next year's Kid Fest."

"It was worth a try."

"So why won't anyone bite? Everybody loves kids."

"Everybody *has* kids." Olivia nods to the phone, where the hold light is blinking. "Who's on the phone?"

I had totally forgotten about the call. "Aimee," I say, reaching for the phone.

"What does she want?"

Aimee is Olivia's friend, not mine. "I don't know. She called just as you walked up."

"Talk to her." Olivia perches on the corner of my desk, interested and prepared to wait.

I lift the phone, brace myself, knowing that a couple of drinks with Aimee doesn't make us pals. "Aimee? Sorry about that. Olivia needed to talk to me just as you rang."

"Is she still there?" Aimee asks, drawling a little. Aimee's a tall, blonde Texan, with Texas-size breasts (implants) and a great Dallas twang. Aimee uses her twang (and implants) the way Olivia uses her exotic beauty.

"She is."

"Tell her I'm working on your social life. That will get her off your back."

I laugh. But Aimee's serious. "Tell her," Aimee insists.

But I don't need to repeat what Aimee said; Olivia has heard for herself. "She's setting you up?" Olivia asks.

"No."

"Yes," Aimee says.

Olivia lifts an eyebrow. "Anybody I know?"

"No," I answer.

"Yes," Aimee says.

This is getting ridiculous. "I don't need to be set up."

"It's not a setup," Aimee soothes. "It's just drinks."

Not bothering even to hide her smile, Olivia rises, gives me a little pat on the shoulder. "Come see me when you're through." She stops, turns back to look at me. "And don't forget the gym. I've got that trial membership all arranged for you, and it's good for the next seven days. You can go every day."

Great. I force a smile. "Thanks."

Olivia leaves, and I put the phone back to my ear. "I'm sorry. Olivia's added my personal life to her Day-Timer. It seems I've become part of her schedule."

"She likes you."

For a moment I don't know what to say. It's not sophisticated to be sentimental; it's not hip or urban or anything remotely cool, but I can't help the big lump blocking my throat. I really needed a job to be able to make the move to San Francisco, and City Events made my move possible. "Olivia's a great person. I appreciate her taking a chance on me."

"Honey, it wasn't chance; it was pity. She knew if she didn't hire you, no one else would."

I open my mouth, drag in air, feel as if she'd given me a one-two punch in the gut when I least expected it.

"You had the worst-looking résumé she'd ever seen in her life," Aimee continues blithely, and I can just picture her at her desk, inspecting her long, polished nails. They're deep red.

At least they should be.

"But you small-town girls never think to put your money where you should. You should have had your résumé professionally done. I bet you did it yourself, didn't you?"

What is she talking about? I like my résumé. Yes, I did it myself, but laser-printed on great ivory paper with cool fonts (Garamond is a personal favorite), listing clearly my education and career objective. I know everything on my résumé by heart: the college degree from University of California, Irvine, graduating with honors; the work experience my senior year in Irvine (that's not including the summer I spent at Disneyland dressed up as Snow White); and then, after graduation, the temp work at the Fresno radio station, the temp work at the PBS station, the temp work at the *Fresno Bee,* and finally full-time work at Grady & Grady Public Relations.

"My résumé isn't that bad," I say in my defense.

"This is San Francisco. If a golf tournament in Fresno is the pinnacle of your achievement—"

"I did lots of PR." I'm chilly now, not just because she's mocking my work, but she's mocking Fresno, and I got enough of that when I went to UC Irvine. Californians love to make fun of Fresno, as if land that's actually fertile and productive (never mind that it feeds millions of people around the world) is an embarrassment to a state famous for artificial tans, breasts, and Botox brows.

"Newsletters for customers," I add, hating that I'm so defensive. I shouldn't care what people say about Fresno. I wasn't born there, didn't grow up there. I just happened to be raised close by.

"I saw samples of your work."

She drawls it out, and I wonder why she feels the need to point out all my failings. Does this make her feel so much better? Smarter? Does it give her great pleasure being right and me being wrong?

Taking a deep breath, I try to calm down. "Is Olivia sorry she hired me?"

"God, no. She's glad you work for her. She thinks you're great. A little misguided, but nothing serious. But that's not why I called. I called because you"—Aimee pauses—"have an admirer."

I nearly choke on my tongue. It's not that I haven't had admirers before—Jean-Marc's good-looking in that French actor way—it's Aimee's tone. Aimee sounds bouncy again, extremely pleased. It's as if I'd just been lifted off the FBI's Most Wanted List of Underachieving Women. "Who is he?"

"Tom."

"Tom?"

"Yes, Tom Lehman. From last night."

I don't remember a Tom Lehman. I barely remember last night. The music was really loud. The bar a complete crush. And I had more margaritas than I should have. Thank goodness I had the sense to cab it home instead of driving.

Too bad I didn't remember leaving my car at work until I'd spent five minutes this morning trying to remember where I parked. By the time I'd hailed a cab, I was in a terrible mood. My mood wasn't improved by Olivia greeting me at the door with a handful of guest passes for her gym.

"Tom's quite taken with you," Aimee adds.

"Tom," I repeat.

"Lehman."

I say nothing.

"He'd love to meet you for drinks Friday."

"Friday?"

"Tomorrow."

Tomorrow? My brain has stopped processing language. Aimee's making sounds, and I have no idea what she's saying. Instead I'm trying to put a face with Tom Lehman. Tom. Thomas. Thomas Lehman. It's a name that smacks of success. And I try to remember the group surrounding Olivia last night. There were quite a few guys . . . "Brown hair?" I hazard.

"Yes."

That was an easy guess. Everybody last night was brunette—Asian, Latino, African-American, Caucasian. "Brown eyes?"

"No, blue. I'm pretty sure they're blue."

Brown hair, blue eyes. Reasonably attractive. "Is he tall?"

Aimee stalls. He's not tall. "Is he short?" I persist.

"No. Not short. Just not ultra-tall."

That means he's short. And he's probably a stockbroker or investment banker—two types I don't have much in common with. "What does he do?"

"He's an institutional trader."

Stockbroker. Great. "Aimee, I don't know if this is such a good idea. I'm not really dating yet."

"It's just drinks, Holly."

"Yeah, but he's going to think drinks are a date."

"Not if you buy the drinks."

My mouth opens, closes. I have to think about that. And while I'm thinking about Aimee's reasoning, she's focused on her mission. "So can I give him your number?"

"Aimee—"

"How about he just calls you there, at work?"

"I don't—"

"Olivia won't care. She gets personal calls all the time."

I'm feeling pressed. Panicked. I don't remember Tom Lehman, and although I'm flattered he'd like to have drinks with me, I can't help wondering about his taste.

I saw myself yesterday. I know what he was looking at. It wasn't my best day, not at all. And if he liked that . . .

"Let me just have him call. You two work it out." Aimee's rushing along, sensing my retreat. "I don't really want to be in the middle of this anyway. I was just doing him a favor, and if you don't want to go out with him, just tell him. He's a nice guy. He'll understand."

"But—"

"Tell Olivia I'll give her a ring in a bit. Bye."

Click. Aimee's hung up. I return the phone to the base and think, she's good. She's really good. I can see why she's the fund-raising director for the Met Museum. She'd get people to part with their money in no time.

And now I get the opportunity to reject Tom Lehman to his face. Or his phone. Which in these days of wireless technology seem to be one and the same.

Tom calls at five minutes before three, just as David, Olivia's boss, is summoning us to an emergency meeting.

"Leather and Lace Ball," Olivia mouths as she passes my desk, arms laden with folders, laptop computer, and more. Even she's looking brittle. David doesn't call many meetings and rarely insists on a whole-company turnout.

"I'm coming," I say, gathering my own folders and notepads and taking Tom Lehman off hold. "This is Holly."

"How're you doing, Holly?"

He says it's Tom, but nothing in his voice resonates. I don't remember meeting him, can't picture him, feel no connection to him now. It'd be pointless to have drinks. Just because he's a man and I'm a woman doesn't mean we'd have anything in common. "Good." What else can I say?

"I really enjoyed getting to know you last night."

Getting to know him? Just how long did we talk? "Yes."

Glancing up, I see everyone file into the glass-walled conference room, and the idea of being the last one to the meeting makes me warm and prickly—and not in a good way. "How do you know Aimee?"

"I don't. She's a friend of a friend of mine. We only met last night."

Oh, God. I really don't want to go out with him. Aimee doesn't even know him. Aimee's just passing out phone numbers because she's bored today. "Listen, Tom—"

"So you've only been here three months?"

"That's right."

"How do you like San Fran?"

"It's good." The glass door to the conference room is closing. Everyone's taking seats at the massive ebony-and-chrome table. Everyone's there but me. "A little chilly."

"It'll warm up. Fall's always nice. October especially."

"You're a native, then?"

"Hell, no. Moved here from Detroit."

Ah. No wonder the weather doesn't bother him. He's used to humidity and ice storms. I didn't have either in Visalia. "Listen, Tom—"

"So we're on for drinks tomorrow night?"

"Uh . . ." I can see Olivia flip open her laptop, watch David take his position at the head of the table while everyone else settles into their chairs, pens lifted, ready to take copious notes. "I've a meeting—"

"You've got to go."

"Right."

"Promise me you'll still have drinks—"

"Tom."

"Promise."

Olivia's looking at me, frowning. I know exactly what she's thinking: *Holly, you get your ass in here now.*

"Promise," he repeats, a singsong in his voice.

Damn it. "I promise."

"Give me your home number; I'll call you later."

I do not want to give him my home number. I do not want to continue talking as if we're old friends, but the meeting's started, I'm terrible at fibbing, and I have to get off the phone.

I rattle off my number, hoping that perhaps he'll write it down wrong, and say a hurried good-bye.

It's not until I'm taking my place at the conference table that I realize I've just accepted—even if inadvertently—my first date in two years.

Two years since I went out with a man who wasn't Jean-Marc.

Eighteen months since I had sex.

I'm in worse shape than I thought.

But David's frothing at the mouth, and it takes me all of five seconds to realize this is not a good meeting; and all thoughts of Tom and drinks and the fact that I've just given my phone number to a man I know very little about fade from mind.

Did I already say this was not a good meeting? I've heard David lose his cool before, but at the moment he's in the middle of a serious rant, and the rant has to do with his highly compensated, overrated staff making stupid mistakes. Fortunately, he's directing most of the flying spit at the staff in charge of this year's Hospice Foundation's Leather & Lace Ball—Tessa and her team.

I catch Olivia's eye. Olivia isn't smiling, but there's a certain fixed smugness at her mouth, which makes me think she's enjoying this. Olivia used to be in charge of the ball—in fact, the ball's wild popularity dates to Olivia's involvement. A couple of years ago she insisted on pushing the edge of the envelope, moving the Leather & Lace away from a '70s Stevie Nicks fantasy to a very urban S and M fetish.

Of course everybody in polite society cluck-clucked, and there were many—and not just the Hospice Foundation's board members—who inundated David and City Events with protests. For nearly ten years, City Events has organized the foundation's ball, including underwriting huge chunks of money, ever since David's partner died from AIDS and David learned the value of hospice care. So David allowed Olivia to overhaul the ball and make her changes.

The Leather & Lace Ball, under the first year of Olivia's direction, *cleared* nearly a million dollars. The second year, 1.8 million. The third year, 2.6 million.

It wasn't just that Olivia got the tickets and tables sold—she managed to sell everything: the concept, the emotion, the suffering, the humanity. People wanted to be part of the ball. They wanted to give. They wanted to be part of something out of the norm . . .

And Olivia, clever girl, turned something wicked— something inherently taboo—into something incredibly beneficial. She made being *bad* good.

San Francisco loved it. David loved it. Rumor has it that he told her if he ever fell in love with a woman, it'd be her. I don't blame him.

As I look at Olivia, the corner of her lovely grape-colored mouth lifts, a small acknowledgment that nobody's perfect. Two years ago David and Olivia had an argument that very nearly came to blows. Olivia wanted a bigger piece of the company pie, and David told her to F-off. Although they patched things up, David took the Leather & Lace Ball from her, handing it over to a new rising star, redhead Tessa Biglione, an Irish-Italian from New York who doesn't give a rat's ass about anybody's feelings, and two and a half years after being hired, Olivia says, it shows.

According to Olivia, Tessa's *team* has the highest turnover at City Events. Tessa's *team* can't stand working together. Tessa's *team* can't stand Tessa.

And right now Tessa's team has apparently run the ball into the ground. The ball is less than six weeks away, and there are no generous corporate sponsors secured, few of the gold and platinum tables have been sold, and even regular-priced tickets aren't moving. Essentially, there's a venue and an event but no money and no one coming.

"I can't have this." David grabs a chair, drops into it. "I won't." He closes his eyes, presses two fingers to the bridge of his nose, and breathes deep.

Medium height, well built, fit, David is a sun-streaked forty-something who looks as if he had jumped out of a Tommy Hilfiger ad, except he's not forty-something; he's fifty-something, but David takes care of himself. David has a new lover, someone Olivia thinks is very good for him, but David can't seem to let go of Tony, even though Tony's been gone ten years. Olivia says it's the way Tony died—awful, so awful—and I think she might be right.

"We spend"—David breaks off, swallows, tries again—"I spend thousands of dollars on this event every year. The Leather and Lace Ball isn't just an event. It's how I remember Tony. Most of you don't know Tony but—" and David breaks off. For a moment he can't speak.

He sits for a moment longer, then abruptly stands. And when he looks at us, all of us, his lips twist, and it'd be a smile if there weren't so much heartbreak in his face. "I don't care what you have to do to make this work. The Leather and Lace Ball funds the Hospice Foundation's annual budget. We can't afford to fail."

The meeting effectively ends with David walking out. You'd think we'd all sit there, pull together the way we should, especially since it's obvious David's really torn up, but Tessa's up and gone, and then various staffers—mostly her staffers—start wandering out, until it's Olivia, Josh, Sara, and me left. Olivia's team.

"So what do we do?" Josh says. Even though he's the only guy on Olivia's team, no one thinks of him as a guy. He's good at this job, organized, detailed, but like Olivia, he also has a great eye, great vision—I've seen him make an amazing centerpiece out of green apples and pussy willow.

Olivia hasn't stirred. "Nothing."

I look at Olivia. "Nothing?"

She suddenly looks old. Older. You can tell she's nearly thirty, and you see something in her eyes you don't normally see: defeat.

I'm not the only one stunned. Josh and Sara exchange

nervous glances. "But you heard David," Josh starts, and Olivia shakes her head.

"It's too late." Her dark eyebrows pull. "The ball is six weeks away. There's no way we can salvage it, not at this point, not when we've so many other commitments."

I can't accept that. I've just listened to David for the last half hour. I've seen his pain. This ball is so important to him. "But—"

"The Foundation's budget isn't our concern," Olivia interrupts, and her voice is flat, tense, ruthless. "Our job is to honor City Events' commitments and protect City Events' reputation."

"But—"

"The ball's been losing money for two years." Olivia turns, looks at me. "It was a good idea ten years ago. We made it more provocative five years ago. But it's old now. It's been done. Attendance is declining because people want something new. You're not going to get the big corporate sponsors anymore."

Sara and Josh gather their things, duck out. I'm still in the conference room, trying to understand. I look at the office, which is virtually deserted. Everyone's gone on home. They've used David's meeting to call it a day.

"Olivia, you could make this work." I sit at the table, facing her, my palms pressed to the ebony-tinted glass. "You're good. Better than good. You could pull this off—"

"Why do you think I let Tessa have the ball?" Olivia leans back, folds her arms behind her head, and regards me steadily. Her expression is calm—calm but hard. She's pulling no punches here.

Forgive me. I'm slow. I'm trying to digest everything Olivia's saying. "I thought David gave Tessa the ball. I thought you were being punished . . ."

"*Punished?* I *let* David take it from me. I knew the ball couldn't sustain that kind of momentum. Everything has its time. Nothing lasts forever." Olivia laughs, low and harsh, and runs long, elegant fingers through her hair. "Rule number one, Holly: know when to say when."

*K*now *when to say when.*

Olivia's words stay with me as I drive home. The fog is moving in, and it's not even that late. It's late August and it feels like winter, and I don't know if it's the cold, damp night or Olivia's fatalism, but I'm definitely depressed.

I realize, too, that my problems seem pretty insignificant compared to David's loss. His partner died. Mine just divorced me. Jean-Marc and I were married for one (unhappy) year. Tony and David had a meaningful decade.

Driving the hilly, congested streets punctuated with the clang-clang and rumble of the cable cars, I can't help wondering what makes couples stick.

Why can some people go the distance? What makes a relationship work?

If only I could identify the ingredient that makes two

people want to be together and stay together despite the problems, the conflicts, the self asserting its needs, then maybe Jean-Marc and I would be together today.

Maybe my mom and dad would be together today.

Maybe half of U.S. marriages wouldn't end in divorce.

I change lanes but fail to signal, and suddenly a white Porsche brakes hard behind me, and the driver gives me lots of attention with his middle finger. Thanks, man. That feels good.

For a split second I feel like Loser Girl all over again, and then I shake it off, thinking instead of David and Tony, of how much David loved Tony and how much Tony—and the Leather & Lace Ball—still means to David. And knowing that the ball is David's tribute to Tony, I can't comprehend how Olivia, who has been so devoted to David and City Events, can detach herself now.

The ball isn't about power. It's about love.

Isn't it?

By the time I've found parking two streets over and hoofed it in damp darkness to my apartment—the tall Victorian gingerbread house, black since Cindy has left for her long weekend already—Tom Lehman is so not part of my thoughts that when I discover two messages from him, I'm shocked.

But what amazes me most is that Tom Lehman has called twice in less than two hours. Two messages in as many hours smacks of desperation even to me. Dropping my coat, I promptly erase both messages.

And then the phone rings.

It's him. I know it is. Simply because I know my luck. I've had this same luck since I started kindergarten, and it's not the kind of luck that's, well . . . lucky. It's more like cursed luck, and it works this way—you don't get what you want, and what you don't want, you get. So when the phone rings now, I know who it is because he's the one I don't want calling.

But the phone keeps ringing, and regretfully I answer. "Holly. Tom Lehman here."

Of course. Murphy's Law meets ancient Chinese fortune. "Hi."

"I've been trying to reach you."

No kidding. "I just walked in." God, I wish I'd never given him my home number. *Big* mistake. I'm so not ready for this, not ready for men and dates and making up polite excuses when I can still barely get myself up and dressed in the morning without bursting into tears.

"How did your meeting go?"

"It was pretty tense."

"I'm sorry."

He doesn't sound all that sorry. He sounds cavalier. "It's not your fault," I answer, trying to think of a way to get off the phone before something truly awful happens.

"Maybe I can make it better. I've reservations at Ovio for tomorrow night." He pauses for emphasis. "Ovio is *the* place to go right now. Great bar. Killer menu. The chef's that Chinese-Brazilian guy everybody's talking about. You can't get reservations."

"How did you?"

He laughs, really pleased. "I'd tell you, but then I'd have to kill you."

Maybe he *should* just kill me. "I thought the plan was to do drinks."

"We'll still have drinks. I have a couple great places in mind. But when Aimee said you're still new to the area, I thought I'd take you out, show you some of the hottest places around town."

I suddenly know the kind of animal I'm dealing with. Trendy Tom's his name. Being seen is his game. "That's really nice of you to offer, Tom, but I don't think—"

"Hey," he cuts me short. *"Holly."* His voice deepens. "I've been there."

We're two guys in the locker room, and he's just given me the halftime pep talk.

"I've been through a big breakup, too," he continues in the same confidential, you-can-trust-me tone that he must have learned when he started his cold-calling career. "I haven't been married yet, so I can't imagine what it feels like getting divorced, but it can't be easy."

I've told very few people about Jean-Marc. I've intentionally kept my marriage and divorce quiet. Yes, there's shame in my silence, but more than that, there's the heartbreak I can't talk about, not with friends, not with family, not with anyone.

It's not that I'm the silent, secretive type. Far from it. My mother used to call me Chatty Cathy, but what's happened to me, what's happened to what I hope, what I believe, is beyond words. Beyond language as I know it.

The divorce—the rejection, the confusion—it all just hurts too bad. Just makes me want to disappear forever, but that's not an option, not when you're only twenty-five and still-young-with-your-whole-life-ahead-of-you.

So I don't talk about it. I haven't talked about it, and no one knows what I went through last year, trying to keep it together, trying to figure out a way to make the marriage work. I changed my hair color four times—went wild with sunny blond highlights, then darkened it, going for sultry; when dark didn't work, I tried red, and the red turned out brassy, overly chemical, and then I tried again and looked Persian with the odd henna purple rinse.

There were diets.

Trips to the shrink.

Agonized phone calls to college friends.

What's wrong with me? How can I change? How can I make him fall in love with me again?

But this is none of Tom Lehman's business; this is something I would never have told him. It's too late now; he knows about my failure. With my pride gone, I give in. "What time are our reservations?"

"Eight. I'll pick you up at six thirty."

An hour and a half of drinks before at least two hours of dinner. Great. I think my first date in two years is going to kill me.

I hang up, head to the kitchen, and curse Jean-Marc yet again.

It's his fault I'm here, back on the market. I didn't want to be on the market. I'd thought I'd escaped all this.

Dating is nothing short of torture.

I know. Some women actually enjoy it, but I never have. I'm so not good at bullshitting. I struggle with having to be nice and make this polite, cordial conversation that sounds horrendous even at cocktail parties. It's practically a miracle to have a good date. It's an out-of-body experience when a man knows how to carry on an interesting conversation.

Jean-Marc was interesting. Talking to him was like playing a game of tennis on a summer morning: warm, flirty, light. Jean-Marc knew a great deal about literature and politics, and yet when he spoke he was dry, witty, self-deprecating. From the first night, I loved being with him.

I loved *him*.

It didn't hurt that marrying him meant I was done with meeting men, done with the awkward conversations and even more awkward attempts at lovemaking. I wasn't a virgin when I married Jean-Marc, but I certainly wasn't an expert, either, yet being with Jean-Marc, making love to him, felt right.

Since Jean-Marc and I spent all our time together, getting married seemed like the natural progression. Marriage meant safety. Security. Acceptance.

In case you're wondering, the sound you hear, that's me laughing hysterically.

Once I've stopped laughing (or crying, depending on how you categorize the sound), I examine the cabinets, looking for something that could pass for dinner, but all I see is my stuff.

Even now, three months after moving in, my kitchen shelves kill me. I have eight Waterford wineglasses but no regular drinking glasses. One set of inexpensive everyday dishes and twelve place settings of Rosenthal china, rich cobalt blue on white, edged with gold. The Rosenthal was four hundred a place setting—so expensive that the lady at the Visalia department store said to my mother (not knowing it was my mother), "Who does this girl think she is, picking out china that's fit for a princess?"

And my mother, bless her, looked that small-town saleslady in the eye. "My daughter."

I really think, in my mother's heart of hearts, she wanted me to be a princess and marry Prince Charming and have the happily-ever, because she didn't. But she and I should have also realized that not everyone in our small town would feel that way. After all, we're not Trumps, Hiltons, or Rockefellers. In Visalia we're Johnsons and Smiths, Morses, Winns, Woodses, and Humpals, but you'd never know it by the gifts Jean-Marc and I received. It was almost as if the entire town wanted the fairy tale, too, because instead of sturdy, practical beige and brown bath towels from Sears, we received the *entire* set of Rosenthal.

I hadn't ever imagined we'd get the entire set of fine china, but that's what happened. We didn't get pots and pans; we got hardly any bath towels; we didn't get ice-cream machines or coffee-bean grinders; but we did get all our Waterford (which Jean-Marc took, except for the eight white-wine goblets). I took the complete set of china.

That's how I started my new life: poor in spirit but rich in extravagant table settings. A girl has to know her priorities.

I never knew mine.

And having been married—for, oh, just about 320 days—I'm going to break the code of silence and tell you all the secret stuff the permanently marrieds would never tell you.

First, be suspicious of anything that is surrounded by the word "shower." The moment the word "shower" is attached to a function, i.e., baby shower, wedding shower, be careful. Really careful.

A bridal shower is usually given by a close friend or family member of the bride, and who attends? All the older women. Mom, Grandma Betty, Aunt Claire, Aunt Carol, Godmother Eileen, plus Mom's bridge group, the friends from Symphony League, PEO, Pi Beta Phi alums, and so on and so on until the young, nubile bride is surrounded by a sea of gray and bottle-brown and blonde fifty-, sixty-, and seventy-year-olds, and what do they do? They shower the bride with presents and pretty cards and lots of enthusiasm when really, on the inside, they're thinking, *Oh, is she in for a big surprise.*

That's right. They know. They know that marriage is a rotten arrangement for women. They know that the young bride will soon be an exhausted new mother and then a frazzled parent and then a stressed-out middle-ager, and, bam, menopause hits, kids are gone, husband is taking cholesterol meds and Viagra, and you know, it's just not a lot of fun anymore.

Thus, the gifts. The gifts are to sweeten the pot, make it all a little more bearable, and while we're toasting your soon-to-be entrapment, we're going to feed you some cake, too.

Good God, this is what we want little girls to grow up looking forward to? Bridal magazines and filmy veils and lavish flowers and so much pretty-pretty before utter bewilderment?

I say, let's just call a spade a spade and show the young bride what's really happening. A death of fantasy, fairy tales, and imagination.

Wait, I'm getting off track. Let's pause for a moment, forget the roomful of old women secretly gloating that another fresh-faced young woman is about to bite the dust. (Come on, you've got to know by now that women never stop being hard on each other!) Let's pull back from the boxes of domestic conveniences, of dish towels and king-size sheets with a 240-thread count.

Let's get away from the nice bows and the silly tradition of how many ribbons broken equals how many babies you'll have, because guess what? You don't have to get married to get presents. You can buy all the stuff yourself.

Let me say that again: you can save yourself a great deal

of stress and strife if you just opt out of the wedding and head for Bergdorf Goodman and buy all the plates, the silver, the crystal, the linens your little heart desires. Never mind "his." "His" doesn't really care about all that stuff, and if he cares a lot, run. Run really fast, because most straight guys don't give a flying fig for towels and mugs.

And speaking of towels and mugs, I suddenly think of all the household items Jean-Marc and I selected together. He seemed interested at the time, looked at all the displays with me, and my gaze settles on the shelf of eight handsome white-wine goblets.

Why did Jean-Marc let me order Waterford instead of Baccarat?

The next morning by the time I arrive at work, Olivia knows about my date with Tom before I even hang my coat up and adjust my turtleneck sweater.

Immediately summoning me into her office, Olivia gestures to the protein bars on the corner of her desk—I pass—and tells me to pull up a chair. "Good for you, Holly. You're smart to get back out there."

I feel like a B actor in a spaghetti Western. "I'm not getting back out anywhere."

"You're right to start dating. You've got to. You can't let what's happened ruin your life. You're only twenty-five. You're still so young."

You'd think Olivia had thirty years on me. And then I remember Tom mentioning my divorce last night. "How did Tom know I'd been married?"

"Aimee must have said something."

No "duh." I try to find a nice way to say this. "It's not something I'm comfortable discussing with people I don't know."

"Lots of people get divorced."

But I'm not lots of people. It happened to my mom, and it nearly broke her. It sure as hell wasn't going to happen to me.

For a moment a cavern opens up inside me, and my whole life seems to be rushing at me: the childhood that seemed relatively normal until Dad abruptly disappeared, the teen years trying to get used to the fact that Mom was never going to be the same Mom she was before Dad left, and the fierce determination that my future would be so much different from (which translated to so much better than) my past.

Wrong.

The cavern opens wider, and I can almost taste the champagne and my white-chocolate wedding cake again, and isn't it horrible how the best night of your life can be someone else's worst nightmare?

Olivia's been studying me. "You're not over your ex, are you?"

Over him? Or over the pain? I realize that the two are

tangled up together now in my mind. "Legally he's still my husband."

"I thought you filed."

"I did. It'll be final by Christmas."

Olivia blows on her chai, expression thoughtful. "Tonight's your first date?"

Somehow I'd forgotten all about Tom Lehman and the fact that we were supposed to be getting together for drinks. "Yes, unfortunately."

"It's good you're going out. This is how you meet people."

I'm not in a good mood. "Even people you don't like?"

Olivia's eyes crease. I must amuse her, but I'm not sure why. "How do you know you won't like him? You haven't even gone out yet. There could be chemistry."

"If I was drunk."

"So drink." She's trying not to laugh.

And I'm trying not to be insulted. "You're kidding."

"You've got to be practical." Her slim shoulders twist, her silk eggplant sweater playing up her dark honey complexion, and she crosses her leg, showing off one knee-high black boot with a stiletto heel. "He has money—"

"I don't care about money."

"Connections."

"So what?"

"Could get you into places where it's good to be seen."

That's another problem. I don't *want* to be seen. I need to lose weight. My hair hasn't been highlighted in ages. I hate men. I don't really like me. This adds up to social disaster.

"So what are you going to wear?" Olivia persists, taking a sip from her tea.

"Clothes."

"Just not too many, I hope."

"He's a dweeb, Olivia."

"Which means he probably has a big dick."

"Disgusting."

She laughs, puts down her tea, and leans across her desk. "You like *little* dick?"

Of course, she can joke about little dicks and big dicks. Her boyfriend is the starting center fielder for the Los Angeles Dodgers and just signed a new contract for what seems like a hundred million dollars. You can have the littlest dick in the world if you make a hundred million dollars.

I stand as gracefully as I can. "Tom Lehman's dick isn't getting anywhere near me."

Olivia laughs again and reaches for the phone. "Maybe an O is just what you need."

I give her a dirty look and exit from her office. I'm serious. Tom Lehman's dick isn't ever leaving his pants.

Returning to my desk, I bury myself in work. Unlike most days, today I don't want time to pass quickly. I pray for interruptions, a heavy workload, annoying problems. Let there be a reason I have to cancel tonight's date: let a meteor fall from the sky; let the San Andreas Fault shift again; let Tom Lehman eat something fishy and foul at Fisherman's Wharf at lunch and end up with a bad bout of food poisoning . . .

But none of that happens. The day sails along, far too quickly for my tastes, and before I know it, it's five thirty and I'm home (not even traffic to slow me down!), changing for my date with Tom Lehman.

If my dread could be visualized, it'd look like something contestants on *Fear Factor* have to eat. Spoiled. Slimy. Maggot-infested.

Stepping out of the shower, I try to give myself a pep talk. Tonight may not be that bad a date. It could be fun. Tom may be less of a pompous ass in real life than he is on the phone.

And yet, as I towel off in my bedroom, I know I'm about as excited as I was last March when I went to the dentist for my second crown and discovered that a root canal was needed, too.

Standing in front of my closet, I try on virtually everything dangling from a hanger. Most of the things I want to wear don't fit, and the things that do fit make me look huge.

No female likes gaining weight, and for me, those extra ten, fifteen pounds equal failure. It's not that I care if I look chunky-ish for Tom, but the extra weight reminds me I've lost control, and good girls never, ever lose control.

Eventually I settle on black jeans and a long, lacy black sweater I wear over a black silk camisole. The soft sweater covers my hips and butt, but the open lace weave shows off my slender collarbones.

I pull on a silver necklace, silver bangles for my wrist, and with the flat iron I go over my hair, flattening it straight. I use more makeup than I have in a while, darkening my eyes, lining my lips, using blush to contour imaginary cheekbones.

The doorbell rings. Butterflies fill my stomach. I look in the mirror, study my now serious face.

I don't know if I can do this. I don't know how to do this. This is a date, my first real date in years, and I'm petrified.

But I can do this. I can, and Aimee and Olivia and everybody say he's a good guy, a really nice guy, so I open the door bravely.

Tom enters my narrow entry hall and checks me out, his gaze sweeping up and down before he gives me a nod of approval. "You look hot."

The guy's word choice isn't my favorite, but I'm trying to be flattered. I haven't felt pretty, much less "hot," in ages, so I smile. "Thanks." I try to find a compliment for him even as I suppress a whisper of disappointment. He's . . . okay. Medium height. Nice features. Dark hair. Except at the back of his head, where he's bald. I shouldn't be disappointed. He could be a wonderful guy. I just need to give him a chance. "You look great, too."

I get my coat, lock up the house, and as we descend the front steps, I see his car, a small BMW model, waiting in the driveway (Cindy would love that), headlights on even though the engine's not running. I reach for the passenger door, but Tom stops me.

"Don't you even think about it," he says loudly, firmly. "That's my job, sweetheart. A woman should never have to open her own door."

"I don't mind opening my own door."

He presses between me and the car. "A man should take care of a woman."

It's a nice idea, I want to tell him, and there's a part of me that would love to be taken care of, but it's beginning to seem like a fairy tale.

Inside the car, Tom fiddles with the music, the dashboard electronically bright. He's changing CDs, flipping through his extensive collection before settling on something that reminds me of Norah Jones.

Mood music.

It's going to be that kind of evening all night long.

I buckle up, tell myself to lighten up, and then we're off, gunning up the hill.

"So what do you like to do in your free time?" Tom asks, shifting gears hard and fast.

We tear around the corner. I grip the edges of the seat. "The usual."

He shoots me a side glance. "What's that?"

"Read. See movies. Hang out with friends."

"What kind of movies?"

"Comedies. Drama—"

"Chick flicks, right?"

He weaves in and out of traffic as if we're in the Indy 500 and the checkered flag's about to come down. I'm glad for the front and side air bags. "Not necessarily. There are all kinds of good movies being made these days, and I love indie films—"

"*Indies?* Like India?" He shifts down abruptly, slams on his brakes, gives the car next to us a look as we're forced to change lanes. "What do you call those movies? Bollywood?"

I'm not even going to go there. Jean-Marc and I used to see all the foreign films we could, and of course, Jean-Marc adored the French films in particular. He collected the older French films, had one of the most extensive black-and-white collections I've ever seen. "What kind of movies do you like?" I ask, determined to get the focus off me.

"Action films. Thrillers. Tom Clancy's my favorite."

"Clancy hasn't done anything in a while."

"I know." He makes another abrupt lane change. "What do you think of The Rock?"

"He's all right."

"And Vin Diesel?"

I purse my lips. "He's good, too."

"Who do you like better?"

"I don't know that I like one better than another. They're both interesting."

"But who would you rather watch in a movie?"

Are we really having this conversation? "I don't think you can compare them."

"Why not? They're both big guys, and they're both part black—"

"So Cuba Gooding and Laurence Fishburne are interchangeable?"

Tom shoots me a blank look. "What does that mean?"

"Well, if you can compare Vin Diesel and The Rock because they're both part black—" I break off as Tom leans forward, opens the sunroof to let the damp San Francisco night in. "Never mind."

Tom laughs, reaches over, pats my knee, his hand lingering longer than I like. "You were getting a little worked up there, weren't you?"

I bite my tongue, hard, as the evening stretches before me. Lengthy. Endless. A Kevin Costner film brought to life.

"Feisty girl," he adds. "I like that."

And then he growls at me.

$\mathcal{I}$ wish I could say the night improved.

It did not.

Tom Lehman liked to talk, especially about himself. Within the first hour of our cocktails, I learned that Tom had attended Brown University, considered going back to school for his MBA, but by then was making so much money as a broker, he passed on higher education to continue building his financial portfolio.

Tom owns his own condo by the water—stunning place, with a view—and has two cars: the BMW and a fun SUV for hauling his toys. He co-owns a "rustic place" in Tahoe with some buddies from the firm so they can ski every weekend in winter (the hot tub Tom insisted they put in has been the best investment ever), and he's decent on skis but kicks ass on the board.

"You look like a skier, Holly," he says, motioning to the waitress that we'd like another round. He's already had two martinis to my one, and I could use another drink, but I can't stomach another sickly sweet-tart apple-tini, which is what Tom ordered for me since all girls like it.

"Can I just get a glass of chardonnay?" I ask, trying to smile at Tom as I flag the cocktail waitress down. I don't know why I feel compelled to ask permission—must be a leftover trait from my good-girl training days—because I really don't care if he approves or not.

"You loved the appletini."

"I know. It's great, it really is, but I don't want to get too tipsy before dinner."

Tom winks. "Gotcha." He orders the wine for me and another Stoli martini for himself, dry, three olives, up. "You don't have to worry," he adds in a whisper as the waitress moves on, "I'll take care of you if you do have too many."

I smile small and tight. "I'm sure you will."

He laughs, ha ha. "So what were we talking about?"

"I don't remember," I answer, because honestly, at that point, I don't. And for a moment there's silence at our bar table, and Tom glances around, drums on the table with his fingertips. He's not bad-looking—decent features, dark sideburns on the short side, blue eyes—but his energy makes me nervous. He continues to scan the interior of the bar as if looking for someone or something.

"I usually know people here," he says abruptly. "It's wild, but every time I'm here, someone I know walks in."

"Really?"

He shakes his head. "It used to piss my girlfriend off. She said we were never alone, we always had a half dozen of my friends hanging around."

"Ah."

"We were going to get married. I mean, we'd talked about it." His gaze keeps darting to the door. "I was the one that broke it off. I felt like shit when it ended. She was a good girl, she really was, and I don't like breaking anyone's heart, but man, she could be clingy. She didn't have any opinions of her own. Couldn't make a decision without asking me what I thought." He sighs, a heavy, tired sigh. "She just *needed* so much."

I find this fascinating. I can't imagine any woman who'd *need* Tom that much. "I'm sorry."

He sighs again, reaches up to pat the back of his head where his missing hair should be. "She took it pretty hard when I broke up with her. I think for a long time she thought we'd get back together."

"How long were you together?"

"Seven months."

I nod because he nods, and for a moment we stare at the table, and I think Tom must still have feelings for her, because his expression is distant, almost brooding.

"Christ, she had a hot body," he says after a minute. "A really great body." His hands rise; they're broad through the palm, fingers medium size, and he shapes his hands as if he's grabbing coconuts. "The sweetest, tightest little fanny ever. I loved her butt. Her face . . . it was okay . . ."

And then he looks up at me, straight into my eyes. "But nothing like yours."

I don't know what to say.

Tom is leaning so far forward that I feel as if we were in prison, exchanging secret information. "You're beautiful."

I pull back. "It's just a face."

"No, no. You have a great face. Really pretty. Beautiful eyes." He's still leaning forward, and he smiles warmly. He's paid me a huge compliment. He wants me to realize that it's significant. "I'm sure you know, there are two kinds of men: the kind that just want a hard body and don't care about the face, and then there are the men that need a pretty face and can put up with a wide ass."

I gather I fall into the wide-ass category. "So you're saying I don't need a paper bag?"

He laughs. Ha ha ha ha. "No. I'd never put a paper bag on your head. I'd want to see those beautiful eyes when I make love to you."

Please let me throw up, so I have a reason to go home.

"Tell me, Holly. I want to know. How old do you think I am?"

I think he thinks he's being deep. I also think he thinks this is a really great conversation. However, I will go with the trivia questions any day if it means we don't have to talk about him making love to me. "Twenty-eight?"

He grins. I guessed well. "Thirty," he says flatly, firmly, clearly impressing me. "You couldn't tell."

"No."

"I work out a lot. Run. Lift weights. Spend a lot of time on the elliptical machine." He looks at me, as if waiting for me to ask the question I'm dying to know, and when I don't (because I haven't a friggin' clue what he'd want me to ask now), he supplies more. "In case you're wondering, I'm in great shape."

"Yes."

"Reaaalllly great shape."

"Uh-huh."

"I've got stamina."

Ah. I see where he's going now. We're back to sex. We get to talk about Mr. Penis now, and I suddenly think of my brother, Jamie, and I can't imagine him ever talking about his body parts. Not on a date. Not even to other guys. Jamie would be appalled. But then, he's never had a difficult time meeting women. They've always fallen all over themselves to get to him.

Jamie was a star baseball player in high school, went to Arizona State on a baseball scholarship, and his senior year he was Mr. October in the Arizona State University calendar the sororities put together to raise money for literacy.

Clearly Jamie never felt his masculinity questioned, although Tom seems quite insecure about his at the moment.

Tom's still talking. "I swear. I can go all night."

This guy's amazing, I think. He's everything I never wanted, and more. "That's fantastic, Tom. You must love night skiing."

"Night skiing?"

"You said you could go all night."

"I'm talking about . . . sex." He leans forward. "In *bed*."

"Oh!" I feign ignorance. "Wow. Congratulations. That's really wonderful. You must be so proud."

Tragically, it seems he is.

We somehow make it from the bar, across the city to Ghirardelli Square. A new restaurant has opened opposite the square, and this is the cool place Tom's been talking about. It's certainly crowded when we arrive, lots of young, glamorous folks standing in the entrance, and even more spilling from the bar. It's a big restaurant, and yet every table is full. The over-the-top lighting—red spotlights only, softened by little votives glowing on all the tables—illuminates the massive statue in the center of Ovio, the statue resembling a Mayan god with a massive erection.

"What do you think?" Tom asks as we're led to our table.

"It's cool."

"I love it here."

I'm not surprised. This is the ultimate in phallic power, and once seated, I realize that at least half the tables are filled with couples that are just men.

"Another drink?" Tom asks, trying to catch the eye of a server.

"No, I'm good."

"One more won't hurt you."

"I don't want to pass out."

"You won't pass out."

"No, but I will be sick, and I'd hate to do that to your car."

That's enough to keep Tom from pushing more liquor on me.

For the next half hour we manage small talk while he has another cocktail and I try not to go mad with hunger. It's nearly a quarter to nine by the time a food server appears to take our order, but before we can actually order anything, the waiter's called away.

I feel like screaming. Or throwing something. I'm so hungry and tired, and have I said really, *really* hungry? But Tom's oblivious. He's happy with his drink, has launched into another discussion, this one about the best private golf courses in Monterey and Carmel, and all I can think about is food. I'm finding it increasingly hard to concentrate on anything Tom is saying.

Please just give me some bread. A little appetizer. One bite of salad. I'll even accept a leaf of iceberg lettuce at this point.

Finally, finally, twenty minutes later, our waiter reappears with a smile. He shakes his head. "It's always like this." He puts his hands on his hips as he surveys us. "Have you two had a chance to look at the menu?"

We've had over an hour. "Yes."

"Any questions I can answer about the menu, or Ovio?"

I'm past hungry. I've hit super grumpy. "Do we actually get anything to eat here?"

The waiter stops smiling, and Tom covers my hand. "Little feisty, aren't you?" he says, squeezing my hand and laughing. Ha ha ha ha. "I think we have to feed Baby."

I pull my hand out from beneath his, attempt to order, but Tom has a different idea. "I know the menu," he says. "Let me handle this."

Why the hell not, Tom? You're doing everything else tonight.

Tom places the order, assures me I'll like what he's selected, and lets the pissed-off waiter escape.

"You were a little argumentative, weren't you?" Tom says. "You have spunk. Fire. I like that."

"I don't think I was that unreasonable. It took him an hour to wait on us."

"But we're in no hurry. We're having fun."

I suddenly think that Tom and I are from two different galaxies, traveling through space at almost the same speed and time. "Did I embarrass you?"

"You can't embarrass me."

I almost believe that.

"I'm confident," he adds. "You can probably tell."

I can.

"But women like confident men." Tom shakes his martini glass, dislodging the olives. "You like confident men."

Again I'm so fascinated I can hardly speak. I have no idea where he's going with this, and I'm dying to know what he'll say next.

"You do," he says, leaning across yet another table, creating yet more intimacy. "You. Like. Me."

"I do?" I say it like a question, I mean it like a question, and yet he takes it as a statement of fact.

"You do. Because women can't resist confident men. It's the number one thing that turns them on."

"I didn't know that."

"Maybe not up here"—and he taps his forehead—"but here," and now he taps his chest, where I assume he thinks the heart should be. As he's tapping his chest, I notice the glint of a blue stone set in a big gold ring on his finger. It looks like a ring from his alma mater.

"You do here," he adds, tapping his chest again. "You know it when you've found someone who can handle the situations life throws at you, who isn't afraid to step up to the plate, who will always look out for you and put your needs first."

This is getting really good. I don't know if it's the martini talking or he honestly believes this stuff, but I'm hanging on every word.

"I like you, Holly."

I'm trying to keep a sober expression. "Thank you."

"I mean it. I. Like. You." He picks up an olive, sucks it dry, chews it. "And I like the vibe we've got going."

There's no vibe. I feel nothing but a desperate desire to escape, and yet I feel like a deer caught in headlights—I can't make myself move.

Tom is popping another olive into his mouth. "I knew when I met you there could be something. I felt the spark, didn't you?"

He doesn't give me a chance to answer. He's already continuing the conversation alone. I admire the energy he brings to the table.

"You're not like most women I meet. There's more to you. There's"—and his hand waves in broad circles—"a lot to you. Inside. You're deep. If you know what I mean."

"That's really nice, Tom, but—"

"No buts." He's leaning on the table, the fire of gin in his eyes. "I'm a take-no-prisoners guy. I won't accept anything less than unconditional surrender."

The waiter—still in a snit—appears with our appetizers. I'm amazed they need sixty minutes to take our order and only five to prepare it.

Tom's reaching for a miniature white corn tamale. "Tell me about your meeting yesterday. What's going on?"

In my favorite Greek myths and fairy tales, the heroes were all the strong, silent type. Unfortunately, Tom seems to be neither. But I can't ignore his attempt at sincerity. "We've an event that's going south."

"Why?"

"Nobody's coming."

"Why?"

I almost smile, my first real smile. This is funny to me. "Olivia says it's been done to death."

He nods, runs his tongue across his back teeth, picking out little bits of shredded chicken. "You need a new angle."

"Exactly."

He points at me. "All you have to do is something new."

I nearly slap the table. "Exactly."

"You can do it, baby."

I hate the "baby." The "baby" needs to die. Fortunately, more food arrives, and for the next half hour we're diverted by platters and samplers, and we eat so much that my waistband starts to cut me in half. And yet Tom really wants me to order coffee and dessert, and I do.

If only to put off what's coming next.

I don't want to get into his car with him. It's not just that he's been drinking, but I have an idea how this is going to play out, and I want no part of it.

I linger over my coffee until Tom's paid the bill, pocketed his credit card, and climbed to his feet. He reaches for my hand and I feel as if he were inviting me to dance.

We walk arm in arm (I'm not happy about this) through the restaurant and exit onto the street.

The fog's moved in, and as the valet attendant runs off to get Tom's car, Tom uses the opportunity to put his arm around me.

I stiffen instinctively. It's been so long since I've had anyone touch me, so long since I let a man get close, and this is not the man I want close. Tom's arm feels heavy. His touch is strange. We're not a couple, and yet he's moving ahead, surging forward, as if everything were already planned.

The cold, damp fog chills me, and I shiver. I don't

mean to; I don't mean to give Tom anything at all, but Tom seizes on yet another opportunity and wraps the other arm around me, sandwiching me between his arms, against his chest.

"Cold, baby?" His voice drops, and he places a kiss on the top of my head. Ugh. And now he's rubbing my upper arm with the palm of his hand.

I shiver again, this time repulsed.

"Poor baby." He brings me even closer. I can smell his dinner. Feel the hair on his chest press through his shirt. His body is sturdy, square, and it probably isn't horrendous naked, but I don't want his body touching mine.

I try to pull away. He doesn't notice. Tom just keeps rubbing my arm, back and forth, back and forth, while the word "baby" screams like a banshee in my head.

"*Baby.*"

I wasn't ready for dating. I know it's going to be a long time before I can think about making love with someone other than Jean-Marc, and even though it's a little thing, I don't want the cutesy nicknames, especially when they mean nothing.

Endearments shouldn't happen on first dates. I've never been comfortable with endearments, but early on, when things are developing, endearments are plain wrong.

Endearments are alienating.

If a man uses an endearment too soon, he's going to be one of those touchy-feely types. And women aren't all that comfortable with touchy-feely men. A lot more women have intimacy issues than folks know, and an indiscriminate use of "sweetie" or "baby" is bound to have negative, and lasting, repercussions.

Tom, for example.

He was trying to do so much so right. And I'm going to give him points for trying, but the "baby" thing is playing in my head, over and over like that annoyingly cheerful kids' song "The Wheels on the Bus" (go round and round, round and round; the wheels on the bus . . .), and I know this is mean, but when Tom says "baby" and rubs my arm, my first thought, after getting rid of the wheels-on-the-bus refrain, is, *Dude, you don't know me.*

But I don't say it; I don't know how to say anything I need. I couldn't ask Jean-Marc why he stopped loving me, and I can't ask Tom Lehman to stop touching me.

Instead I fixate on the use of endearments and think maybe Arnold Schwarzenegger (before the whole governor thing started) could get away with a "baby" and still seem masculine, but unless you're built like the Terminator, or you're Tarzan and still mastering human language, "baby" is out.

And so is "honey," and "sweetie." They're icky.

If there are rules for good girls, then there should be rules for singles, and the number one rule would be no endearments outside serious, monogamous relationships. Casual endearments make the user look (a) weak, (b) desperate, and (c) cheap.

Valet pulls up with Tom's BMW, and the uniformed

kid climbs out from behind the wheel. "Nice car, isn't it?" Tom says about his own car to the kid from valet.

The kid nods but doesn't look as impressed as Tom probably thinks he should be.

We get in the car, and before we pull away, Tom leans over and kisses me. This is not a tentative kiss; this is big and wet and hard, right on the lips. His mouth feels funny against mine, and the hair on my nape tingles.

I try to dislodge myself, but Tom's plunging ahead, pushing his tongue into my mouth, and my nails bite into the palms of my hands.

I don't want the kiss, can't imagine how he could feel one thing and I feel absolutely nothing, but I can't say this, just as I've never been able to say what I really need. My eyes burn hot, a salty stinging, before I finally wrench away.

His thumb strokes my cheek. "You're so sweet."

I'm so not.

And then he guns the engine a little and pulls away from the curb. I'm disgusted, not with him but with me.

Tom turns the music up, cranking it all the way, and after he opens the sunroof again, he accelerates like mad.

Michael Andretti on his way home.

For a few minutes Norah or Sade or whoever she is fills the BMW with longing sound. I don't buy CDs like this. I don't find that this husky, throaty singing does any-thing for me.

Tom's another story. His head is back against the seat;

he's driving as if all the blood in his body were rushing to his pants. I can feel the tension build. Something's going to happen, and it's not good.

Please just get me close to home before he makes a move. Please, God, just get me within walking distance. Please . . .

Tom's hand settles on my thigh, a good six inches above my knee.

Obviously God's not listening to me right now.

This is my fault. I married to avoid all this—married to sidestep the stuff I didn't know how to do—and yet suddenly I'm alone again and even more vulnerable than before. How am I supposed to handle men if I don't know how to handle myself? Or worse, if I don't even know who the hell I am?

I'm screaming inside my head now. I don't want to be divorced. I want to be married. I want to have kids and make pot roasts and string popcorn and cranberries for the most wonderful old-fashioned Christmas tree ever.

"I enjoyed tonight," Tom says.

I try to make myself go numb, because hysterics are pretty much overrated and the screaming in my head doesn't help my sense of calm or control.

And while I try to be numb, I try not to obsess about his hand, but his fingers are resting on the inside of my thigh, and they're gently kneading the muscle—if there were muscle.

"Yes," I say, and it's strangled.

"You're a lot of fun, Holly." His hand is sliding up, his fingertips stretching.

What do I do? What do I do? I try to calm myself; I force myself to think.

Cross the legs, Holly.

Good idea. I shift, cross my legs, trapping his hand between my thighs. He doesn't seem to have noticed. I wiggle, trying to dislodge his hand. He uses the shift of my hips to try to go in for the kill, and this time I forcibly remove his hand. There's no point in subtlety. "I'm flattered, Tom, and as great as you are, I'm not ready for anything more than friendship."

"But I can take care of you." His hand lands on my thigh again, this time the other one. "You need someone like me. Someone strong, sure of himself, someone—"

"Confident," I conclude, knowing where this is going, thinking he's got persistence on his side, that's for certain. I remove his hand again. "As you know, I've just gotten out of a serious relationship, and I'm not ready to start anything new."

Tom takes the corner fast, and I suddenly recognize my neighborhood. We're not far from my apartment now. Just a couple of blocks.

"Tell me about your ex," he says. "What's his name?"

"Jean-Marc."

"Jean-Marc? What was he? French?"

"Yes."

"Meet him in France?"

"No." I don't want to get into details, not with Tom. When I don't say anything else, Tom looks at me quizzically. "Are you still in love with him?"

"No."

"I think you are."

"No."

"You sound hung up on him."

How would he know? I look at Tom, his face lit by the blue dashboard lights, and I wonder at his audacity, or what he calls confidence. I couldn't ever be like him. Couldn't force my opinions on people.

"Why didn't it work out?" Tom persists. "Did he cheat on you?"

"No."

"So he didn't have an affair?"

"No." My hands are clenched; I feel so tight and tense on the inside, I can hardly breathe.

"Most men can't stay faithful. They're dogs," Tom adds helpfully.

"Are *you?*"

"No. I'm one of the good ones."

God help us women.

For a moment the car is silent except for the longing and craving coming out of the stereo. Then Tom clears his throat. "What made him so special, this Jean-Luc—"

"Jean-Marc."

"Whatever." He pulls up in front of my house, turns to face me, waits for an answer.

I want to tell him that "whatever" is rude and that I find him incredibly boorish and that even Jean-Marc had impeccable manners. But I don't. I hug the car door instead, fingers inching toward the lock. "I don't know."

"Was he gay?"

God, I hate Tom. *"No."*

"You're sure? Did you have sex?"

That pretty much does it for me. I fling my door open, and Tom is quickly coming around his side of the car, but before his lips can get anywhere near my face again, I'm running up the front steps, waving and shouting good-bye.

Tom shoves his hands in his trouser pockets. "I'll call you."

The horrible thing is, I think he means it.

$\mathcal{J}$t could have been worse. He could have been an ax murderer.

These are my waking thoughts the next morning, and perhaps they could be a little more cheerful, but I'm depressed that Tom has intruded into my morning already. I don't want to think about him. It was bad enough he took over my Friday night. He doesn't get Saturday.

Still lying in bed, duvet pulled firmly to my chin, I know that Tom is the reason I married in the first place. The Toms of the world scare me. I don't understand them. I don't know what they want from me (besides my vagina), and that's not a prize buried in a box of Cocoa Puffs.

Rolling over, I press my face into my pillow and close my eyes and will myself to think of happier things. And not a lot comes to mind.

Waking up and knowing I'm the only one here, that even when I get out of bed I'll still be alone, and that unless I go out for breakfast I'll continue to be alone, depresses me almost as much as remembering my night with Tom Lehman.

This is a terrible thing to admit, very immature and antiprogressive, but I'm not great at being alone. When I'm alone, I have too many thoughts and too many feelings, and I don't know what to do with them.

I could shop. Lots of people shop. I could exercise. Lots of people run and work out incessantly.

Or I could try to get used to being alone and to how it feels to have more thoughts and more emotions than I want.

Eating is really a lot simpler, isn't it?

Considering my options, I decide to go out for breakfast. Eggs and coffee are cheaper than shoes and still cheaper than my favorite reasonably priced Benefit cosmetics (which I love and wear almost exclusively because the company was founded by two cool chicks in San Francisco, which means you must ignore all the bad things I say about the city's predilection for turtlenecks and my difficulty finding parking, much less successfully parking, on steep hills), and eating out means I get company of sorts.

So I throw on some jeans, much baggier, more comfortable jeans than I wore last night, a favorite oversize men's shirt in a great shade of blue (of course it was Jean-Marc's), and the cowboy boots I can't give up even though I'm not in Hicktown anymore. The truth is, I like wearing my cowboy boots; I like that they're not hip, not fashionable, not pretty. I like the pointy toes, the low stacked heels, the battered, faded brown leather. I also like the fact that Jean-Marc hated them and now I get to wear them. When I wear my boots, I feel tough and interesting and far more together.

Cow Hollow, like most neighborhoods in San Francisco, has its own little center of business, plenty of corner coffeehouses, cool restaurants tucked into the ground floors of various renovated houses.

I head for one of those hole-in-the-wall restaurants, buy a Saturday morning paper on the way, and with the sun shining and the sky a wispy Northern California blue, I feel almost human.

A real person.

And the real-person sensation stays as I order coffee, juice, scrambled eggs. The real person reads the paper, savors a second cup of coffee, and suddenly feels so good about herself that she smiles, thinking that life's not so awful, that maybe, just maybe, everything's going to be okay.

"Can I borrow your sports page?"

It takes me a second to register that I'm hearing a voice, and that the voice is talking to me.

Looking up, I see Gorgeous Guy sitting at a table across from me. He's leaning on the table, elbows braced, looking rough-and-tumble in a way you don't often see in this city.

For starters, he's big. Tall. He's got shoulders. And from what I can see of his right thigh—tight, hard quads—he must have tight, hard legs.

He's wearing a denim shirt open over a white T-shirt and a pair of well-washed, well-worn Levi's.

"You want what?" I ask, unable to focus on anything but his legs. I had no idea I was so damn visual, and for a moment I think this is what it must feel like to be Tom Lehman.

"The sports section."

I nod to show that something has finally registered, and quickly riffle through the paper. Fortunately, with Jamie for a brother, a rabid sports fan since his terrible twos, I know where to locate the sports page. "Here."

I'm blushing as I give it to him, and I've no idea why I'm blushing, or adjusting my collar, or brushing the tip of my ponytail. But I know that the moment I adjust something, touch something like my ear, my hair, my mouth, I'm attracted. I'm sending out some physical, biological signal. I don't know the specifics, but I'm transmitting "you male, me female," hormones engaged. I'm sure my cousin who works at the Bronx Zoo could do a better job explaining this.

"Just for a minute," he adds.

"No hurry." And there isn't. I've got no plans for the rest of the day, and so I just stare. His teeth are straight and white, and I swear, he's a bona fide Gap model.

Why wasn't I out with *him* last night? I would have

been charming. I would have been eager, happy, funny. Candy-floss appletini? Why not? Al Unser Jr. behind the steering wheel? Bring it on. Hours between courses? Who needs to eat when your heart's in your throat and everything in you is wishing for happily-ever-afters?

He's far too good-looking for me. Far too sexy. Far too everything. But after last night, when I felt like a slab of meat in cold storage, I welcome the wash of heat.

"Damn," he says, and shakes his head. He's frowning now, and he closes the paper.

I take the paper back. "Didn't like what you saw?"

"Nope. They lost."

They? "Your team?"

"My high school."

The guy's at least thirty. Maybe even thirty-five. Yes, he's gorgeous, but he's not a kid, and I can't see him still trying to follow his high school team. I open my mouth to ask a question, but he's already standing and heading for the door.

I watch him walk out, the tail of his blue denim shirt flapping, and as the café door shuts behind him, I feel a moment of utter loss.

We could have been so good together.

My coffee isn't as tasty as it was, and I don't feel quite as buoyant as I did. I slowly return to my apartment, open and close the door, and head into the kitchen, tossing the newspaper and my keys onto the little table beneath the window.

For a split second I picture a life with him. Gorgeous Guy.

Isn't there some ancient Asian philosophy that says you are often confronted by the same problem over and over until you've mastered it? If not, there should be.

The whole reason I picked this apartment was because it looked perfect for a couple. Even though I was still reeling from the divorce, in the back of my mind I was already keeping my options open.

I saw the apartment's possibilities. Yes, the crown was thick and glossy white, and the living room's large bay window overlooked a sunny street, but I also saw the big bedroom (big enough for trading up to a king-size bed if need be), the fireplace for romantic evenings, the space in the kitchen beneath the window, where a cute table would go.

I saw it all.

The good-looking guy sprawled on the sectional sofa I'd soon buy. The weekends, when he'd be reading the paper or idly flipping through the TV channels, watching three different football games simultaneously. I saw me preparing extravagant Sunday brunches, dazzling him with my culinary skills, slipping him incredibly tasty food while I slipped into something sexy. (I do have all that lingerie that's never been worn.)

This idea of me, this vision for my future, is what made me sign a year lease on an apartment that I couldn't afford and that wasn't all that convenient. I could have gotten apartments for far less—newer, more modern apartments that came with parking—but this apartment had charm. This apartment had style. This apartment shouted, *She's worthy!*

And so the movers left my boxes in my newly leased apartment, which has twenty-three steps to the front door, and the smallest, narrowest toilet-in-a-closet I'd ever seen. But I'm not complaining, because I don't cook or eat in the bathroom; I do that in the kitchen, and the kitchen might not be ideally laid out, but it is spacious and has new appliances and, of course, room for that table beneath the window.

Now you know everything about me. I'm not just impulsive and romantic; I'm dumb and broke, too.

Dumb, because once again I signed on for something reason and responsibility should have told me I couldn't afford.

Broke because when Jean-Marc and I divorced, I asked for nothing since I came with nothing, and it seemed wrong to ask for a piece of his house or his bank account when he'd never wanted me in the first place.

That thought alone stops me, and sinking onto the back of my sofa, I stare blankly at my fireplace's pink marble surround. Why didn't I know that Jean-Marc didn't want me?

Why couldn't I tell how he really felt about me? Surely there were signs. Symptoms.

I rack my brain yet again, trying to discern what must have been there, true, obvious. But before the wedding we seemed so happy. We didn't fight. We took trips together. Jean-Marc spent more time at home with me than he did in his campus office.

There was a distinct lack of sex, but I thought . . . I thought . . . what?

The phone rings.

Panic floods me. I tense. Every muscle knots, locks. Who is it? I don't know, and therefore I can't answer.

I wait through the six rings until my answering machine picks up. But when the machine picks up, the caller hangs up.

I stare at the phone, hating it. It could have been a good call. Could have been someone I wanted to talk to.

I should have gotten caller ID, like the saleslady at Pac Bell suggested when I first moved in. All I had to do was buy a new phone.

So that's what I'm going to do. I'm going to go to Circuit City and buy a phone with caller ID, because if I'm going to date, I need to know who is on the other line.

And *then* I'll go to the gym.

On Monday morning, I'm back at work, sitting in an early morning team meeting. Olivia is briefing us on a new event we'll be coordinating—the seventy-fifth anniversary of the Beckett School in Hillsborough. The Beckett School is one of the most prestigious academies for boys— impossible to get into, and yet an education at Beckett

ensures lifelong success, if not due to personal achievement, then due to the extremely loyal network of alumni.

Olivia is enthusiastic. Even though her African-
American Georgia-born father, Terrell Dempsey, would
never have been allowed within a hundred feet of socially
restrictive Beckett, Olivia embraces old money. But to be
fair, she also embraces new money. To Olivia, money is
opportunity.

Olivia is one of the reasons City Events is so successful. Olivia isn't just an event planner; Olivia is the company's top account executive. She's not afraid to go after
business, not afraid to ask for what she wants. She's smart.
Tough. Teflon coated. She's learned to separate herself
from her work, learned that rejection isn't personal, and
that just because someone says no now, it doesn't mean
they'll say no later.

I wish I could be smart like that. Not to mention a lot
more Teflon. I still can't say what I want, what I need. I
don't ask. Instead I've hoped that being good, being just,
being fair would reward me.

I'm not so sure anymore.

"How did you get the account?" Sara, the fourth person on Olivia's team, asks, Olivia's team consisting of
Olivia, Josh, Sara, and me.

Olivia nods at Josh. "Josh's connections."

We all look at Josh. He shifts uncomfortably. "My dad
went there," he said after a moment.

"Josh did, too." Olivia's sitting on the edge of her desk,

and we're facing her like kids in a schoolroom. "He's third generation."

We're all still staring at Josh. Tuition to Beckett is around seventeen thousand a year. And we're all thinking approximately the same thing: does that mean Josh's family is loaded? And if so, why is Josh working here? A job at City Events is creative and diverse, but it doesn't pay. You don't really start making anything until you're a director, like Olivia or Tessa.

Speaking of Tessa, I saw her summon her staff together earlier this morning for their weekly meeting, and I prayed she'd had a brainstorm over the weekend about how to save the ailing Leather & Lace Ball. Somebody needs to save the ball—

"Holly?"

The sharp edge in Olivia's voice brings me back, and from the expectant faces facing me, I know I've missed whatever they've been discussing.

"You have anything to contribute?" Olivia asks, and as I look at them—blonde, pixielike Sara; silent, gender-neutral Josh; vivacious, exotic Olivia—I see us all fast-forwarded into the future; I see a story that hasn't yet been written, but the ending is the same. We all will age. We'll all get sick. None of us shall live forever.

And I know I must do something about the Leather & Lace Ball. Not because I'm heroic, but because I'm afraid. When I'm ill and dying, preferably when I'm *old* and ill and dying, I don't want to be alone. I hope someone will be there for me the way David was there for Tony.

"I'm good," I say, and I am, because I know I'm going to get involved with the ball, and I know it must be kept quiet. Olivia and Tessa are at odds lately, and I don't know why, but I'm not going to go there. This isn't about Olivia or Tessa. It's not even about David. It's just me.

Back at my desk, I get on the phone, call the Beckett School's administrative office to request their alumni database. Planning an anniversary celebration for a school is a lot like planning a reunion. Putting on the actual event is easy. No one needs to be sold on the school. It's more a matter of letting everyone know the where and when, and the more advance notice, the better.

Olivia and Sara head out at lunchtime for an appointment with the Palace Hotel off Union Square. Sara was in charge of a wedding being held at the Palace Hotel on Valentine's Day, but the wedding, although still six and a half months away, is way over budget, and the father of the bride is panicking, and the bride is covered in hives, and Olivia is stepping in to see if she can't get a handle on the costs before the bride's hives turn into full-fledged eczema.

With Sara and Olivia gone, I've got a good opportunity to speak with Tessa. She's in her own office—she and Olivia and David having the only private offices with doors and windows—and I approach, knock gingerly on her open door.

She looks up, her red hair cut in a spiky bob, her short bangs dyed a magenta hue, and as she looks up, she runs one hand wildly through the spikes. "Yeah?"

She knows I work for the other team.

"Do you have a minute?"

"No, actually." She folds her arms in front of her, and she looks at me long and level. "Besides, your director won't want you in here."

"She's not here."

"I'm not interested in any complaints 'bout her."

"I'm not here to complain. I love working with Olivia."

"Then . . . ?"

Tessa makes me feel like a beetle-bug, and I'm afraid she's going to jump up and squish me any second. "I wanted to offer you my help."

"I don't need help."

"David says—"

"David was out of line."

I stand there for a moment and feel nothing. I'm very good at moments like this. I go numb, all cool and empty and hollow as if I never had feelings and nothing could ever hurt me, touch me; and I stay there until I can shrug. "If you say so."

But I don't leave.

I should, but I don't.

The Hospice Foundation depends on the ball. David says the ball is the foundation's primary source of income, and I believe him, and maybe this is why Jean-Marc fell out of love with me. I get stubborn at all the wrong times, for all the wrong reasons.

Tessa's dark red eyebrows flatten. "If you're done . . . ?"

I feel really stupid, but I'm good being stupid. I hang on doggedly; I hang on and don't let go. "Olivia doesn't want me involved with the ball. I'm coming to you behind her back, and she wouldn't like me coming to you. But this ball means everything to David, and I respect David. A lot."

"Olivia would fire you if she found out."

The cold feeling's back, but so is a hotter emotion, one I can't name. The hot threatens to swallow the cold. "David signs the paychecks."

She leans back in her chair, eyes me for a moment. "So what do you want to do?"

"Whatever needs to be done that I could help do— away from the office, of course."

"You don't want Olivia to find out?"

"I don't *want* to be fired."

She puts her feet up on her desk. "We only have a quarter of our tables sold. We don't have any high-end sponsors. I'm working on sponsorship, and the rest of my team is trying to approach various companies about buying tables, but . . ." She shrugs, and it's the shrug that says she's losing faith.

The event's been done to death.

"Let me try the media," I say, and Tessa smiles. I know

she's thinking that this is San Francisco, not Fresno, but she doesn't say it. "I'll see if there isn't a way to generate some excitement that way," I add, trying to sound convincing.

"Go for it." And she's still smiling, but she's less antagonistic. "You'll be our media queen, only stealth." She reaches for her iced mocha, shakes the cup, rattling the ice. "So keep me posted. Let me know how it goes."

It was a bold offer on my part, but it doesn't take me long to discover that being media queen (even stealth) has more lows than highs.

During the next week I make endless phone calls that go nowhere, leave messages that never get returned. I turn to Outlook Express, which isn't as effective as a personal call, send a flurry of e-mails, introducing myself, asking for a moment of so-and-so's time. Half the e-mails get ignored. The other half come back with a "thanks but no thanks, not newsworthy, not groundbreaking, not interesting," the underlying message being that people already know about the Leather & Lace Ball, and people don't care.

I stare at my computer screen, reading the latest one-line rebuff. At least it's not as curt as the last.

I rub my eyes, tired. It's a little after five, and with Olivia leaving just after lunch today, heading down to L.A. to see her boyfriend, I've been trying to make some headway on the media list I'd been given.

Maybe people don't care about the ball anymore, but

once upon a time they cared. Once upon a time the ball was fun. Intriguing. A novelty.

Why can't it be fun, intriguing, a novelty, again?

Maybe the mistake wasn't in continuing the ball for ten years but in allowing the ball just to endlessly repeat itself without offering anything new or unique.

I can't really blame people for not wanting to attend again. If you've been there, done that, why persist unless you can (a) guarantee a great time or (b) discover something new?

Is it too late for the ball to reinvent itself? Too late for City Events to put a twist on the ball, come up with something new? Or would dramatically changing the ball at the eleventh hour smack of desperation?

My phone rings, and I reach for it. "Holly Bishop."

"Tom Lehman."

Oh, no.

"You haven't returned any of my calls," he says.

"It's been frantic around here."

"The market's been worse."

I'm sure it was. I hunch my shoulders, attempting to stretch. "Bad week?"

"You didn't return my calls."

"I'm sorry."

"How sorry?"

Not that sorry. I grit my teeth. Close my eyes. *Be strong, Holly. Just get rid of him. Tell him you're not interested. Tell him good-bye and be done with it.*

I don't, which gives him a chance to talk next. "What are you doing tonight?"

"Working late," I answer.

"After work?"

"Going to bed."

"Sounds like fun."

I shudder. I should know better than to use a word like "bed" or "night" around him. "Alone."

"You'd like me in your bed. I'm a big cuddler. Love to spoon."

I nearly hang up. The verb "spoon" has always turned me off. There's something unsavory about two people calling themselves silverware. "Tom, I hate to be rude, but I've got to go; I've got another call holding."

"Oh." He pauses. "Who?"

"A reporter from the paper," I fib, but it's a good fib.

"Which paper?"

"The *Chronicle*."

Tom's quiet now, and I want to get off the phone before he asks me out for tomorrow night. "I'll talk to you soon," I say, trying to sound cheerful but not too encouraging.

But he jumps on it, like a dog on a stick. "When?"

Never. "Next week."

"I'll hold you to it."

I've no doubt. I hang up. I still have Tom to deal with, but at least I'm off the hook for now.

Josh appears at my desk. He's attractive in a nearly

invisible sort of way. Slender frame, about six feet, lightish eyes, light brown hair. He probably was a very sweet child.

I can't imagine him attending Beckett. Beckett has more than money. It's been investigated twice in the past ten years for its "history of hazing."

I don't know if Josh is gay. He might be; he might not be. But I can't imagine him wild in high school, pumped by testosterone surges.

"You're leaving," I say, seeing he's got his brown leather barn coat on.

"Going to meet friends for drinks."

"Sounds fun." I sound wistful. I didn't mean it to come out that way, either, but suddenly I dread going home, dread being alone again, dread the moment my front door closes, shutting me inside an empty apartment that reminds me far too much of my newly empty life.

Josh hesitates. "You want to come?"

I actually feel sorry for him now. I'm not much better than Lehman, am I? "No," I answer brightly, far more brightly than I feel. "I'm good. But thanks for asking. That's nice of you."

He laughs uncomfortably. "It's not a date, and I'm not making a pass—"

"No, I know." I cut him off, mercifully short. I don't think either one of us can handle this. I don't know if Josh is gay or straight, but he's the one person at work who hasn't gone out of his way to make me feel like a complete idiot. "But thanks. Really."

He just looks at me, his expression curious. Surprisingly thoughtful. His eyelashes are long and thick, and as they drop, he looks almost beautiful, in an androgynous David Bowie sort of way.

"The person you want at the *Chronicle* is Fadden," he says after a moment. "Brian Fadden. I forget his exact title, but he's a features editor and has a lot of seniority."

"Thanks."

"Fadden can bark, but he doesn't bite."

I nod, but on the inside I've hit the red panic button with both hands. Just what does Josh know? He's been here three—four?—years and will probably be the next to be promoted to events director, if Tessa or Olivia should leave.

"She wouldn't like you doing this, Hol. Be careful."

I know who and what he's talking about, and he's giving me fair warning. I wasn't sure if he knew what I was doing, all those calls I was quietly making, but now I do. I shouldn't be surprised. Josh is quiet at work, often goes unnoticed, but he's usually aware of everything.

And he also sits just two cubicles away.

My face feels hot, the skin prickly. "You won't say anything?"

"It's none of my business."

It may be none of his business, and he doesn't want to get caught in office politics, but he did give me Fadden's name. Warned me to be careful. I'm touched. Grateful. And even more determined not to go home and sit in my apartment, lonely and alone. "So where are you going for drinks?"

"The Mission."

The Mission district's the in spot in recent years. Josh looks at me, thick lashes lifting, his brown eyes half-smiling. He dangles his car keys. "Don't worry, you're not my type. I don't drink a lot. And I'm happy to drive."

I'm hugely tempted. I really don't want to be alone. "Your friends won't mind?"

"I wouldn't have asked if I thought they would."

I had no idea that Josh was so interesting.

And I don't just mean interesting because Josh gave me the name at the paper or promised not to say anything to Olivia, but interesting as in intriguing. The guy's a poet. He's had a collection of his poems published—he claims no one read it, but his friends say Josh is too modest.

His friends are all artsy types—there are three novelists (one Spanish, one American, and the other is Middle Eastern), a short story writer, a playwright, a sculptor, a photographer, a graphic artist, painters, and so on. They're men and women. Diverse, international, and heavy smokers.

And I like the idea of them, the idea that I'm part of something intellectual, weighty, of substance, particularly because Jean-Marc used to say after we'd been married a couple months, *Why don't you read a real novel? Why don't you do something with your mind?* Or, if I was leafing through a magazine at night, *You should read a real newspaper. A European paper. Your American newspapers are all so biased.*

We're at a Greek restaurant for drinks—we're supposed to be going elsewhere for dinner later—and everyone's loose, enjoying their beer and wine and taking turns going outside for a quick cigarette, cursing San Francisco's ridiculous antismoking laws as they come and go.

Even though I'm sitting next to Josh, I spend most of the evening talking to an intense novelist named Paul Petersen, who could be any age between twenty-five and thirty-five. Paul doesn't actually have a book published yet, but he gave up his day job two years ago and takes his work very seriously. He doesn't write genre stuff, only "good fiction."

I've nursed the same beer for over an hour because I want to keep my wits about me—I am starting to watch my weight a little more—and Paul is fiercely argumentative about what constitutes great writing. I think he thinks he's an authority on great writing, and apparently he's crafting something that's very dark, serious, and relevant.

Although I'm not sure what that means.

I do know that critics and reviewers love novels filled with unhappy people searching for meaning. The search for meaning speaks of human nature. And suffering. But my problem is, I've lived suffering, and I'm just about suffered out.

I think it's time to order another beer.

By the time I head home, I've had shish kebab and dolmades, fried cheese and pita bread. I grew up on Greek and Armenian food in Central California, and the kebabs and pita bread remind me of home. As I unlock the door to my apartment, the city feels a little smaller, a little friendlier, and I've even agreed to have dinner sometime with Paul so we can continue our discussion on the great American novel.

It's probably not the smartest thing I've done, but surely it can't be as bad as going out with Tom Lehman.

Speaking of Tom, he calls over the weekend. Twice on Saturday. Once on Sunday. And then when he fails to reach me on the phone, he drops by in person late Sunday afternoon.

Thank God I'm actually out when he stops by, and he's forced to leave a note on the back of his business card, which he slid under the door.

I return from the Laundromat (Cindy has a washing machine and drier in the garage, but it's hers, not her tenant's) and find the business card, feel as if I've escaped the death penalty, and am about to close the door when Cindy's footsteps echo on the stairs above me.

"Holly."

It's a command. I'm to wait. And shifting the laundry basket onto my other hip, I do.

She's in khakis, a tight black top, and casual khaki Skechers, and her dark hair is in a trim, immaculate ponytail. "Your friend—I don't know his name—stopped by." She sounds disgusted.

He must have parked in the driveway.

"I told him you weren't here, and Drew was trying to move his car."

I was right. It is about the driveway.

"Drew had to wait for your friend to leave."

Just how long did it take for Tom to write his note? It was only a business card, for Christ's sake.

"You know the garage and driveway are reserved."

For your use only. Yes, I know that. But I don't say it. I don't say anything. I've had a great day at the Laundromat, sorting my whites and folding my underwear while being watched by a group of freaks.

For a moment I wish the freaks had followed me home. I wish they'd come up the stairs, entered Cindy's pristine hall, and I wish Cindy had seen them here, about to enter my apartment.

She would really love my *friends* then.

"I'll apologize to Drew," I say, and smile, a kind smile, the one I'd give Drew if he were here, and Cindy's mouth tightens.

"I don't want to be a jerk," Cindy says.

"I know." I smile more kindly. "It's so not you." And hitching my basket higher on my hip, I go into my apartment and gently, firmly close the door.

Monday morning, new week, which means the Leather & Lace Ball is now only five weeks away.

In our loft office, Tessa looks calm, and her staff is working intently while we have a loose, loud team meeting in Olivia's office—with her door open.

Olivia has brought in a tray of raspberry and lemon sugar scones, along with our favorite Starbucks coffee drinks. "To thank my team for their excellence and dedication," she says, passing out the coffees and lifting her chai in a friendly little toast.

I feel a prick of guilt, and it's all I can do not to look at Josh. What's he thinking right now? Does he feel any of my disloyalty? But my guilt is cut short by Olivia's shift to the morning's agenda.

The Schlessenger wedding's back on track.

The Beckett School anniversary is moving ahead.

Olivia's been asked to put together a proposal for a big shindig to thank Oracle's major investors.

We all have tasks, plenty to do, and we return to our desks with a sense of renewed purpose.

Fifteen minutes later, Olivia stops by my desk and stands there for a moment without saying a word. I was just grouping my files on my desk, and so I organize a second longer, waiting for her to start.

As the silence grows, I feel her disappointment. I've let her down. Something's happened. I can't help my reaction, but my stomach knots, and I feel terrible. Olivia's been really good to me, extremely supportive. I don't want to upset her.

I look up at her, battling dread.

She meets my gaze, holds it. "You never did use the guest membership at my gym."

Is that it? My legs feel weak. "It's been hectic."

"It'll always be hectic. You have to make time for yourself." She extends a hand, points to my Day-Timer. "Open your calendar; schedule gym time now."

"I will."

"Do it now." And she waits, giving me no alternative but to reach for my Day-Timer, and as I do so, I uncover my notepad.

Olivia's eyes narrow; her gaze settles on the chunky notepad with the City Events logo on top.

She's reading what I've written. "You've talked with Brian?"

"Trying to reach him," I answer, as she can see the name Brian Fadden, "Features Editor," written in big block letters, followed by a phone number.

"That's not his direct line," she says. "That's the main switchboard number."

"I'm hoping the switchboard will put me through."

"They won't. Not to Brian. They'll send you to voice mail, or another journalist who will just screen you." Olivia curves her finger, gestures for me to follow. "Come, I've got his direct line. He hates calls from us, but once he's on the phone, he won't hang up. At least not immediately."

In her office she scribbles down a number and hands the sheet of paper to me. "You know, he's single again."

"That's nice."

"He's attractive."

"You said the same thing about Lehman."

"I didn't. That was Aimee, and she was drunk off her ass."

"Still not interested."

"You might change your mind if you actually met him."

"I doubt it." I glance at the paper, see the number, feel like a traitor. She doesn't even know why I want to call Brian Fadden in the first place. "But thanks."

"Now do me a favor."

I look at her, and she's serious. "Get yourself to the gym. Do twenty, thirty minutes solid cardio. Try the weights"— and she lifts a finger when it appears I'll interrupt. "It's not just good for the bod, girl. It's good for the head."

"Got it."

She smiles, and I leave. But instead of returning immediately to my desk, I walk on shaky legs to the little kitchen we have at the back of the loft, make myself a cup of inoffensive herbal tea, and lean against a counter, still trembling, staring out at nothing.

Things are starting to get complicated. My personal life has always been confusing, but at least work was simple. Straightforward. Show up, do a good job, go home. But it's not just about doing a good job anymore. It's about putting myself out there, committing myself to something I shouldn't have.

Olivia will be so angry . . .

Tessa won't keep it a secret . . .

My stomach flip-flops, and I hate this feeling, hate the nerves and dread. I don't know how to handle tension or confrontations. I do anything to avoid conflict, going so far as to stay married for a year to a man who doesn't want me, won't kiss or touch me, just to put off admitting failure publicly and filing for divorce.

Tessa, apparently in a Celtic Goth mood, enters the kitchen in her all-black ensemble consisting of leggings, long skirt, black knit top, and massive silver Celtic cross. She opens the mini fridge, pulls out her second can of Dr Pepper this morning even though it's not even eleven. Tessa is one of those unfortunates who need caffeine but don't like coffee. Actually, she likes hardly anything, but that's neither here nor there.

"How is your intrepid leader?" she asks now, popping open the tab.

"Fine." I don't understand the bad blood between Tessa and Olivia. These are two smart, creative, ambitious women. They should be on the same team. They'd be so much stronger that way.

"Any progress on the publicity side of things?"

It's been a week, and I've achieved next to nothing. "I'm hoping to meet Brian Fadden for coffee later."

"Brian Fadden?"

She sounds dubious, and I take a sip of my tea, nod nonchalantly. "Why so surprised?" I ask, wanting more information and yet not wanting to sound as if I'm digging.

"No reason. Except he hates City Events, thanks to Olivia."

"What did Olivia do?"

"What does she always do?"

I don't know the answer to this. I haven't been around long enough to see a pattern of behavior. My silence irritates Tessa, and she gives her head a short, impatient shake. "Forget it. You're still in the naive, I-just-want-everybody-to-like-me stage."

"I do want Olivia to like me."

"Why?" The freckles on Tessa's narrow nose stand out. She's a lucky redhead; her freckles are few and pert and rather pretty, but she has a sharp temper and an even sharper tongue. You can hear the Long Island accent if you listen for it. "Why does it matter what anyone thinks of you? All that really matters is what you think of yourself."

Again I don't have an answer, and Tessa swears, something with an expletive and "stupid women," before walking out.

Feeling sick, I return to my cubicle. As I fumble with paperwork, I become conscious of Tessa in her office at her desk and conscious of Olivia in her office at her desk, and I think it's just a matter of time before I ruin everything.

Thankfully, both Olivia and Tessa have afternoon appointments, and the minute Olivia steps out, I reach for the phone.

I'm terrified of calling Brian Fadden, since it's obvious that everyone at City Events knows him (and it sounds as if there's history of sorts between him and Olivia), but I'm more terrified of failing, and I battle terrors. If I were someone else . . . someone like my brother, Jamie, I'd be fearless. If I were Jamie with his string of social and athletic successes, I could pick up the phone with impunity, dial Brian Fadden's number, tell him what I want, why I'm calling, without suffering this enormity of fear.

But I'm not Jamie, and I only like calling people when I'm in a position of granting favors. I like to be in control, not dependent on others, and clearly, in this case I am dependent on others. I'm very dependent on the kindness— or at least civility—of strangers.

Think about David. Tony. All the people like them who've been helped by the Hospice Foundation.

I punch in the number before courage, and opportunity, fade.

"Fadden."

My God. He answered, himself. First ring.

For a moment my jaw works, and I see him at his desk. I know the inner workings of newspapers (okay, the *Fresno Bee*, but a paper is a paper is a paper), and I realize that these guys' desks are crammed together and they all have more work than money and, frankly, everyone calls in, bugging them. Wanting something. And I'm the one who wants something this time.

"My name's Holly Bishop. I'm with City Events," I plunge in, going for it before he can stop me. "We organize the Leather and Lace Ball—"

"Oh, that."

Not an auspicious beginning. "Have you been?"

Snide sound. *"No."*

"You should. It's a great event—"

"Have you been?"

"Not yet, but I'm going to this year."

He says nothing. I picture him tapping a pencil on his desk. He wants off the phone. I don't blame him. "I've got to drop some artwork by your building later today," I lie. "I was hoping you'd have ten minutes free for coffee."

"I'm sorry . . ." He pauses, searches; he doesn't remember my name. "I've got a lot on my plate right now. We're hiring a new editor; I'm covering for someone else—"

"Five minutes."

I hear his sigh. I feel his irritation. He doesn't want to talk to me, doesn't have the energy to waste, but Olivia's right, he's not quite rude enough just to hang up on me.

Poor guy. He's a nice guy.

"I know what you want," he says, "but I can't give you the editorial space. And we already have something about the event in the Calendar section."

"Why wouldn't you go to the ball?"

"What?"

"You've lived here how long?"

"Ten years, give or take a few."

"In ten years, why didn't you ever go to the Leather and Lace Ball?"

"Not my thing."

"You don't like costumes?"

"Don't like costumes, don't like yuppies, don't like forking out a couple hundred bucks to be with a bunch of people I don't know and won't like."

"You've made some good points."

"Good. And, um . . ." He's searching for my name again. "I wish there was more I could do, but the economy's hurting, people are being selective in how they spend their money, and frankly, I couldn't endorse the ball if I tried—"

"Not even though it helps hundreds of people who are dying?"

He splutters. Laughs. He must have been drinking something. "It's not about dying."

"It is. The ball benefits the Hospice Foundation."

"Very little goes to the foundation. We ran an article a couple years ago, and the majority of black-tie fund-raisers spend a dollar for every dollar they earn."

"Eighty-two percent of every ticket sold to the ball goes straight to the Hospice Foundation—"

"That's impossible."

"David Burkheimer underwrites the ball."

Brian Fadden isn't saying anything, and I'm not sure what he's thinking, but I keep going. "I don't think people know what the ball is for anymore. I think the event has been around long enough that people have lost sight of the need, of the suffering. AIDS isn't gone. It's still an epidemic, and it's still taking the lives of young people—men, women; destroying families."

"Okay."

"Maybe the ball isn't new and exciting, but it practically funds the foundation every year; and maybe the foundation will need to find alternative sources of funding, but they don't have it yet, and they need the ball. San Francisco needs the ball. It's not an event that should be dismissed."

"Okay."

"Nobody should have to be alone or in an institution at the end. People should be allowed to die with dignity—"

"Okay. Got it. Enough." He's finally silenced me. "Coffee. Ten minutes. But today's no good. How about tomorrow?"

I'm grinning. I feel as if I had just won the Tour de France. I practically pump the air. He said coffee. And he said ten minutes. Not five. Ten. "Wonderful."

"How's three?"

"Great."

"Have the front desk let me know you've arrived. I'll warn them that I'm expecting you." He pauses. "And who did you say you were?"

"Holly Bishop." And I'm still smiling.

At home that night I have a message from Tom and a message from Paul Petersen. I delete Tom's message and call Paul back.

He's called to see if I've got time for dinner on

Saturday night, and the words "dinner" and "Saturday night" are enough to make my blood run cold.

I like Paul. But I don't want to date him, and I also don't want to hurt him, because I don't yet have enough friends to start alienating more than one a week. "How about Thursday?" I propose. Thursday night isn't a date night, and it's near enough the end of the week to sound better than a Tuesday night dinner, which always sounds rather like Shrove Tuesday regardless of the time of year.

He counters with Friday night. I counter with Wednesday. We settle on Thursday, and then we chat a while about a book he's reading that was heralded as brilliant and groundbreaking but is really just crap. When I finally hang up, I see I was on the phone for nearly a half hour.

If we can talk for a half hour on the phone about nothing, dinner shouldn't be a problem.

Morning arrives too soon, and with my venti Starbucks nonfat white chocolate mocha sans whipped cream in hand, I settle at my desk and get to work. I'm so immersed in what I'm doing that I forget to take lunch (which was meant to be spent at the gym), and am only roused by the ringing of the phone.

It's Brian Fadden. He's called to cancel our meeting. "Okay," I say, and I must sound very small and sad and pathetic, because he suddenly sighs.

"How about on Thursday? I'll be in your vicinity late tomorrow morning. I could do a quick coffee then."

Thursday, two days from now. Thursday, which is getting quite busy with my two engagements in one day—Brian Fadden in the morning, and dinner with Paul Petersen at night. "Sure."

"Mr. J's?" he suggests.

"Perfect." It's a funky coffeehouse not far from the office.

Before I know it, it's Thursday, and I still haven't been to the gym or produced the numbers Olivia needs for the Oracle proposal, but I'm at Mr. J's, trying not to look anxious, trying not to look as though I'm looking for someone, although of course I'm looking, since I have no idea who Brian is or what to expect.

"Holly?"

I turn abruptly, look up. It's a long look up. He's tall, easily six three, possibly six four. "Brian?"

"You sound surprised."

I do, because I am. Brian Fadden is the name of a short, wide writer, not a guy who looks as if he could have played basketball at Cal. Brian's not handsome, but he's also not at all unattractive. In fact, with that little smile he's smiling now, he's quite attractive. Wavy brown hair, light blue eyes, a pair of wire-rimmed glasses, and a face that looks smart, literate, competent.

So he's handsome.

I rise, stick out my hand, shake his. "Thanks for meeting me."

His mouth quirks. "You don't look like Olivia's usual girl Friday."

I didn't know Olivia had girls Friday. "What's the usual?"

"Hard, tight, I'm-going-to-nail-your-ass-to-the-wall."

"So I do need to get back to the gym."

He grins a broad, crooked grin, and his light brown hair kind of flops across his brow, and he's looking more literate by the moment. "Coffee?"

I reach for my wallet. "My treat."

"Not necessary—"

"Brian, if I thought a cup of java would buy you, I'd be sending coffee to your desk. I'm just being polite."

His eyebrows lift, and we both order. I pay. He's a cheap date. Seven dollars and fifty-eight cents total, and that includes tax.

We sit down with our coffees, and Brian leans back in his rattan chair, stretches his long legs out. He's wearing jeans and a funky tweedy blazer over a T-shirt. He could be a college professor on a campus somewhere.

"Where did you go to school?" I ask, intrigued by his glasses, his height, the way he fills out the blazer. He doesn't look muscular big, but his shoulders are wide and there's no obvious gut.

"Yale."

"Yale?"

"It's on the East Coast, New Haven, Conn—"

"I know where Yale is," I interrupt, thinking I like the way he speaks. It's his delivery, his expressions. He has a dry, wry wit, and it's been a long time since I talked with someone who made me feel like smiling. It's been since . . .

Jean-Marc.

I don't feel like smiling quite so much anymore.

"So you're new in the city?" Brian asks.

I nod. "Been here three and a half months."

"You're still counting in terms of weeks, I see."

"It's been an adjustment."

"Where are you from?"

"You'll make fun of it."

"I won't."

"You will."

"I won't."

"People like you always do."

He pushes his glasses higher on the bridge of his nose. "Now, that's just offensive. You don't even know me. You can't categorize me yet."

I hold my cup in two hands, blow on the steam. "I've moved up from Fresno."

His lips twitch. He takes off his glasses, makes a show of polishing the lenses. "I'm sorry."

"Fuck you."

He laughs. Slides his glasses back on. "That's terrible language, Miss Bishop—" He breaks off, looks at me. "It is Miss, isn't it?"

"Ms."

"Never been married?"

I look down at the table. "Going through a divorce."

"How long were you married?"

"A little over a year."

"I made it to ten. My divorce was final last week."

I look up at him, see if he's smiling but he's not. His eyes are sober behind the wire-rimmed glasses, and he's looking at me intently, as if trying to see whatever it is I won't let him see. "It's hard, isn't it?"

"Yeah." And I can still see my wedding dress so clearly, see the pale ivory silk, the crystal beading, the snug skirt with the bustle at the back. It was like a turn-of-the-century evening gown, all Wharton-James style, so elegant, so foreign, so dreamy me.

What a mistake.

I can never pass that wedding gown on to a daughter, can't ever do anything with it, can't try it on again, remember it, love it.

It's a dress I wore to nowhere, and stupid me, my eyes are burning.

I wish I'd never been a bride if it meant there'd be no marriage.

I wish I'd just shacked up with Jean-Marc and not worried what my family would think.

I wish . . . I wish . . . and looking up, I meet Brian Fadden's gaze, and his expression is strangely compassionate. But this isn't a social visit; this is business, and I have to pull myself together.

"I used to be the features editor at the *Fresno Bee*," he says, as if this is a peace offering.

I'm not sure, but I could have sworn he said the *Fresno Bee*, as in Fresno's morning newspaper, as in Fresno's only newspaper. "The *Bee*?"

"For nearly a year."

"When?"

"A couple years ago."

"How did that happen?"

We're both kind of smiling, and he shrugs. "I'd been working at the *Chronicle* for a couple years as a staff writer, got a call from someone down in Fresno, did some interviews, was offered the job, took it."

"And then realized you were trapped in a one-horse town?" But I mean this in the best sort of way because I was raised in one-horse towns, and I understand them, but then, I didn't go to Yale, and I didn't live in New Haven, and I'm not a senior editor at the *Chronicle*, either.

"It wasn't *that* bad."

"So why, then, did you only last a year?"

"Eleven months and one week. But that's because the *Chronicle* brought me back. Lured me with a promotion."

"I can't imagine it took much luring."

"Fresno was a little slow for my tastes."

"I bet."

His cell phone rings; he checks the number, apologizes to me, and takes the call. He's only on the phone a moment, but when he hangs up, he looks ready to go.

"Problems?" I ask.

"Always." He grimaces, and I think I really like his

face. It's a comfortable face, a good face, and I was right about him on the phone. He's a nice guy.

"If you can bring me something new," he says now, putting away his phone, "give me something to work with, I'll see if I can't get someone to do a little write-up, but there's no way I can advocate editorial space if it's not newsworthy."

"Understood." We both stand, and I extend my hand again. "Thanks so much for taking time to meet me."

"My pleasure."

I think he's reaching for his keys, but instead it's his business card. He hands it to me. It's got his direct line on it, along with his e-mail address. "Stay in touch," he says.

I quickly dig out a card of my own and give it to him. "I will. You, too."

And we leave Mr. J's. Brian turns right; I turn left, and as I walk the couple of blocks back to the office, I study his business card.

Brian Fadden.

Brian Fadden.

It'd be great if he called, invited me out sometime. But knowing how things work in my world, he probably won't.

★ . 8 ★

$\mathcal{I}$'m still studying Brian Fadden's card when I step off the elevator and into our second-floor loft office. So engrossed in Brian's name and number am I, that I walk through the office reception without looking up.

"Holly." Josh's voice stops me as I head for my cubicle.

I look up, not entirely pleased to be pulled from my wishful thinking. Fantasies are so much more pleasurable than real life, and I can guarantee a happy ending. "What?"

"Olivia's been looking for you," he says, and although the words are innocuous enough, his tone conveys a warning. Something's not right.

My stomach free-falls, and I quickly drop Brian's card into my purse. "Do you know what she wants?"

"The Oracle info."

Right. And of course it's not together. "I don't have it yet."

"So she discovered." He pauses. "When she went through your files." Another uncomfortable pause. "You are careful with your files, aren't you?"

I know what he's saying, what he's asking, and I manage a sickly smile. "Definitely." *Not.* And I start for my desk, tugging off my coat. "Is she here right now?"

"No. She had a meeting with the Beckett board, but she should be back soon."

"I'll get on the Oracle stuff now. Maybe I can have it done by the time she returns."

"It's a nice thought." And Josh clears his throat. "Um, Holly, one more thing."

I look up at him, trying to hide my panic because I'm freaked, freaked that Olivia went through my files, freaked that she might have seen something she shouldn't have seen. Like the notes all over the inside of a folder, regarding staff writers contacted at the various papers. "What?"

His expression is downright apologetic. "Your mom is here."

He might as well be speaking Greek. "What?"

"Your mom arrived just after you left to meet Fadden. She's in David's office."

He's got to have it wrong. He's thinking of someone else. My mother doesn't leave the San Joaquin Valley. Those foothills and mountain ranges keep her from getting lost. "My mom?"

He points toward David's office. David's been gone all week on a trip back east, but the light is on in his office, and, brow furrowing, I stare into the office. And yes, Josh is right. A lady sits in there, hands folded in her lap, studying the wall of awards and blown-up press clippings, the clippings now huge, colorful posters, mounted, laminated, hung up for all to see.

She's medium height. Medium build. With medium graying brown hair. In a glaring pink and turquoise dress.

Mom.

For a second I feel as if someone had hit me over the head with a two-by-four. Seeing her here, sitting in one of David's mammoth leather chairs, makes absolutely no sense.

And then she looks up, and her expression lightens, and Mom's on her feet, arms outstretched, waving madly. But the wave isn't enough. Her fingers—all ten of them—are wiggling delightedly. "Holly!"

The wiggling fingers have stilled, and her arms flap now. She's guiding traffic or trying to take off in flight—I'm really not sure which—and I dart a quick glance in Josh's direction and am relieved to see that his expression is courteously blank.

I can't help wondering if Josh's Beckett School alum father married a woman like my mom, and somehow I doubt it. People with serious money dress with serious intent: understated, sophisticated wardrobe pieces, expensive understated footwear, shimmering yet unassuming makeup and hair color. I love my mother, but she's far from understated. She's like that girl in high school who tries too hard—and is still trying too hard nearly forty years later.

But maybe it doesn't have anything to do with trying so hard. Maybe it's just survival. We couldn't afford a cushy house or car, clothes that didn't come from Target, JC Penney, or Mervyn's. There were no trips to posh hair salons or weekly appearances from cleaning people, yard people, child-care people. Mom did everything.

And now Mom is in David's doorway, and she's still waving, but it's become a big two-arm wave, like the guys at the airport on the tarmac directing pilots and their planes. *Come this way, right this way, easy, that's nice, slow, slow, okay, almost there, yes! Engines off . . .*

I drop my coat and purse on my desk, tucking a loose bit of hair behind my ear before I head toward David's office. "Mom."

Josh discreetly fades into the background, and my mother throws her arms around me. "Holly." She squeezes me hard. "Holly. Holly. Hol—"

"Hi, Mom." I give her a quick, panicked squeeze back before letting go. Mom's voice is loud enough that I'm certain everyone can hear her maternal proclamations of love, and I appreciate the love—we all need love—but in my four-plus months working at City Events I've never seen another parent put in an appearance.

"Holly, this is quite an office," Mom says, adjusting the strap of her purse on her arm. "Very, very impressive."

I look up and around. "It is, isn't it?"

"Look at all these awards," she adds, gesturing to the wall of awards and blown-up news clippings. "Obviously a successful company."

I'm pleased she thinks so, and I beam. "Yes."

Again she glances up at the wall and then looks back to me, and a hint of puzzlement creases her eyes. "So what do *you* do here?"

I hesitate. "Events." Her puzzlement hasn't cleared so I add, "*Plan* events."

"Plan events?"

"I'm an event planner."

The creases deepen in her forehead and around her eyes. "You know how to do that?"

I'm beginning to feel a little prickly. "It's what I did in Fresno, Mom."

"You *did*?"

"That's all I've ever done."

She makes a little sound, a puff of air as she exhales in utter surprise. "I had no idea."

I swear, this has been our relationship from birth. I smother my frustration. Can't be frustrated with Mom. Love Mom. She's my mom. Mom needs love.

Take a deep breath, Holly, I say to myself. *Think nice thoughts.* "So what are you doing in the city?"

A new, fine frown line puckers between her brows. Her eyebrows are thinner, sparser, and for a moment I'm worried—cancer? Stress? And then I realize she's just overplucked them.

"I love San Francisco," she says.

She hasn't been here in years. She hates driving in cities, has the same phobia I do about steep hills, runaway cable cars, and earthquakes.

"Did you come to see me?" I ask.

She looks startled, draws her purse against her middle. "No."

Things feel hot inside me, hot and tight, and I want to hug her, if only to keep from throttling her. Mom and I have issues going back to, well, birth. It's been this way since the beginning. I was her hardest delivery. I was her colicky baby. I was the dark, hairy girl when she wanted a beautiful blond boy named Jack. Apparently I never did figure out how to latch on properly and I wouldn't nurse right, and then when she'd burp me, I'd spew. Apparently I hated her singing voice. And the way she walked me. And the clothes she bought me. And we're still talking the first year of my life.

But hey, that's all history. "When did you arrive, Mom?"

"Just a few minutes ago."

"Did you fly?"

"Fly?" She has that slightly bewildered look again, which sends my blood pressure spiking. Airplanes are not generational. They had airplanes when she was a child, too. "Mom. Did you drive?"

"Of course."

This is my mother. I don't know what else to say. Everyone has a mother. And I love my mother. It's just so . . . complicated . . . and I don't want to feel this way. I don't want to be angry or frustrated. I don't want to sound irritable with her, either. I just wish she had called me, let me know she was coming. I would have at least been . . . prepared.

Or at least had the chance to advise her on her wardrobe. No bright colors, loud patterns, elasticized waistbands.

No open-toe heels in shades of pink or green.

No oversize purses that don't match anything.

And I don't know whether it's her bright geometric/ floral/neon dress, or that she's sitting in a chair big enough for a pro basketball player, but she looks so much smaller than I remembered. When *was* the last time I saw her? Memorial Day weekend? Easter?

Josh's head suddenly appears in the doorway, his brown eyes extremely apologetic. "Sorry to interrupt, but, Holly, you've got a call." He grimaces. "Olivia . . ."

Olivia. "Mom, I've got to take that call. It's my boss—"

"That's fine." Mom waves grandly. "I'm in no hurry and I've got"—she gestures to Josh—"your friend to talk to."

I look at Josh, smile weakly. "I'll be right back."

Olivia's terse on the line. "I can't believe you didn't have those numbers for me." Her voice is low, clipped, furious. "I'm in the middle of a presentation without any of the numbers I needed. I look like a damn fool!"

I feel little prickles of heat. "Can I give you something now?"

"It's a little late."

"I'm sorry—"

"I needed those numbers today."

"I'll have them for you today."

"You'll e-mail them out this afternoon and then follow up with a FedEx hard copy before you leave tonight. Understand?"

"Yes."

Olivia slams the phone down in my ear, and I more slowly replace mine.

It's going to be a long afternoon.

Returning to David's office, I walk in on Mom regaling Josh with stories of my awkward youth. "First time in high heels and panty hose, Holly slips—"

"*Mom!*"

Mom ignores me. "Slips in her new heels and falls in front of the entire church congregation." Now she looks at me. "You were fourteen?"

"Thirteen," I say flatly, mortified.

"She put a huge hole in her panty hose and burst into tears."

"I hurt my knee, Mom."

"I know, but it wasn't the grand entrance you'd hoped, was it?"

No, Mom, it wasn't. Tripping and falling in front of three people is embarrassing, let alone in front of a hundred. I was so excited about those shoes. My first real high heels.

I've never forgotten that day, and I wouldn't even remember those shoes, if I hadn't slipped and gone down the church's brick steps.

This had been my big moment. New, fashionably short beige skirt, suntan-colored panty hose, and heeled pumps—I was so sure everybody would look at me and think I was beautiful.

Instead old people rushed to help me while my own sister, Ashlee, laughed hysterically.

I'd wish bad things on Ashlee, but she's still struggling to get through college (starting her fifth—sixth?—year), so I can't be too unkind.

But Mom's moved on, and she turns to Josh. "So you do events, too?"

Josh nods, glances at me. "Yes."

Mom shakes her head in wonder. "I had no idea Holly did this kind of thing. I always thought she was a secretary—"

"Mom!"

"Personal assistant?"

"No, Mom. Never." My face is burning up. I'm so hot, so frustrated, so angry. Doesn't Mom listen to anything I tell her? Would it be too much trouble to get her facts right about the one daughter who *has* a job and continues to be financially self-sufficient? "I've never done clerical work. I've always been in marketing and public relations, even at a junior level."

"There's nothing wrong with clerical work." Mom

suddenly sounds injured. "I've been a bookkeeper for twenty years. It's paid the bills. Put a roof over your head. Even paid for that fancy fairy-tale wedding you wanted!"

Please, please, ground, open up—San Andreas Fault, shift now, and swallow me whole. I can't bear this. Can't bear to be reminded of all my faults and shortcomings. "You did," I say, wanting peace, wanting to move past this painful topic. "You have. I'm sorry."

Josh puts out his arm, extending his hand toward Mother. "It was a pleasure meeting you, Mrs. Bishop."

Mom visibly relaxes a little and shakes his hand. "It was a pleasure meeting you, too, Joshua."

She watches him leave, and I watch Mom's face. I can see she's still upset with me, and I'm not sure what I'm going to do with her. I glance up at the clock on David's wall, see that it's nearly two, and I still have Olivia's mandate hanging over my head.

"Have you had lunch, Mom?"

"Are you going to lunch?"

She sounds so hopeful, and I feel terrible because I'm going to disappoint her, just as I've disappointed her ever since that traumatic birth and latching-on nightmare. Apparently Ashlee and brother Jamie had no problem nursing, or keeping their milk down, or sleeping through the night. They were, by all accounts, dream babies. "I hadn't planned on it. I've just come from a meeting, and I have this Oracle account I'm working on—"

"Don't worry about me."

She says it too quickly, and the problem is, I do worry, and the fact that I can feel so much worry and angst on her behalf doesn't make this relationship any simpler.

"I'm fine," she adds, her voice airy, casual (she's *not* casual), and everything inside me bunches up.

We've been in this odd partnership for, oh, twenty-five years, and I think she should know how much I love her, but I don't think she does, and being me, I don't know how to tell her. I don't know how to talk to her. "If this account weren't a problem at the moment, I'd take you to lunch now. I would—"

"Of course." And she's smiling at me, fiercely determined to be kind and patient, but I see something else in her eyes. I see that hidden puzzlement I've witnessed all my life, ever since Dad left, and it breaks my heart in a way that Jean-Marc never did.

Mother shouldn't have been left. No woman should be left, but especially not my mom. I don't want to, but every time I look at her face, I see her past, see the childhood, where they didn't have a lot and there wasn't always security, or love. And I want her to have that security, and the love, but she didn't get it from Dad, and she isn't getting it from me.

"Maybe I can get off early," I say, feigning optimism because there isn't a chance in hell I'll be going anywhere soon. I don't have Olivia's numbers, because before I met with Brian Fadden, I spent the morning trying to connect with Perry Zeeb from one of the TV stations, and Melinda

Martinez at the *Examiner*, but she never returned my calls. So although I worked all morning, it wasn't what Olivia wanted me to accomplish, which is why the info for the Oracle proposal was never pulled together, which is why Olivia is going to be livid when she returns from the Beckett meeting.

"Don't worry if you can't, honey. I understand."

"Thanks." For a moment I'm not sure what to say, or what I should suggest. If I gave her directions to my apartment, would she find her way there? If I offered to treat her to a spa manicure and pedicure at the Vietnamese nail salon down the street, would she agree? (No. And no.)

"I was hoping I could meet some of your new friends," she says after a moment, clutching her purse again, smiling shyly. "Just so I could get a feel for your new life."

I glance back at my cubicle, see no one stirring. I think half the office is gone (since David is), and the rest doesn't want to be visible. This office isn't into family visits. Most of us moved to the city to escape our families, nearly all having issues with our past, and to be brutally honest, unless someone in your family is an extremely important person, that person probably doesn't matter.

Just as my mother doesn't matter.

I know this, recognize this, and hate it all the same. Everyone knows my story—at least where I'm from—and while they don't know where Mom was born, they can guess.

Mother was raised in Coalinga, California, and has spent her life making sure she knows people, the right people, people who will get her out of Coalinga and keep her out.

Which explains Father.

However, the essential thing to know about Coalinga isn't Father—I really try hard not to think about him, and he makes it easy by behaving as if we kids never existed, except for his showing up at my wedding late and then leaving early—it's that if you can survive a life in one of Central California's little cow towns, you can survive anything life throws at you.

I'm not trying to be cruel. I'm the girl who grew up thinking a good party was a two-kegger in an orchard. Growing up provincial had its merits.

Like Mother's ability to be outwardly calm when disaster strikes. The sky could fall, and my mother would be the only one not running around screaming. Okay. Maybe she ought to be running, if only to look for shelter, but she wouldn't panic. Because she wouldn't do anything.

Mother certainly didn't do anything when Dad left all those years ago. She didn't take to her bed. Didn't drink, pop pills. Didn't vow to clean him out by going to court. No, Mom was very controlled. And civil. She wrapped her pride around her nice and tight, kept her chin up, attended all the usual social functions, and managed to convince everyone she was better off without Ted.

She was so convincing that in no time she had everyone thinking that Ted's leaving was a godsend and that the only tragedy here was that he didn't do it years earlier.

It wasn't, of course, that easy. Mom suffered. I know she did. I just don't know how, as she's kind of a mystery lady. She's present but not. Kind but defensive. Positive but petrified.

I suppose I don't know her at all.

"Everybody's in meetings," I say, trying to ignore two of Tessa's girls turning the corner and walking down the hall to the break room. "It's really crunch time right now around here."

"I shouldn't have come. I'm sorry."

This is why I wish Mom had remarried. A new husband might have kept her off San Francisco's streets and from blurting misery-inducing things like this. But Mom never did remarry, nor did she ever get serious again. In the beginning there were a string of casual dates, but eventually even those faceless, nameless men disappeared.

"Don't say that, Mom." I'm already assailed by guilt. I haven't seen my mother in months. We never really talk, even though she tries to call once every couple of weeks; but she usually calls me at home during the day, and I'm not at home during the day—I'm at City Events—and she'll leave messages like this: *Oh, Holly* (sigh) *it seems I've missed you again. We never do seem to connect.*

That's right, Mom. Because you call me at the apartment when I'm working, and you call work when I'm at the apartment. I almost want to give her a crib sheet, a little chart, marking workdays and weekends and attaching the right phone number to the right day.

There's no reason for her to be so confused. Childbirth couldn't have taken that much out of her. Sometimes I even wonder how she managed to snag Ted, my so-called dad (it's not nice, but I'm more comfortable thinking of him as a sperm donor than as my father), because she can be pretty damn clueless.

But I'm now feeling bad for having bad feelings, and the guilt grows. "I can't get away now," I repeat, "but maybe I could round up a few people and we all go to dinner." I don't even know where this thought comes from. I don't know how I let it pop out of my mouth. It's not as if I even have friends to round up, but I'm desperate to feel like a nicer person again, and Mom does appreciatively brighten.

"That sounds like fun."

Not really. I don't know where I'm going to find friends, and I don't know where we should go to dinner, and I feel like Tom Cruise in *Mission Impossible VI*. Why are we even making this film? "I'll work on firming dinner plans."

"Where will we go?"

"Let me think about it." I'm already feeling claustrophobic. She's a dear, dear lady, but she should have had a good, sweet daughter. Not me. "Why don't you go to Union Square, do some shopping, maybe get tea at Neiman Marcus?"

"I'd rather have tea with you."

"Then shop! You know I hate shopping."

Mom's expression falls. "I do, too."

She sounds forlorn again, and I'm Cruel Joke for a Daughter. "Why not wander around a little, take in the sights, and then we'll meet up for dinner?"

"But where?"

I struggle to think of a place near Union Square that Mom would like and that I could convince some of my colleagues to go to, because the people here at City Events are the only people I even know in the city. Immediately Josh comes to mind. I'll approach him first. He'll have a hard time telling me no if I get down on my knees and weep.

"I'll think of something." There are lots of little places by Union Square, lots of big, expensive hotel restaurants, lots to choose from, but right now I can't think of one.

Suddenly Mom's eyes light. Her mouth opens. She has an idea.

"What?"

"The Tonga Room," she breathes reverently.

The Tonga Room at the Fairmont? There's no way in hell I'd ever get anyone from work to go there. Not even Josh. Although . . . if Josh *is* gay, he might like it. But I don't think he's gay. I think he's from a wealthy, oppressive family that lacks a sense of humor. "Mom—"

"We went there when you were little."

"I remember."

"You loved it, Holly."

I did. But I was eight.

"It rains from the ceiling, Holly."

Yes, it's a Polynesian tropical paradise complete with a band playing on a floating raft, thunderstorms, exotic bird calls, and outrageously priced Chinese food, but it's also my last memory of dinner with Ted—Dad—before he packed up and left.

"Oh, Holly . . ." Mom's eyes are shining, and clearly she doesn't remember the Tonga Room the way I do. "It'd be so fun. With your new friends it'd be a party."

She doesn't know I haven't made friends yet. She doesn't know I'm barely able to cover my rent and, worse, that my landlady's a bitch. She doesn't know I get parking tickets right and left. She doesn't know I still get lost when I drive around the city.

But she's smiling. And I feel a pang, the way her eyes light up. I hate seeing her like this. Girlish. Excited. Hopeful. It reminds me of how she must have been, once upon a time before she married Ted and had us.

Ted's a bastard.

Ted left her with his three little Bishops (Jamie, Holly, and Ashlee) and a houseful of heartbreak in the middle of Central California. He moved south, somewhere sunny and beachy in Southern Cal, and with the help of some mind-science church he discovered his true self. (Praise the power of the mind!) And Mom continues to struggle along, doing her best, which means instead of being on some cruise ship in the Panama Canal meeting sex-starved sixty-year-olds (preferably male, but hey, I'm open-minded), she's in San Francisco for some mother-daughter bonding time.

I'd say it's a fate worse than death, but that's actually reserved for my night out with Lehman.

"Call the Tonga Room," Mom says.

I really want to be a good daughter, I do, but I'm dragging my feet here. "I don't know if I can get reservations."

She lifts a hand, a careless wave. "I'll go there myself. Speak with the manager. See what I can do." She winks, suddenly self-important, suddenly surprisingly pretty. Even if her dress hurts my eyes. "How many should I say, Holly?"

How many? There's a good question for you. How about two, Mom? You and me. But I'm going for broke; I'm going to be outrageous here. "Let's say four—"

"Just four?"

"It's Thursday night. Lots of people work late, and they still have to get in early tomorrow."

"Okay." Her smile returns. She leans forward, presses a kiss to my cheek, and then a little pat with her hand. "What time shall we say?"

"Seven thirty?"

"That's so late!"

I think about the work waiting for me, I think about Olivia's temper, but this is also my mom's first visit to the city in years, and I know she's excited. "Six thirty?"

"*Holly.*"

"It'll take us a half hour with traffic."

"But Nob Hill's not that far!"

"It's the city, Mom." I can't say no to her. I hate that; I hate that I can't say what I want, or tell her what I feel. "Fine," I say with a small sigh. "Six o'clock."

"Six o'clock," Mom repeats. "For four." Her purse changes hands. She looks invigorated, almost young. "See you then, honey."

Mom leaves, and I go back to my desk, and immediately the office is a beehive of activity.

Tessa appears at my desk, soon followed by Josh and then delicate little Sara.

"Your mom?" Tessa asks, leaning against my cubicle wall, downing a little silver can of Red Bull, but it's not a question; it's a statement, and I can't help thinking that Tessa's the last person who should be drinking Red Bull. She's by far the most creative director with her wardrobe. Today she's wearing a short red vinyl skirt, red tights, a black leather vest, and black combat boots.

"Yes."

"She wasn't here long," Tessa adds, taking another hit from her can. "You should have taken her on a tour around the office, introduced her to everyone."

Mom would have loved that. She would have been thrilled by a guided tour, getting the official "Here's my desk, here's the break room, here's where we make coffee, and that's where I make my photocopies" description.

My throat suddenly feels lumpy, and I swallow hard as a big red neon sign, like those applause cues in TV studios, blinks BAD DAUGHTER over my head.

Everybody's waiting for me to say something now. "I was worried about Olivia returning," I say, feeling lame, and it is lame. "I'm behind on work and didn't think she'd appreciate my mom hanging around."

Tessa crunches her now empty can. "Olivia doesn't own the office."

Josh nods.

Sara just continues to monitor everything like a little whatever-she-is. I have not figured Sara out yet. She might be a lot of fun (if she ever talked), or she might be a drone (which I think everyone thinks I am), or she might be someone dangerous, which I doubt, but you never know.

"I know, I—" and I break off, feeling even more like a lame-ass because my mom never comes to the city, we never do "girl things" together, and yet I've been really lonely, and good company would be nice.

And maybe that's why I'm nervous about Mom being here. She's good, and she's company, but I wouldn't exactly call her good company. I just get so uptight around her, my insides knotting, and somehow I go from zero to sixty in no time flat. "I wasn't sure about protocol."

"If my mom were here, I wouldn't give a flying fuck

about protocol or what anyone might think," Tessa answered, tossing the smashed Red Bull can into my trash bin. Two points.

"Is your mom in New York?" Sara asks Tessa.

Sara doesn't usually speak directly to Tessa. It's kind of an unwritten team rule. Each team has its own members, and members fraternize with one another, not with the enemy team. But somehow, now that Tessa and I have broken the ice, Josh seems just as comfortable talking to Tessa as he does with Olivia.

"No," Tessa answers flatly, and Josh, in his brown cords and nondescript beige shirt, is listening intently.

"Is she in New Jersey, then?" Sara persists, and Tessa gives Sara a drop-dead look.

"No." Tessa tugs on her red tights, pulling them higher on her skinny thighs. "My mom's dead. She died when I was four." And then she walks away, combat boots clomping violently as though she's a hotheaded Irish looking for a fight.

For a moment no one speaks. Sara just looks at me and then Josh before slinking away.

Josh remains. "That explains a lot," he says after a moment, staring after Tessa.

"Does it?" And in Josh's face I see something new, something different, something . . . protective.

He doesn't like Tessa, does he?

"She's like a character from a Hemingway novel," he says, and I try to follow this figurative leap, because it has to be figurative. Hemingway didn't really write about women, did he?

I look down the corridor toward Tessa's office. "I wonder what she'd do if I invited her to join Mom and me for dinner."

"Where are you going to dinner?"

I'm jerked back to the stark reality of a weekend alone with my mother. "The Tonga Room."

Josh nods. "I love that place. I'm really into the old tiki thing. I used to collect hula dancer dolls."

Okay, he has to be gay. That's *not* a heterosexual man talking right now.

"You're welcome to come," I say, fingers crossed that he'll say yes, but I don't want to come on too strong, for fear of scaring him away. I have to have at least one friend attend dinner with me tonight, or Mom will think I haven't made any friends yet (which is true), and she'll worry about me more (which would mean more visits and phone calls). "My mom is hoping to meet some of my . . ."

My voice trails away, and Josh looks at me, then deadpans. "I'll be your token friend."

"You will?"

"Mmmm. After hearing that pitiful story about you falling as a kid in your new high heels—beige Naturalizers, your mom said—I think you need one."

And I smile, a funny, crooked smile because gay or straight, Josh has been nicer to me than anyone else I've met since I've moved to the city. "Thanks." My smile grows. "I'll go talk to Tessa."

"You better do it fast. Olivia will be back soon."

I can see Tessa through her open door. She's sitting cross-legged in her chair, staring intently at her computer screen.

"What do you want?" Tessa asks brusquely without glancing up from the computer.

She's uncomfortable. I realize she hadn't meant to say anything about her mom and is angry that she did.

Asking her to join me and my mom and Josh for dinner is nothing short of stupid and insensitive. I shouldn't do it.

"Well?" Tessa sighs with exaggerated patience, giving the edge of her desk a push, rolling her chair backward.

Don't be stupid, don't be stupid, don't be stupid—

"Would you like to join my mom and me for dinner?" I ask brightly, eyebrows lifted as if to convey *Fun! Excitement! Good Times for All!*

"Jesus, Mary, and—"

"My mom thinks I have friends," I say fast, cutting her short, mortified that I'm giving her the true version of events, but unable to lie. "She's going to a lot of effort to make dinner reservations for tonight, and . . ." I exhale, take a brittle breath. "I already feel like a schmuck for sending her away without the office tour. And now if I show up at her meet-Holly's-friends party without any friends, she'll think I'm mad at her, or embarrassed."

"Which you are."

Damn, Tessa's tough. "Not mad." I hesitate delicately. "Well, maybe mad. And maybe embarrassed."

"She's your *mom*."

"It's not that simple."

"What's to be embarrassed about?"

"It's not one thing; it's little things, lots of little things."

"Name one."

I stay silent. I don't want to do this. In high school it was cool to put your parents down, but I don't like criticizing my mom. At least not out loud.

"Come on." Tessa pushes for a reason.

Fine. If she wants a reason, she can have one. She can have ten. "My mom doesn't remember anything I tell her. Like what I do. Today she said she didn't know I was in PR, or that I'd handled events, and yet I invited her to a half-dozen different things when I worked in Fresno."

"What else?"

"She's always compared me to Ashlee, my younger sister, who starred on her volleyball team, never missed a prom, was crowned homecoming queen as well as Miss Congeniality in the local Miss America pageant."

"Wow." Tessa's impressed. "Quite a girl."

"Yes, she is. And that's how my mom wants me to be, but I'm not extroverted like that. I'm not a social butterfly. I don't even want to be a social butterfly."

"Then don't be. Be yourself," Tessa answers, unfolding her legs, dropping her feet on the floor so the heels of her boots thump, *boom-boom*. "God, I could use a smoke." She opens up her desk drawer, slams it shut, and then opens it again, fishes out some orange Tic Tacs, and then throws the Tic Tacs back into her drawer. "What time's dinner?"

"Six."

Tessa's dark red eyebrows arch. "Early."

"She's eager."

Tessa laughs, a surprisingly deep belly laugh. She may have an Irish temper, but she's got the Irish humor as well. "So where are we going?"

I gulp air. I can't believe she's going to go. "The Tonga Room."

And Tessa just laughs some more. "See you there."

I leave Tessa's office, and her laugh follows me down the corridor, all the way to my cubicle, where Olivia is sitting in my chair, filing her nails.

"Hey," I say, my face twitching from happy smile to horrified, petrified smile.

"Hhhheeeeey." Olivia mocks my greeting before blowing dust from the tip of one perfect nail. "So how are things, girl? Having a good day?"

I'm suddenly glad Mom's gone. I would not want Mom here for this. I'm going to get my butt kicked, and I'm going to feel pretty bad pretty quick.

"Okay," I say, trying to keep my smile. Olivia's also smiling, but her eyes are hard and she's pissed. I've seen her pissed before—not nice—but never at me until now.

Chilly smile. "How are my Oracle numbers coming along?"

"Pretty good."

"Can I see what you've got so far?"

I'm panicking, scrambling, thinking I've done it now, backed myself into a corner with a big fat lie. "I did have until five, didn't I?"

Her expression hardens. She studies me for an uncomfortably long time. "What were you talking to Tessa about?"

So that's what has set Olivia off. Not the fact that I don't have the Oracle info together. Not the media phone numbers on the inside of my file folder. Not my disappearance at eleven when I went to meet Brian Fadden. It strikes me that there's a lot I could get in trouble for—and it all has to do with me helping out on the Leather & Lace Ball. "My mom's in town. I invited Tessa to join us for dinner tonight."

"Tessa."

"I'm inviting everyone."

"Why?"

"My mom wanted to meet my . . . office colleagues."

Her eyes narrow. "I don't understand."

"Understand what?"

"Why she'd want to have dinner with the people you work with. And why you'd think it was appropriate to ask City Events staff to join you for dinner." Her hands with the long slim fingers flutter. "Holly, you're not in college. This isn't a sorority. This is business. Act like a professional."

I feel my jaw harden. I'm getting angry, and I don't want to get angry, not with Olivia, and not now, because

I can't hide my temper well and I'm not in a good position for an argument. I'm overwhelmed by my workload. I've made Olivia wait for information. I haven't acted properly obeisant. "I was simply being nice."

Olivia slowly rises from my chair. She's the most graceful woman I've ever met. Everything she does is beautiful, and as she turns to look at me, I'm reminded of a big cat before it pounces. "'Nice' is irrelevant. Success is important. And if you're not successful here, you won't be at City Events long."

She walks away, all long-legged, loose-hipped, the walk of a model on the European runway. For the first time, I think I could hate her. But I don't want to hate her. Olivia's brilliant. She's definitely got "it," and people respond. They can't help responding. Even I do.

I turn around, reach for the chair that Olivia has just vacated, and spot Sara standing not far from my cubicle. Her eyes are wide, and I wonder how long she's been there and how much she's heard. Plenty, I think.

I give Sara a long, unsmiling look.

"You're going to dinner with Tessa?" she asks, breaking the awkward silence.

Sara's blonde, a delicate Ivy League–type blonde, who favors black, gray, and navy cashmere. Everything she wears on her top half is cashmere. It's a nice look for her. But I'd never, ever buy two dozen of the same sweater. "It's an open invitation," I say. "You're welcome to join us."

"Josh is going?"

"Yes. We're meeting at the Tonga Room at six."

Sara casts a furtive glance around. "Is Olivia going?"

I let my eyebrows lift. "Did you hear our conversation?"

She colors, then mumbles something like, "I better not. I've got lots of work. The Schlessenger wedding and the, um, other things."

"Right." I pick up my pen and hit a key on my keyboard so the screen saver disappears, returning me to the Excel spreadsheet on my monitor. "Have a nice evening with the wedding and other things."

But Sara doesn't leave. She takes several steps toward me, leans over the edge of my desk. "You don't want Olivia mad."

She's right. I don't want Olivia mad, but I also refuse to be intimidated by Olivia's office politics. I've always done my own thing, made my own decisions, even if they're disastrous. "I'm not uninviting Tessa." I start scrolling through the spreadsheet. "I think it's great that Tessa wants to be supportive."

Sara stands there another moment. I can feel her frustration, as well as her indecision. And then, heaving a sigh, she walks away. I don't even glance up. I'm starting to realize that I can't make everybody happy today, and I'm not even going to try.

Josh and I end up driving together. The Fairmont is on Nob Hill and probably my favorite place for catching a cable car.

On Powell, at the top of the hill, you can see in all directions, and as the cable car descends, it rolls and grinds, hums and clanks, and the street and the cable car shudder as the conductor rings the bell, *ding-ding-ding*, and the brakeman works the gears.

After parking—a slow, painstaking process of inching up and back until I've squeezed into the spot on the street—I join Josh on the curb just as a cable car climbs the hill.

When I was little, I thought it was the shape of the cable car that made it so evocative, but now I know it's not the shape, or color, but the sound. That busy, cheerful hum-and-clank-and-ding sound is so San Francisco, at once festive and old-world, exciting and comforting, like Ghirardelli chocolates, clam chowder in sourdough bread bowls at Fisherman's Wharf, or the glimpse of the deep-orange Golden Gate Bridge poking through the morning fog.

The doorman at the Fairmont holds the door for us as we duck into the grand gilt-and-marble hotel lobby. I ended up in San Francisco because it was north of Fresno, not south, and because my father lives in the southern half of the state, and because I went to college down there and this time I wanted—needed—the unknown. The unknown was north, so that's why I'm here, but now that I'm here, I'm grateful.

We take the elevator downstairs, and as I walk through the hotel's hallway, I know San Francisco's right for me. It can't quite be classified as a fairy-tale city, because I've seen too many homeless people sleeping on corners and been chased once too often by deranged persons when leaving the theater in the Tenderloin district, but there is a fictional quality to it.

Maybe it's that whole western frontier movement, with the California gold rush and its infamous forty-niners (not the football team but the men and women who swarmed San Francisco in the height of gold rush fever), the hardy American novelists like Mark Twain and Jack London immortalizing life in the glorious new state of California, or the great earthquake and fire in 1906 that razed the city, but San Francisco is and always will be larger than life.

Mythical.

It's the mythical I relate to, and the mythical I feel as Josh and I enter the Tonga Room's exotic world of Polynesia. Tessa is already there, sitting with my mom, and they're both sipping enormous drinks festooned with spears of fresh fruit, garish paper umbrellas, and little plastic monkeys. Mom waves to us from across the room, and for a second all I can see is a blinding flash of turquoise and pink. *Please stay seated; please wave from a sitting position,* I pray silently, and miraculously, my mother does.

"We're having a great time," she says as we reach the table, and I look at Tessa for confirmation. Tessa smiles, shrugs, and I think that's about as warm and fuzzy as I've ever seen Tessa.

Mom has stories to tell tonight. She'd tried to drive here earlier and got lost and somehow ended up on some bridge but it wasn't the Golden Gate; it was the other one, the big gray one that was severely damaged in the last big earthquake, and the traffic was impossible, traffic like you don't believe, but she did finally get back across the bridge after paying the toll, and now here we are.

Yes we are.

I need a drink bad.

Drinks arrive, and I'm very happy with my ultra-smooth piña colada. I know piña coladas are the wimpiest of all blender drinks (perhaps only a chi-chi is lower in terms of verve), but it's tasty and smooth and it goes down easy, and soon I'm a little mellower.

We order pupu platters and expensive entrées you'd find in many Chinese restaurants for a quarter the price, but we're paying for the atmosphere and the band that's setting up on their little island/raft bandstand. But wait, there's mist and a storm, and then the rain passes and the sun comes out again, and the tropical drinks keep rolling, and we keep eating.

The band doesn't start playing until eight, and we've pretty much wrapped up eating by then, but once the music starts, my mom looks so positively blissful that I resist the urge to rush her home and into bed.

Why shouldn't she enjoy herself? She certainly can't do this in Visalia. And as the waiter brings a third (fourth?) round of drinks, I look at Tessa and Josh, who've got their heads together, deep in conversation, and I think, we might have a couple here—but then I overhear bits of their soulful conversation.

"There's nothing wrong with the Yankees loading their team. If George can pay the salaries, he should bring in the best. Other cities are just jealous."

But Josh isn't buying into Tessa's argument. "Yes, because other cities don't have the population base or the tax revenue New York does."

"Tax revenue, pooh! If other teams could afford our players, they'd have them—"

"But other teams can't—"

"That's not the Yankees' fault, and they shouldn't be penalized."

"But there should be some equality."

"You don't mean equality; you mean parity . . ."

Their voices are getting louder, which is why I can hear every word. And the louder the voices, the closer they come to blows.

Suddenly Josh is standing and grabbing his coat. "It's late; I better go," he says grimly, reaching into his wallet for cash, but my mom refuses to take his money.

"My treat," she says, hands clasped, although she's anxious about the new tension at the table, and her eyes dart from Tessa to Josh.

"Thank you for dinner, Mrs. Bishop. I had a wonderful time." Josh leans forward, gives my mother a kiss on the cheek and, with a nod to me and hardly anything at all to Tessa, leaves.

Tessa sticks around another five minutes, but the mood has changed, the fruity tropical cocktails seem dense and sickeningly sweet now, and even the band is playing the crowd favorite, "When a Man Loves a Woman," which makes me want to gag. It's definitely time to go home.

Tessa tries to give Mom money as well, which Mom again adamantly refuses, firmly conveying that this is her night, her party for my special friends (I cringe at that part), and Tessa goes.

Mom settles the bill. She won't let me contribute, either, and tonight was expensive, each cocktail around ten dollars, but Mom's in her element. She loves being able to provide, loves feeling useful and needed. But even though she's paid, we don't immediately leave.

Instead we sit there, listening to the band and the rain and what I'm sure are exotic birds, but that could be the fizz of rum in my veins or in my brain.

"Ah," Mom sighs, a pleasant, perhaps slightly tipsy look on her face, "this was fun."

"It was. And thank you for being so nice to my friends."

She gestures with a don't-even-mention-it shake of her hand. "I hope you're happy." She tips her head back, regards me for several seconds. "Or happier. Although I really don't know what will make you happy."

Something in her tone hits me funny, and I sit up in the red booth. "What do you mean?"

"I just don't think anything will ever make you happy, Holly."

It's funny, but when I get mad at work, I feel as though I can explode, fast. Sharp and hard. But when my mom upsets me, it's so different. With Mom it's an intense heat, a slow, hot burn that comes from deep inside me.

"You had everything," she continues. "The most wonderful man—handsome and charming, kind and generous—"

"He didn't want me, Mom."

"Why not? What did you do?"

I look away, hurt, so hurt. What did I do? "I didn't do anything wrong. I was just myself, Mom."

"But it doesn't make sense. He loved you! He married you. It was a beautiful wedding, and you two made such a lovely home together."

"It was a lovely home, but we weren't happy." I stand up, reach for my coat, my purse. "We should go. It's getting late and I have to work in the morning."

Leaving the Fairmont, I realize that neither of us should be driving after so many drinks, so I tell Mom we'll leave the cars and we'll get them in the morning, and we hail a cab to my apartment after Mom retrieves her suitcase from her car.

Mom and I sit stiffly side by side in the back of the cab until Mom finally breaks the silence. "I don't know why you're mad at me."

"I'm not mad," I say wearily. "I'm hurt."

She makes a soft, hurt sound of protest. "Why are you hurt? I was just trying to reach out to you, Holly."

I tense, close my eyes, hands in fists in my lap. I know her too well. I know every sound she makes—the way she swallows, breathes, eats, exhales.

I know maybe too much about her. And there are times I think I could annihilate her with my knowledge. Destroy her with my hands, or with the cruelty of my tongue.

It's terrifying to feel that kind of emotion, that kind of power, particularly toward your own mother.

I don't know if it's the same for other mothers and daughters, but my mom and I hurt each other sometimes just by being alive. And yet it'd kill me if she were dead.

"You make it sound like I was so lucky to get a guy like Jean-Marc."

"You have to admit, he was really special."

"Yes, but maybe he was lucky to have me. Maybe he should have been more grateful for me."

Mom lapses into silence, and I push a hand through my hair, feeling increasingly blue. This always happens when Mom and I get together. We can't seem to speak the same language, and I don't know why. Mom doesn't have this problem with Jamie (he doesn't talk) or Ashlee (she smiles at everything). Just me. I don't want her hurt, and I don't want to hurt her.

And I don't want her to hurt me.

But this is also why I don't call her, or ask her advice, or even try to confide in her. It's impossible to take my problems to her. She doesn't understand me, or what I need.

The cab pulls up in front of my apartment, and I pay the cabdriver, and Mom and I enter my apartment.

I show my mom around and offer her my bed, but she refuses, saying she'd be perfectly happy on the living room couch. I've got the start of a killer headache, and I'm in no mood to argue with her now. "I'm not putting you on the couch, Mom—"

"I prefer the couch. I sleep better there than in a big bed."

"That's silly."

"I sleep on the couch all the time at home."

"You do?"

She steps out of her shoes and lines them up perfectly straight between the couch and end table. "Yes. I do."

Somehow she's managed to sound righteous and defiant all at the same time, and I watch her adjusting the pillows on the couch.

"Why do you sleep better on the sofa?" I ask, picturing the old sofa with the faded pink and burgundy cabbage roses in the living room at home. I think the upholstery was once vaguely Laura Ashley–like, but that was the '80s, and cabbage roses were everywhere for a while.

"It's more comfortable."

"But the sofa is small. It's not even full-size!"

Mom shrugs and turns. "I don't mind." She's unzipping her small suitcase and takes out her nightgown. "I'll just watch a little TV and be asleep in no time."

"Are you sure?"

"Positive. Just give me a blanket and I'll be fine."

"I'll make the couch up properly."

"No. A blanket's all I need. I can use one of the pillows from the couch."

I have a rather terrifying picture of how Mom lives at home. Dinners alone in front of the television, and then later she pulls the afghan from the back of the couch and covers herself, watching TV until she falls asleep.

It is such a lonely life, I think, and I wonder yet again why she stopped dating when, in the early years after Bastard Ted left, she went out a lot. Those were the years she did anything and everything to meet other singles. She even took up square dancing, heading out twice a week in the ugliest yellow-and-aqua-checked dresses with enormous starchy skirts beneath.

I look at her now, really look at her, and see the face that I've known forever, and it's older; it's changed. The skin is less taut; the circles beneath the eyes are permanent, shallow hollows of lavender; the corners of her eyes droop more. So do her lips. Her brown hair, once my exact shade, is faded and heavily laced with gray, and I think, this is what I'm going to look like in thirty years. This is me at fifty-five.

It scares me. I don't want to look faded or rumpled; I don't want to be so tired that I fail to color my hair, or so poor that I can't buy clothes without a heavy polyester thread count.

This all sounds so petty, but I'm afraid of aging. Afraid of dying. Afraid of my own mortality. No one in fairy tales really gets old; they just go to sleep—think of Sleeping Beauty and Snow White—but this is real life, and I'm twenty-five, a good third of the way through my life, and

I don't know if it's going to get any better or easier. I don't know if I'll ever have more happiness than Mom did, and I don't think Mom had a lot.

And my mom should have. She was a good girl, too.

Tears suddenly sting my eyes, and I turn away, close the shutters at the big bay window so the whole world doesn't watch Mom watching TV on the couch.

And I'd hate Bastard Ted more if I thought he was truly happy in his little Orange County townhome. It's all very nice that Ted's so spiritual and in touch with his true essence, but what about his kids? What about us? Dads aren't supposed to freak out on their families. Dads are supposed to be dads to their kids. Dads are supposed to be . . . good.

"You know where the bathroom is," I say, double-checking the dead bolt on the front door, "and the kitchen. Help yourself, and if you need anything, ask."

$\mathcal{J}$ give Mom an awkward hug good night and wash my face, brush my teeth, and pull my hair into a loose pony-tail, but once in bed, I can't fall asleep despite the piña coladas.

Fairy tales always started with "Once upon a time," and they always ended with "happily ever after." And in between there's struggle and tragedy, love and loss, heart-break and triumph. But in the end, love conquers all. In the end, everyone is happy.

Why did I ever love fairy tales? And why did my mom love reading them to me?

And why does my mom still think Jean-Marc was Prince Charming when he has so completely rejected me?

She's my mom. She should be on my side. She should think Jean-Marc was a jerk—a villain, not a hero!

I close my eyes, put an arm over my face, trying very hard not to get teary and upset. I'm still so ashamed about the whole wedding and divorce. It was—is—such a fiasco. It was so not anything I thought it would be, and I thought it'd be beautiful. Wonderful. I thought I'd be a perfect princess bride.

I take a rough breath, and my throat burns and my eyes burn and the tears are coming anyway. What is love anyway? Why do we need love? Is wanting to be loved, *needed*, a weakness, or a necessity? Is wanting someone to love you, maybe even validate you, bad?

When I first met Jean-Marc, I swear, I felt like Cinderella. I felt important. Exciting. *Transformed*. Jean-Marc's love made me feel strong. With his love, I could do anything.

But then he took his love away, and I was turned back into the old me again. The magic's gone. And I'm scared. I'm scared I never was good enough, or pretty enough, or smart or strong enough.

Lying in my ridiculous girly princess bed, I pull my sheet over my head so Mom can't hear me crying. No wonder Jean-Marc wanted out. He saw through my mask to the real me.

I wake early the next morning, my head pounding like mad. Damn, damn, damn. I didn't need three piña coladas. I should never drink more than two of anything.

It hurts to stand. Staggering to the bathroom, I pop some Advil, and seeing it's not even six yet and still dark,

I struggle to put on running shoes and sweats and sneak Mom's car keys from her purse. Leaving my apartment, I zip up my sweatshirt hood and blow on my fingers and begin walking up California, toward the top of Nob Hill, where we left our cars.

I always forget this city is built on hills, until I have to walk. I'm half walking, half jogging my way up the hill, and it takes me twenty minutes to reach Mom's car. Wheezing, I climb into her car, start it, and drive it back to my apartment. I'm home in minutes and sweating profusely.

I find a spot for Mom's car just a half block from my apartment. Checking my watch, I see it's now six thirty, and I slowly begin the second jog/walk up Nob Hill.

If I thought it was hard the first time, it's even tougher the second. My legs remember how steep the hill is and how it just climbs endlessly. But I don't stop. I keep puffing and moving my feet, one after the other, and eventually I reach the block where I left my car, and soon I'm home again.

I don't go inside the apartment after parking my car. Instead I go to the nearest Starbucks and buy two lattes and blueberry scones and carry them home.

Mom's still asleep, and I leave the coffees and scones on the kitchen table while I shower, but she's awake and in the kitchen when I get out. Her hair's all rumpled, and she has a deep crease in her cheek from the pillow's welting.

"You've been busy," she says, yawning.

"I got your car." I'm still wrapped in my towel, but I

need some coffee. I take a sip even as I slide her keys across the table. "Your car's parked just a half block down, same side as the house. When you go out the front door, take a right and you'll see it."

Mom wraps her arms around me for a hug. "Thank you," she whispers, and I stand in my towel, awkwardly receiving her hug.

"My pleasure," I say, but I can't warm up, can't feel anything with her arms around me. I don't know why I'm all numb and cold inside. I don't know why I can't reciprocate or feel anything other than regret. I step away, breaking free. "I better get dressed. Can't be late."

And it's not until I'm heading out the apartment door that I realize it's Friday. And I was supposed to do something on Thursday. What?

Brian Fadden coffee meeting. And something in the evening . . .

Something . . . something . . . oh, *shit!*

Dinner with Paul. I stood up Paul.

Racing back inside, I check my message phone, and sure enough, four calls. All from Paul. Last night he called every fifteen minutes from the restaurant, each call increasingly agitated, until the last is downright scary, a rambling tirade about how I could have at least had the courtesy to call and cancel, and how he had a life and it'd been a sacrifice for him to leave his book when he was in the middle of writing a difficult scene, but he'd done it and he'd appreciate some respect, please.

His tone and word choice give me the weebie-jeebies, but I have to give him credit. He did wait nearly an hour before accepting that I wasn't going to be meeting him.

But Mom has also heard the last message. She looks at me, alarmed. "He doesn't sound very nice."

"He's upset," I say, deleting the messages even as I pick up the phone. "I was supposed to have dinner with him last night and I spaced. He waited at the restaurant for an hour for me."

But Paul doesn't answer. He's probably already left for work. (But wait. Didn't he give up his technical job somewhere to be a full-time unemployed novelist? So he works from home, right?) I leave him a wordy apology with the general theme being, "I goofed, I owe you, I'm sorry."

Paul ends up calling me late in the day. I'm at my desk at the office and surprised to hear his voice, wondering how he got my work number, then remember that he's one of Josh's crowd, so of course he knows the office phone number. It's a tense call—Paul's still fuming—but I grovel some more, and eventually he accepts my apology under the condition that I make it up to him soon.

I tell him my mom's in town and try to schedule a make-up dinner for Tuesday or Wednesday. Paul doesn't want another weekday night. He wants Saturday. I don't want Saturday but, feeling guilty, succumb to Friday. So one week from today we're going on what now seems to be a date.

The rest of the day has been anticlimactic. Olivia has pretty much acted as though everything's normal, so I trust everything's normal. Josh and Tessa never mention dinner, and I actually get a lot of work done. By the time I leave the office for the weekend, I feel as if I've finally accomplished something, and return to my apartment to find Mom waiting at the door with her purse and coat.

I look at my mom, dressed in her second-favorite color combination, licorice red and cobalt blue paired with white running shoes, and think, *You've got to be kidding.* There's no way I can go out right away. I'm beat. And I can't take my mom out to dinner somewhere in my neighborhood wearing the American flag. It's fine to be a tourist. You just don't have to look like one.

"Mom, did you bring anything brown, or black?"

"Black?"

"Like a black T-shirt or turtleneck?"

"I don't wear black." She sounds almost traumatized. "You know I never wear black. I love bright colors."

I noticed. "Let me change into jeans," I say, trying to hide the wilting note in my voice. I swear to God, I feel as if I'm back in high school and Mom's raining on my parade. I try to remember Tessa's attitude. I'm lucky to have a mother. It shouldn't matter what she wears, what she says, or what she thinks I need.

"How does Italian sound?" Mom shouts through the half-closed bedroom door. "I thought we could go to North Beach. I found a little restaurant that has an early-bird special—"

Oh, no.

"And if we get there before six thirty we can get a free appetizer or drink with my happy-hour coupon."

Sunday morning arrives, and it's time for Mom to head home. She doesn't like to drive after dark, and it's a good four-and-a-half-hour drive—or longer if you go the speed limit, and Mom always does.

But before Mom does go, I take her to one of my favorite cafés, and we have a great brunch. Mom keeps smiling at everyone and everything. "I feel like I'm in Paris," she says for the third or fourth time whenever someone wearing black enters the café. Mom thinks wearing black is something of an artistic statement, but whispers that it also reveals a certain instability of character.

"I don't know, Mom," I answer, compelled to defend the color black. "People like it because it's understated—"

"It's not understated; it's dramatic."

"—and sophisticated at the same time."

"Black's boring."

"How can black be boring and dramatic?"

"It's boring to look at, and dramatic because people who wear it want to appear like something they're not."

"No."

Mom leans so far across the table, I think we're going to bump heads. "What child wears black?"

My mouth opens, closes. I'm genuinely stumped.

"My point," she concludes, straightening. "No child wears black. Children reach for color. Jamie would wear only yellow and royal blue T-shirts. His favorite sweatpants were St. Patrick's Day green. Ashlee loved pink. Pink underwear, pink skirts, pink sweaters, pink hair barrettes, pink everything. And if pink wasn't an option, she'd grudgingly choose lavender."

"And me?"

Mom hesitates. Frowning, she shakes her head. "I forget."

"You don't remember?"

"You liked all the colors of the rainbow."

"But I had to have a favorite."

Her frown deepens. She's thinking. Her shoulders finally lift, fall. "I don't think you had a favorite, or if you did, I don't recall."

As we walk back to my apartment, Mom takes my arm, gives me a little squeeze. "I really enjoyed having a girls' weekend with you, Holly. It's so fun doing girl things together."

I nod, and I'm completely conflicted on the inside, but I'm glad I was able to spend time with her. I probably don't see enough of her. "Thanks for driving up."

"You were surprised!" She laughs.

"It was a good surprise."

She pats my arm. "I'm glad. I did want to see you. I've been worried about you . . . you know . . . since separating from Jean-Marc and moving up here alone. I just felt so much better when he was taking care of you."

We've reached the steps to my building, and I stop on the sidewalk. The sun is high and shining warmly, having decided to act like summer after all. "Mom, I'm not a little girl. I didn't need Jean-Marc to take care of me."

"I know, but it's nice to be treated special . . . have someone do things for you. Protect you. That sort of thing." And she sounds wistful, full of longings and regrets she never talks about with me.

"I can do things for myself."

She nods quickly, too quickly. "Of course you can."

"I *can*."

"I didn't say you couldn't."

"But you look completely dubious, Mom, as if I haven't managed to do anything right in my life."

Mom reaches for me, gives me a swift hug. "Now, that's silly. You do lots of things right. And someday you'll meet someone new and even more wonderful and he'll sweep you off your feet—"

"*Mom.*" I cut her short, and I'm not gentle and not patient. "I don't want to meet anyone new, and I certainly don't want to be swept off my feet, or rescued. I don't want or need another Prince Charming."

Mom's features pinch. "I was trying to be supportive."

Christ. I cover my face, take a breath, fight the twenty-five years of shared history. She's my mom and I love her, and I'm her daughter and she loves me; this is okay; everything's okay; conflict is normal between mothers and daughters . . .

"You're very supportive," I say after a moment, dropping my hand and forcing a smile. "You're great. You really are."

I carry Mom's suitcase down to her car, which is still parked down the street where I left it two days ago. As Mom climbs into the car, I ask her to call me, let me know that she's made it back safely; sometimes I'm not sure who's the parent and who's the child.

Then her car pulls away, heading down the street, and she puts on her blinker, signals she's going to turn at the corner, and as her car disappears around the corner, I feel something break loose inside me.

It's terrible. Sad. *I feel so sad.*

I want to run after her, chase her car down like a five-year-old on the first day of kindergarten, crying, "Don't leave me, don't leave me, don't go!"

And I think I've missed her my whole life, and I'm not even sure what that means, but I wish I could go back in time and undo whatever has been done so I'm not hurt and scared any longer.

Cindy and Drew emerge from the Victorian even as I head back in. Cindy nods at me, and I nod back as I climb the front steps.

In the apartment I face the empty living room, the empty hall, the emptiness beyond. It's okay to be alone. I'm not lonely—Mom was just here—but right now I don't want to be in the apartment all by myself, and I have no money to blow, so I change into my sweats and put on running shoes (an optimistic purchase for me when I've never done much more than jog/walk) and head out for a jog. Walk.

And I'm going to keep jog/walking until I can handle the emptiness and loneliness, because this is my life.

Back at work Monday it's busy, which helps the time pass, and our usual Monday morning team meeting is smooth, without any obvious tension.

I spend the week doing everything I should, plus following up with phone calls to the media, and although I'm tempted to call Brian Fadden, I don't. I can't—won't—call him until I really have something for him, and right now my interest is more personal than professional, so I definitely can't call.

Despite the rather frenetic pace at the office, I do finally manage to use Olivia's gym guest pass, going every day, even though the time isn't consistent. Some days it's before work, other days it's after work, and on Tuesday and Wednesday it's during my lunch.

I even see Olivia Thursday morning before work, at the gym. She's just finished the hybrid yoga-Pilates class, and though I've heard it described as a ninety-minute torture fest, Olivia walks out of the class as if it were kids' play. She's wearing a cropped brown athletic top and bootleg brown velvet yoga pants, and she looks as if she were still a model. I envy her. I can barely do a circuit in the weight room, and I don't look anything like a model in my navy blue workout gear. I'm short and hippy and relatively flat-chested. But I'm here, I tell myself, and that's what counts.

In the women's locker room Olivia makes some small talk, but she's fairly distant, and it's a reminder that she hasn't totally forgotten last week's Tessa incident. I can't help wondering what would happen if she found out I am actually helping Tessa with the Leather & Lace Ball.

And I don't like the thought, because I know I'd hate the consequences.

Friday afternoon around three, Olivia calls me into her office. "You can shut the door," she says, but it's not really a suggestion; it's a directive, and I do.

I sit down in one of the chairs opposite her desk and wish I'd brought a notebook and pen just so I'd have something to hold, because right now I feel like a kid called into the principal's office.

I hate this feeling. I only ever went to the principal's office once (no, make that twice), but the time that stands out in my memory was in seventh grade, when I put a mean note in a girl's locker because I was jealous of her. The girl was pretty and had great hair and great clothes and tons of friends, and the cutest guy in junior high for a boyfriend. I didn't think it was fair that she should have so much when I had so little.

So I typed up this mean letter that suggested ways she could die (I'm not proud of this). The note was typed and anonymous. But she took it to the school office, and the

English teacher recognized my fluency with language (as mean notes go, it was very creative), and that visit with the principal was followed up by a meeting with my mom, followed by several sessions with the school counselor, followed by an apology to the girl, followed by a final meeting with the principal, the girl, my mom, and the girl's family.

I learned several important things from that painful incident: (1) You won't become more popular by telling the popular girl she should die. And (2) if you're going to write mean things, use small words and bad grammar instead of proper syntax and diction.

"What's going on?" Olivia finally asks after leaving me in suspended silence for nearly a minute. "You don't seem like you're happy here anymore."

I'm surprised. "I'm very happy here."

"I don't know. Something's different."

I try to keep my mouth from falling open. I'm genuinely bewildered. I've worked really hard all week, and handling numerous events at the same time is like juggling bowling pins. There's always something big and awkward coming up (and down), and the only way to survive is to focus and keep moving. "I think I've had a great week. I've gotten a lot done, and the Kid Fest proposal is ready to go out first thing Monday morning . . ." My voice trails off, and I look at Olivia and try to understand what she wants me to say, what she wants me to do.

"You've changed." It's all she'll say, and she lapses back into silence.

I've changed?

I think this over, feeling obligated to think this over. Have I changed?

I'm finally going to the gym regularly. I've lost a couple of pounds. And I do feel more settled in San Francisco than I did a month ago. But have I changed?

"Is it a bad change?" I ask.

She shrugs. "You're different. That's what I'm saying." Olivia picks up her phone to make a call. "You can leave the door open."

I've been dismissed.

Back in my cubicle, I'm troubled by the brief meeting with Olivia and would very much like to discuss it with Josh, who I think has a better handle on office politics than anyone else on the payroll, but he's down on the Peninsula, meeting with some of the Beckett School folks, and there's no one else I trust enough to talk about this with. So I force myself to finish up what I'm working on, and at five I stop in at the gym for a fast workout before my dinner with Paul.

But the fast workout takes a little longer, and although I shower, I don't have time to wash my hair, and it's not looking all that hot as I try to style it at home. I shouldn't have worked out. And I should have washed my hair. But now I'm late, and I'm making mistakes as I do my makeup—my shaking hand means a big blob of mascara right in the middle of my eye, and now my eye is tearing up and my eyeliner is smearing and I've got a grayish streak in my foundation beneath my eye.

Damn it.

I don't want to be going to dinner with Paul. I don't want Olivia being short with me. I don't want any more problems for the next twenty-four hours.

But I've agreed to the date, and Olivia is mad at me, and I can't control life, only my attitude, so I finish dressing and try to spray more hair spray on my hair in hopes of giving it some lift before dashing to my car.

As I drive, I panic. Tonight is starting out all wrong. You should never forget you've made plans and then stand your date up. And then when you book a makeup date, you should not be late. I know this, and yet I am late, and although I'm driving as fast as I can, it's not fast enough. Traffic is heavy, and I'm impatient and tempted to lean on my horn, but I don't.

Calm down, I tell myself. Be calm. Nothing bad is going to happen.

By the time I reach Formaggio, I'm twenty minutes late, and I lose another five to seven trying to find parking for the car since there's no valet. I've never been to Formaggio before but have heard plenty about the cuisine. It's a hip Italian-Mediterranean place that's always packed.

The first time I circle the block looking for parking, I see no sign of Paul, which could be good—or bad, depending on how you look at it. By the time I park and jog toward the entrance (thank goodness I've started to work out; I can actually jog a block without blowing up), Paul's waiting out front, wearing a black turtleneck, black jeans, and black boots. It's his literary look, but I'm reminded of "Sprockets," an old *Saturday Night Live* skit.

I rush toward Paul, apologizing profusely, and his cheek muscle pulls, and I'm crossing my fingers, hoping this is a smile.

He opens the door for me, tells the hostess his date has finally arrived and we'd like to be seated.

The hostess, a pretty young Italian girl, most likely a local university student and not Italian at all, studies the restaurant layout a moment and then, with her wax pencil, assigns us a table at the back.

Paul leans over the desk. He's seen where we were going to be seated. "Isn't there another table somewhere?"

Pretty hostess looks up, smiles. "No."

Paul has seen all the empty tables beyond her shoulder in the restaurant, as well as unmarked tables on her layout. "The restaurant isn't even half full."

The hostess doesn't even glance down at the layout. "Those are being held for specific reservations."

"We have reservations."

I tense. The energy doesn't feel particularly good, but the hostess's glossy smile never wavers. "A half hour ago."

Paul leans farther across the stand. "I *was* here."

She doesn't budge even though Paul is clearly invading her space, a conscious or unconscious attempt at intimidation. "As I've already told you, our restaurant requires all parties must be here before being seated."

Paul shoots me a look. It's what could be called a dirty look. I feel like shit. If I'd been here on time, none of this would have happened. "I'm sorry," I pipe in. "It's my fault. I was late getting off work—"

"Not to worry," the hostess says, tone friendly again. "We have a table for you, and I can seat you right now."

"But I don't want that table," Paul says, pointing to the numbered table on her floor plan. "I want a good table. That's why we made reservations—"

"We're going to honor your reservations," the hostess interrupts, "if you'll just come with me."

Paul stares her down. "To a center table."

This is not going to be a good evening, I realize, and every instinct is screaming for me to run. Get away. Survive. But I don't run. I'm too worried about hurting Paul's feelings, which worries me, because the atmosphere here is crap.

"Sir," the hostess attempts.

"No," Paul cuts her short. "I was here. I want to be seated at the table I requested."

"I'm sorry, that table has been reassigned." The hostess is looking beyond us to the couple entering through the front door now. "Good evening," she calls cheerily. "Welcome to Formaggio. How many, please?"

Paul plants himself in front of her. "What about us?"

The hostess looks almost surprised to see Paul still standing there. "What about you?"

"Our *table*."

"You'll have to wait a moment now. I'm going to go ahead and seat these people now." And she takes two stiff menus from below the desk and escorts the couple to a center table.

Paul splutters. He's mad, very mad, and I don't know what to say or do. I barely know him. We've had just that one night as a group, and then our conversation earlier in the week.

"I'm sorry," I say to Paul, watching the hostess from the corner of my eye, anxious for her to return and seat us. Paul's practically frothing at the mouth now, muttering things about incompetent waitresses and women, and how he ought to ask for the manager, and this wasn't the kind of treatment he expected from a place like Formaggio.

The hostess doesn't seem to be in any hurry to return, though.

In fact, as I watch, she settles her hand on the back of the woman's chair and laughs, shaking her head a little. She looks serene. Happy. Relaxed.

Just the opposite of Paul, who is about to blow a head gasket. I will say this for Jean-Marc. He might not have loved me, but I never had to worry about how he'd behave in a public place. And I'm worrying very much right now about Paul.

More people arrive, crowding the small entryway. Formaggio isn't a big restaurant, and the only way they accommodate a crowd is by squeezing the maximum number of tables into the small corner space, taking advantage of two narrow walls with lots of little tables sandwiched between hard wooden chairs and a long upholstered bench.

The hostess finally leaves the couple she's seated and returns to the podium at the entrance.

"Ready?" she says brightly.

"Yes," I say.

"No," Paul contradicts, lifting a hand to slice me in two. "I'd like to speak to the manager immediately."

The hostess's eyes have gone cold. "Then you'll have to wait a minute—"

"I've already waited nearly thirty minutes."

"You'll have to wait one more. As you can see, I have people to seat."

And picking up more menus, she warmly greets the four people standing behind us.

The foursome get a center table, too.

"It's a power play," Paul mutters furiously. "This is just a goddamn power play." Then he stops a passing busboy. "Where's your manager? Get your manager. I want to talk to him now."

"¿Cómo?"

"Your manager." Paul's getting even hotter. He speaks louder. "Man-a-ger."

A fifty-something-year-old man in a dark suit appears. "May I help you?"

"Yes." And Paul is suddenly mollified. You can almost

see his ruffled feathers smoothing. "I had a reservation for seven and—"

"What time did you arrive, sir?"

Paul's look of satisfaction fades somewhat. "Seven."

"You were here together at seven?"

"No. I was here. My . . . date . . . was running late."

"I see. And did we not have a table available for you?"

"You did. It's back there somewhere," and Paul gestures to the wall at the back. "But I don't want to sit back there. I want a center table. It's what I requested when I made the reservation."

"Table thirty-seven," the hostess murmurs, having returned. She leans across the podium, pointing to the diagram of the restaurant interior.

The older man nods. "There isn't the center table available, but we've a lovely table for you waiting, and we can seat you right now if you'd like."

"Yes. Well . . ." Paul swallows, looking far from comfortable. "Okay."

The manager takes the two menus from the hostess. "If you'll come this way," he says, and leads us to our table. Table 37. Right in the middle of the long wall, right where Paul didn't want to be.

Paul hesitates at the table as the manager waits silently, expressionlessly. This is what he does for a living. He can wait all night if necessary.

"Where would you like to sit?" I ask Paul, desperately ready to move beyond the seating stage of dinner. I hate tension—avoid conflict like the plague—and I can't bear to continue in this vein.

Paul shrugs. "I don't care."

"I'll sit on the booth side, then," I offer, and I slide carefully between tables and settle into the booth, the seat sinking slightly.

Paul sits in the chair opposite me. The table's small, we're practically touching, and the restaurant is beginning to fill up. The hostess seats a couple on one side of us. The middle tables are virtually full.

As I pick up my menu, Paul mutters, "I can't sit here."

I look up at him. "Why not?"

"I can't face the wall. I always sit with my back to the wall. I have to be able to see the door. I have to see who's coming and going."

If I had known Paul was going to be such a pain in the ass, I would never have agreed to dinner. "Would you like to switch places with me?"

"Yes."

I get up and give the hostess an apologetic smile as I have to squeeze past the couple she's now trying to seat on the other side of us. And now Paul's squeezing past the couple, and it's a four-way traffic stop with everyone backing up, moving forward, turning a corner, sitting down.

It's a damn production, and I'm roiling on the inside, but I take his chair. His chair is hard. And warm. For some reason that gives me the creeps. I suppose if I liked him, if I were more attracted, it'd be a nonissue, but right now, thinking of my butt sitting where his butt has just been is making me feel a little squirmy.

But Paul's still not happy. "Now you're too tall."

I look across the table, try to avoid my reflection in the big mirror running behind Paul's head. "What?"

"Can you scrunch down a little?"

I smile, but I feel peculiar on the inside. I'm not understanding. Something's happening, and I don't understand what it is.

"People are going to think I'm short." He's talking again, probably because I'm just staring at him, my mind blank, my face blank, unable to process anything.

"People will think you're taller than me," and he's still talking. His mouth is moving, and I'm watching his mouth, thinking this is weird, he's so weird, but I can't seem to say or do anything. "But you're not taller than me, Holly. I'm taller than you."

"I know. And nobody is going to think that."

He gives a little bounce on the bench, and yes, okay, he is rather low, but he's no lower than I was, and I never worried about who was taller or shorter.

"I can't sit this low." He bounces on the bench again, up and down in his black "Sprockets" turtleneck, and with his pale hair combed all the way off his forehead, I feel as if I were in a German postmodern play. Abruptly he leans across the table, tries to get the attention of another unfortunate busboy. "Yeah, hi," Paul says as the busboy approaches. "I'm too low. I can't sit this low."

The busboy stares at Paul and then me, uncomprehendingly, but I say nothing, too fascinated with my glass of ice water.

"I need something to sit on." Paul's voice carries, and I slink lower in my seat, knowing that people are going to think Paul is my boyfriend. They're going to think we're together, because, well, we're together, and that's humiliating, so I practice detaching myself from my body and floating above the restaurant.

"I need something to sit on," Paul repeats, and I'm no longer floating anywhere but crashing back into our table headfirst.

Something he can sit on? Like what? A booster seat?

"You want something to sit on?" The busboy repeats haltingly. He doesn't speak English as a first language, either, and I curse Paul silently for putting young immigrant males through this torture with me.

But Paul's pleased. He's been heard. *"Exactly!"*

The busboy leaves, and Paul looks at me, hands folded on the table. "We're going to get this fixed."

Oh, yes, we will. And my thought is that I'm just going to stand up and leave—I don't owe him an explanation; I can just go—but before I can move, the manager returns with the busboy in tow.

"What seems to be the problem?" the manager asks.

Paul bounces on the seat once, twice. "I can't sit here. I'm too short. I can barely see over the table."

"Why don't you change places?" the manager suggests with exaggerated politeness, pointing to me.

Paul shakes his head. "My back would be to the door."

I glance down at the napkin in my lap and think calming thoughts.

"So what do you want me to do?" the manager says.

"Don't you have something I can sit on?" Paul holds

his hands up, showing a good twenty inches of space. "You know, something tall?"

"Like what?"

"Phone books."

"You want to sit on phone books?"

"Three or four."

The couples on either side of us are listening. They're not even trying to hide their interest. Both couples, one young and chic and the other older and silver, are following the discussion now.

"I'm sorry, sir," the manager answers, "but we don't have phone books."

"You *have* to have phone books. Every restaurant has phone books."

"But not for people to sit on."

"I just need—"

"*No.*"

Paul flushes. "You have to have something in the back. Something I could use."

"And what do you suggest?" The manager's voice drips ice.

Paul glances around, his gaze traveling across the restaurant, over the tables, the linens . . .

"Napkins. Towels. Something like that."

If I were boneless, I'd slide beneath the table right now.

"You'd like *towels*," drawls the manager.

"Or tablecloths."

"*Table*cloths."

"Yes, tablecloths," Paul repeats stiffly. "If you don't mind."

The manager bows and walks away. I lower my menu. Paul glowers at me, and I rise. I've had it, absolutely had it, and I want to be polite and find a cordial way to make my escape, but before words leave my lips, two busboys return with a stack of tablecloths, still wrapped in plastic from the cleaners.

"Wonderful!" Paul enthuses, as if this were entirely normal. I stand next to our table as he takes half the tablecloths, places them on the bench, sits down, tests the tablecloths, and then stands and takes three more.

And that's when I go. I don't even say a word. I can't. Holding my coat and purse close to my body, I run from the restaurant and all the way to my car as if the devil himself were chasing me.

That was horrible, horrible, and I will never, ever endure another bad date—or rude man—just because I'm supposed to be a nice girl.

I'm not that nice.

God help me, I'm honestly not that nice.

I'm so upset driving home—upset with Paul, upset with Tom, upset with me—that I can hardly see straight.

By the time I reach my apartment, I crack, absolutely crack, and do the worst thing possible. I pick up the phone and make the absolutely worst kind of call.

A call of need, a call of desperation.

I phone Jean-Marc. Late on a Friday night, no less. Even worse, he picks up.

Jean-Marc is quiet on the other end of the line, and I wonder if I've gone too far, said too much, sounded too broken, too exposed, too pathetic.

I know the worst mistake is ever to need too much, and yet I need too much.

This much I know.

I'm the way I am because I feel so hollow, and the only way to fill the emptiness is by getting something.

Something like attention. Something like warmth. Something like . . . love.

I've read all the magazines and books you've read, watched the same TV shows, too. I know what the experts and talk show doctors say. No one will ever love me the way I need to be loved. No one will ever want me the way I want. No one will ever give me everything, so I've got to do it for myself. I have to like myself more. Have to love myself so no one else will ever have to do that job.

But I want someone to do that job. I want someone who will find it not a job but a pleasure. Someone who will want me, like me just because I'm likable.

"Maybe it'd be better if you didn't call anymore." Jean-Marc sounds quiet, distant, so coolly, completely detached. I say nothing. I'm pressing my nails into the palms of my hands. Not call? "I don't—" My voice breaks. He hasn't been a proper lover, proper husband, proper anything at all, but he's still somehow important. Significant.

He ties me to a life I don't have anymore, the life I'd thought I wanted, the life I thought I was getting.

"It'd probably be better," he says, and I wonder how he could say that. Better for whom?

Him?

And I see him—us—on our first date, the beautiful French restaurant, the champagne he'd ordered, and me sitting there smiling like a fool as the bubbles rose up inside me, dancing in my head even as the bubbles fizzed and popped out of my flute onto the back of my hand. It was magic: the place, the night, the dreams.

I even remember what I wore—a turquoise silk blouse, black leather pants, something sparkly at my ears—and I felt just as sparkly on the inside, felt beautiful and together as if the world were my oyster.

"You don't want me to call anymore."

"I just don't think it helps. You always get upset and I—"

I hang on his words, wondering, hoping, wanting him to finally say something that will help, something that will make sense.

"You're using me as a crutch," is what he does say. "But I can't help you adjust. I can't help you through this."

"Why not?" And this time I can't keep the anger to myself. "Why not, Jean-Marc? You helped make this."

He makes a rough sound in his throat, very guttural, very French. I've heard my favorite French actors do this, and they sound intelligent, gorgeous, sexy, but it makes me see red now.

"You are a part of this," I say, and I'm practically shouting. "You married me. Whether you like it or not. You walked me down the aisle. You said the words 'I do.' You put the ring on my finger—"

"Only because you wanted me to."

I grab for air, mouth opening wide.

"You pushed," he continues, his voice bitter, more bitter than I've ever heard before. "You pushed and pushed and there you are, living in my house, sleeping in my bed, and what was I to do? Hmm? Tell me, Holly, what was I to do?"

Love me. Be *glad* I was in your house, sleeping in your bed.

My eyes sting, and I look away, can't focus, turn my head the opposite direction, trying to escape the pain inside me. I did this. I did this. I did this.

But how?

"I loved you," I say at last, and the words are almost laughable between us. What the hell does "love" mean? What the hell does love do?

"Holly, you're a good girl, a sweet girl, but I didn't ever . . ." He sighs. "*Cherie*, I didn't love you."

Oh. It was bad the first time, but it's no better this time. No, not at all. "You said you did," and my voice comes out small, and I sound no better than a kid. Hurt, disillusioned—this isn't the me I want to be.

He's not saying anything, and for a minute there's just this awful silence and emptiness, and I know this place. I know this feeling well.

"You wanted me to love you," he continues. "You

wanted something I didn't have, something . . . I don't know . . . something I just couldn't give you."

"So it—we—were just sex?" Not that the sex lasted very long, either.

"And friendship."

Fuck. You.

I'm seething. Raging. The friendship was obviously lacking, and for your information, the sex wasn't that good.

"We made a mistake." Jean-Marc, who never wanted to talk, can't seem to shut up now. "So we're fixing it."

Leaving me is his idea of fixing.

Jean-Marc must have gone to Dad's class, Abandonment 101: Agony for the Whole Family.

"I won't call again," I say, but I don't want to say the words, don't want to make anything so final, so definitive. Like death, I think.

Or divorce.

But that's what this is. And the realization slams into me, swift, harsh—divorce.

Finished. Kaput. Over. Dead.

"Take care, Holly."

Is this it, then? It's really over, the final tie cut, the relationship truly dead and buried?

I want to say his name; I want him to be kind; I want warmth, but I can't tell him what I want, can't humiliate myself again with what I need.

"Be happy," he adds, and before I can say "Good luck, good-bye," he's hung up.

The tears want to rush my eyes. There's a half-scream hanging in my throat. I can't bear it when people hang up on me, can't bear it when people walk away from me, can't bear feeling so helpless. Feeling so . . .

Abandoned.

Thanks, Dad.

I leave my apartment to keep from dissolving into the mess I tend to be, and walk, and walk. It's dark, and the cold bites at me, and I should have brought a coat, but maybe it's better this way, better to keep me icy and alive than warm and fragmented.

I can't call him anymore, I think; he's told me not to call. He's told me to leave him alone. That's essentially what he's saying.

Stay away.

Leave me alone.

I don't want to deal with you anymore.

And even though I'm chilly, the tears well up and they fall, but I keep walking up Fillmore, and I wipe the tears as they fall, but I don't stop walking. I just bundle my arms across my chest and stagger up a hill and down a hill and past the big beautiful houses in Pacific Heights, and back down the street toward Japan Town. I'm so full of missing, so full of loneliness and broken dreams, that I don't know what to do but walk.

And walk.

And walk.

Missing is the hardest thing I know; missing is so much

harder than not thinking and not feeling, and now that I've started to feel, I'm afraid to be alone with all my emotions.

If I knew how to talk to my mom, I'd call her right now. I know she was just here for a weekend with me, but she loved Jean-Marc; she thought he was the answer to everything, thought he'd whisk me away, save me from myself. And yet here I am—alone and single again and not quite certain that I can take care of myself despite all my indignant assertions.

But of course she'd think Jean-Marc was the answer. She's the one who craves the fairy-tale ending even more than I do. She's the one who believes it's a man who will, and must, save us . . . that women need to be rescued, as if we were all helpless, fragile maidens locked in towers and dungeons or lying asleep, poisoned.

Rapunzel had to let down her ridiculously long hair so the prince could climb up it and free her.

Cinderella needed a fairy godmother and glass slippers for Prince Charming to save her from a life of misery.

Snow White needed not just one but a *bunch* of little men—seven, to be exact—to protect her until the prince could stumble through the woods and discover said maiden, unconscious and waiting for him. A gift offering on ice.

No, can't call Mom, can't tell her what I'm feeling, or let her close to my pain. I don't think she knows what to do with pain. She doesn't even know what to do with *her* pain. For God's sake, she's fifty-five and sleeping on the living room couch in front of the TV every night!

I lost my husband and I lost my dad, and in so many ways I lost my mom, too.

The losses, added up like that, are rather horrifying, and there seems to be a pattern here, and the pattern requires examination, but that's the one thing I can't do. I'm afraid to pull out a mirror and inspect all my flaws and wounds. I'm scared. What if I'm not a real human being after all?

What if I'm an alien?

A two-headed monster from Mars? Something from one of those old sci-fi films I used to watch at the Tower Theater in Fresno back in high school?

I bundle my arms across my chest. It's colder, and I'm chilled all the way through. My teeth have begun to chatter, and the chattering teeth have helped dry up my tears.

I make another turn, climb another hill, and return to my neighborhood.

I reach the café where I went to breakfast a couple of weeks ago and order a cup of decaf cappuccino, and I sit at a table by the window with my grande cappuccino and stare down into the oversize cup. The tears are so close to the surface but there's no one to call, no one to tell. I've spent too much time trying to be okay; I don't know how to ask for help.

I reach up to swipe tears, and somehow I hit the rim of the big mug with my elbow, and the cappuccino tips, spilling. Suddenly there is someone shoving paper napkins at me, a whole handful. I say a muffled thanks and clean up the coffee. As I move to throw away the soggy napkins, I realize that the person who shoved the napkins into my hands is Gorgeous Guy, the one who looks like a Gap model, the one who wanted to see the sports section.

"Hi," I say. "Thanks."

"You didn't get burned, did you?"

I'd forgotten what a great voice he had, forgotten that it's slow and a little sexy. "No. I'm fine."

"Good."

He stands next to my table for a moment, staring down at me. "You look familiar," he says.

"Oh." I reach up, push hair out of my eyes. "We talked once, briefly. You asked to borrow the sports section."

He seems to remember, or at least almost, because there's still a funny line between his eyebrows. "Right."

"You wanted to check your high school's score."

He smiles, expression clearing. "You have a good memory."

You're kind of hard to forget. But I don't say that, because it goes without saying, and I wonder how genetics does this—makes someone so strong and clear, all clean lines, perfect geometric planes, and then throws in the thick hair, the deep-blue eyes, and the intelligence on the inside that makes it come together, the energy that makes the person more than beautiful, but intriguing. "How's your school doing?"

"Okay."

"You're not in high school."

He laughs. "No. I teach in San Mateo, at the high school. Science."

"Science?" I look up at him briefly and look away, a hint of heat in my face. I would have loved science if I had a teacher who looked like him.

"Biology, advanced biology, that kind of thing."

I nod, trying not to think too much about the birds and the bees—reproductive science I'm sure he covers at some point, somewhere in the curriculum. And I think we've just about wrapped up our conversation when he gestures to the chair across from me.

"Mind if I join you?"

"Yes—no." I swipe the rest of my tears away. "I mean, that'd be great."

He sits, and he's even handsomer up close. His eyes are really blue, Hollywood blue, and I'm reminded of that actor, the one who played the southern hunk in *Sweet Home Alabama*.

"Where're you from?" he asks, leaning toward me, one hard thigh jutting out from beneath the table, the shape of a strong knee just barely outlined against the faded denim.

"Visalia," I say, knowing he won't have a clue.

"Exeter," he answers, and we both grin.

Exeter's just nine miles east of Visalia. You take Highway 198 toward Kaweah Lake, jog right off the highway before you reach Badger Hill, and there it is.

I can't believe he was raised nine miles from my

hometown. He's too good-looking to be from Cowville. "You moved away from Exeter when you were a kid, right?"

His eyes crease. "Sometimes I wish I did, but nope. Graduated from Exeter High School. I'm Alex."

"Holly." I shake his hand, and I'm tempted to ask what class he was in, but I hold back. I know he's older than I am; I peg him to be early, maybe even mid-thirties, as his bones are settled, his frame big, solid, and there's something in his eyes that indicates he's comfortable. Relaxed. He knows who he is.

Instead I point to his feet. "So those are real boots?" I ask. "Not just Needless Markup wannabes?"

He laughs low and husky and, stretching one leg out, lifts the hem on his jeans, showing the genuine stitching on the leather. "Real boots."

"You were an aggie?"

"Yep. You, too?"

"Nope."

"No Four-H? No FFA sweetheart queen?"

I shake my head as the knot inside my chest eases. I can already breathe a little easier. I feel a little better. Just knowing that Gorgeous Guy is from my neck of the woods makes everything okay. "I lived in town. I left the ag stuff to my friends."

"Smart girl."

"You're a country boy."

"Citrus."

"You must love fog."

He laughs, and it's deep, sharp, distinctly male. "Far better than cold snaps." And we both know we're talking about the cold, clear winter nights that send farmers rushing through their orchards, lighting the oil smudge pots to keep the fruit from freezing.

"So what are you doing in the city?" he asks, changing the subject.

"I'm in PR."

He lifts an eyebrow, so I hurriedly add, "I work as an event planner."

"That's great."

And then I blurt things I shouldn't. "I can't believe you're a teacher. I thought you were a model."

He laughs again, a great big belly laugh, but before he can answer, I hear a voice. "Holly?"

I recognize the voice, even the incredulous tone, and immediately flash back to my freshman year of high school.

I turn around, and it is Katie. Katie. Katie from freshmen PE, Katie from honors English, Katie from AP history. Katie Robinson. For a moment I do nothing but grin like an idiot, and then I'm launching myself up out of the chair and I'm hugging her. "What are you doing here, Katie?"

"I live in San Francisco."

"Where?" I let go, step back, glance at Gorgeous Guy and then Katie. "She's from Visalia, too." I can't stop beaming at her. "Do you live near here?"

"Up the street, three blocks over," she says, pointing toward Lombard. But Katie's not alone. She's with a friend she introduces as Kirk. Alex stands up, and we all shake hands.

With introductions over, I turn immediately back to Katie. It's been so long since I last saw her . . . seven years . . . eight . . . incredible.

"So how are you?" I ask for what seems like the fifth time.

"Good," Katie answers. "Really good. And you?"

"Great." I'm still grinning. I can't help it. These past few weeks have been really hard, and tonight was just the worst, and when I feel at my lowest, Kate Robinson appears. Kate—Katie—and I go way back, to all those geeky years when we washed our faces with Noxzema and slapped on Clearasil like it was going out of style.

"When did you return to California?" I ask. She'd moved away in the middle of our senior year. Her father had been transferred to the East Coast—Boston? Philadelphia? (It's terrible, but all those places sound the same to West Coasters.) And even though she'd begged to finish her year at Redwood, her parents had decided it'd be in the best interests of the family to move everyone at once. So they'd all gone, Katie and her three younger brothers.

My God. *Katie*. Katie Robinson.

And she's even more gorgeous than before, less whole-some, more sophisticated; cheekbones have emerged from adolescent baby fat; her eyebrows are darker; her blond hair highlighted and precision cut. She looks like the ultimate California girl, even though she's New Jersey born and partially bred.

"Two years ago. I work for Intel, but here in the city."

Alex is still standing, but he's reaching for the coat he'd slung over the back of his chair. "Sounds like you guys have a lot to catch up on. I'll let you chat, but, Holly, can I get your number?"

I think he's joking and then I see he's got a pen out and a scrap of paper with his number on it. I tear off the part with his number and then write my number on the other part. I look at him and think he's so out of my league—I mean, he is Gorgeous Guy after all—but I hand him my number, knowing he'll never call, knowing he's just trying to be nice since I was bawling my eyes out.

And then he's gone, gorgeous Alex walking out the door.

Katie is riffling through her purse, digging out a business card. "Kirk and I are on our way to a comedy club; he's got front-row tickets, so we can't be late." She pulls out a pen and scribbles a number on the back of her card. "But call me in the morning. Let's get drinks tomorrow night or meet on Sunday for brunch."

"Great." I put her card in my pocket but don't let go. It's a lifeline, something good from my past, something good in my present. "I'll call you in the morning."

She and Kirk are heading to the door. "Don't forget!" Katie shouts to me, raising her hand to her ear, thumb and pinkie extended. "Call me."

Katie and I meet for brunch Sunday morning. Brunch in the city is still something new to me. Growing up, we didn't belong to any country clubs, and brunch wasn't something we did as a family. It's not that Mom didn't ever make a big breakfast late in the morning, but there was no rushing out of the house on a Sunday if it wasn't for church. And after church there was usually housework and yard work to do. Not brunching.

But I swear, everyone in San Francisco does it, and on a nice day like today, dozens of people cluster outside every city café, talking, smoking, reading newspapers or novels, while waiting to be seated.

We put our name on the wait list and stand outside our corner café with everyone else. Lots of people wearing black, and leather barn coats, turtlenecks, boots, jeans, cords. I'm wearing a skirt. I don't know why I'm wearing a skirt. Maybe it's the old good-girl upbringing. Good girls don't wear jeans to church; good girls dress nicely for social occasions; good girls try to make an effort.

Or just possibly, good girls don't know any better.

Katie's telling me about her work. She travels a lot for business, is on the road a couple of weeks every month, but she likes the travel, loves accumulating mileage points, because it allows her to keep up with her friends on both coasts. She's between boyfriends at the moment but isn't worried, since there always seems to be someone new on the horizon.

A cool breeze blows, and I hug my coat tighter. "You like dating," I say, torn between admiration and horror as the restaurant door bangs open and a big group leaves. How can *anyone* like to date?

"Dating's fun. It's an adventure. You never know what's going to happen."

I flash back to my last two dates—my first two dates in years, and both scored very high on the Richter scale of horrible encounters. I'd have to give Tom a 6.8 or 6.9 for yucky company, and Paul . . . oh, he gets at least a 7.3, maybe even a 7.6, for boorish behavior and the booster seat request. Men should never ask for a booster seat on a date. That might be fine when you're out with Mom, but not with another woman. "And you like that feeling?"

Katie, who is wearing jeans, a dark turtleneck, and a suede coat, shrugs. She looks urban. Hip. *Cool.* How did she learn to do that? "Why not?" she answers, tucking straight blond hair behind her ear. "It's fun meeting new people, getting to see if you're going to click or not."

I really wish I hadn't worn a skirt. "I never click."

"Then you haven't been out enough. Dating's like the lottery. You've got to up your chances of winning by entering more times."

The black restaurant door opens again, and the hostess comes out, calls our name, and we get seated inside at one of the little tables next to the window. Normally a window seat is ideal, but today it means we get our sunlight blocked by a half-dozen people on the other side of the glass.

"So, Hol, what's new with you?" Katie asks as we sit down and rearrange our place settings more to our liking.

I nod to the busboy who has come to fill our water glasses. "Not much."

She laughs, a burst of short, explosive sound. "Not much? Holly. I got your wedding invitation."

"Mmmhmm."

"But you're not wearing your ring anymore. And you've made no mention of Jean-Paul—"

"Jean-Marc."

"Jean-Marc," she corrects impatiently, "and that means . . . ?"

"It means we're not together anymore."

"You're getting divorced?" Katie asks, eyeing me over her menu, but I can't say much more, because our waiter has arrived and he's giving us the specials, and I'm barely listening because I saw disappointment in Katie's eyes. Disappointment and . . . what? Disapproval? Sadness? What?

I order pancakes—easy enough to eat with knots in your stomach—and wait for the waiter to leave. "Yeah, we're getting divorced."

"You've filed."

"Yes."

Katie doesn't say anything for a minute. She just taps her spoon against the wooden table. Finally she drops her spoon and leans back in her chair. "You were the first from our crowd to marry."

And the first to divorce, I mentally add.

"So what happened?" she asks.

"He . . . we . . ." I try, and I stop. I honestly don't know how to explain, and I feel that wave of confusion and helplessness, the same one I felt in St. Tropez when I lay on the chaise longue in the sun and everyone was drinking and smiling and I felt cold and sick in my gut, knowing that something was wrong but not knowing how to fix it. "He wasn't in love with me."

Katie shoots me a you've-got-to-be-kidding look. "What?"

"He didn't want to be married. He told me on our honeymoon." I swallow. "Told me on the fourth night. Said he didn't . . ." I smile. I don't know why. I guess I figure if I smile, laugh, no one else can laugh at me; no one else can hurt me, because I've done it first. "He didn't feel that way about me. We were better friends than lovers."

"I don't understand." Katie shifts in her chair, arm hanging over the back. "You're smart, pretty, funny—"

"You'll change your mind after you marry me."

"Holly, I'm serious."

"So am I. But it's okay. I'm okay with the divorce."

But Katie doesn't move; she just stares at me, but her expression is serious, and she looks hard. Fierce. "It's not okay."

I bite the tip of my tongue. I'm not going to cry anymore. I'm sick of crying, sick of sad feelings. It's time to move on. "I can't blame him, Katie. I should have paid attention . . ."

"Attention to what?"

"The signs . . . the signals . . . I rushed him. Rushed the relationship. I was just so happy to be in love. I couldn't wait to get married."

Katie gestures curtly. "Don't ever say that again. Jean-Marc, Paul, whatever his name is, didn't have to marry you. He's a man, has all kinds of degrees from all kinds of prestigious universities, and he bought you a ring, and he showed up at the church, and paid for a honeymoon. *Blame* him. He screwed you over!"

"I know, but—"

"No. No buts. No more. Holly, stop being a frickin' doormat. You've always been too nice for your own good. Stop letting people walk all over you. Get off the floor and get a life!"

I start laughing. Coming from anyone else, this would have hurt me, but from Katie—formerly pimply, somewhat stocky Katie Robinson, who looked hideous in the bright blue polyester gym shorts we used to have to wear for PE (her thighs were so white, even I couldn't look at her when she ran)—it's a relief.

Katie can speak her mind with me and I'll listen. Katie knows my world—knows my mom, my family. (Heck, Jamie even came from college and took her to our senior prom when neither of us could get dates!) She practically grew up sleeping over at my house, or vice versa. If anyone has insight into my strengths and weaknesses, it's her.

"Why Jean-Marc?" she asks after a minute. "You never liked having a boyfriend. Why did you settle down so quickly with him? You're the one who never wanted to be tied down in high school."

She's right. It was pretty much the same in college, too. At UC Irvine I liked the idea of having a boyfriend, until I got one, and then I felt . . . trapped. Bored.

So why was I so desperate to marry Jean-Marc?

Because I thought he wasn't like American guys. He seemed more intelligent, more interesting, more sophisticated, more of everything. And when I thought I had found the right one, the Prince Charming I'd always been looking for, I jumped. "I was confused," I say after a moment, when the silence has stretched for an uncomfortably long time. "I guess I thought I was marrying a hero, someone foreign and glamorous, and I thought if someone sophisticated likes me, then well . . ." I shrug, and my voice fades away.

In the dim light, with her pale oval face and her long, straight blond hair, Katie's a study of contrasts: tough and tender, fragile and fierce. "You thought you'd be sophisticated, too," she concludes as our breakfast arrives.

We pause, allowing the waiter to do his presentation with a flourish and leave before we continue.

"I wanted to be special," I say in a small voice, staring down at my pancakes, and there's a pound of butter melting into the top of the stack. I really should scrape some of the butter off, but I like butter.

Katie's cutting into her corned beef hash and eggs. "A man doesn't make you special. You're special because you're you."

I finally, reluctantly push some of the butter off the stack. "So you feel special?"

"No." Katie cuts another bite, then looks up at me with a wicked smile. "But it's what all the experts say. No man will love us the way we need to be loved. We have to love ourselves before anyone else can love us."

And I suddenly see my mom, stretched out on the sofa in front of the TV night after night. Maybe that's why Mom is alone. It's not that she couldn't have company, but maybe she doesn't love herself and can't let anyone else love her.

"You're a genius," I say.

"No. I just watch a lot of Oprah and Dr. Phil."

I laugh. I can't help it, and yet, laughing, I realize how long it's been since I did this—felt something like this—

and as my laugh dies away, I know I want to laugh more. "It's good to see you, Katie."

"Definitely meant to be," she answers with a firm nod.

The waiter comes by with a pot of fresh coffee and refills our cups, and with our coffees refreshed and our plates nearly empty, Katie leans away from the table, fiddles with a bit of her hair. "I am sorry I missed your wedding, though. Heard it was beautiful. Jean-Marc's family all flew in from Paris, didn't they?"

"Provence," I correct. "And it was beautiful. Very formal. The wedding cost my mom a fortune." I think of the bridesmaids, the fresh flowers everywhere, the seven-tier wedding cake with delicate spun-sugar blossoms spilling down the side, and remembering makes me sick inside. So much money for so little love. "We should have just run away. Eloped. Done something private and cheap."

The corners of Katie's mouth lift. "But you're a princess, and you know it."

Once this might have made me smile, but it doesn't, not now, not after the past horrible year. I wanted to stay in the valley. I never intended to be living in the city. I like farm towns, and cows, and simple things. I wanted marriage and babies. How does that make me a princess? How did I become a princess?

I didn't go to an Ivy League college. I don't wear designer clothes. I don't own any nice jewelry. I don't even care about the kinds of cars men drive.

But I did want a "happily ever after." I did want the

storybook ending. I wanted happiness. I just don't know how to get it.

Monday at work, there's another team meeting, but this one is long and intensive. There are lots of upcoming events, lots of client appointments, lots of potential sales meetings. Olivia dispatches duties swiftly. We're all to bring in new accounts by the end of the quarter.

After the meeting Olivia takes off for an appointment with David. I don't know where they're going, and I don't really care. But once they're both gone, the office relaxes, and Tessa and Josh head downstairs together. I briefly wonder what's up with them before I check my e-mail in-box.

There are some boring business e-mails, and then—surprise, surprise!—an e-mail from Brian Fadden.

It's short, so short it shouldn't even be called an e-mail, but it makes me smile nonetheless.

"How's life in the jungle?"

He didn't sign his name, but it's there in his signature line, including all his various work contact numbers. "Life in the jungle," indeed. I smile at the computer screen. Chew the tip of my nail, wonder what I should say. I don't want to say too much—his e-mail was very short. And I can't be boring, as his e-mail was amusing.

So not too wordy, not too dry . . .

I think about it a little longer and then decide just to go for it. I type a quick reply. "It's actually a zoo, Mr. Fadden.

We have one of everything here." I hit "Send," watch the e-mail disappear in my out-box, and as I do, I feel a flutter of nerves and anticipation.

Let's see what happens now.

Then I do something I should have done ages ago: I go through my e-mail address book and delete Jean-Marc's e-mail addy. I delete every record of his phone number and mailing address from every place I've written it. I delete him from my cell phone. I delete him as much as I can from my life.

Finished, I sit back and look at my desk, stacked with folders and files, Post-it notepads filled with scribbled scrawl, and I feel better.

I feel good.

Mom was wrong. I wasn't lucky to have Jean-Marc. Jean-Marc was lucky to have me.

I leave my computer, grab a diet soda from the break room, and take the elevator downstairs, in need of fresh air.

Tessa's nowhere in sight, but Josh is still downstairs, smoking a cigarette.

"Hey," I say, joining him on the blue-painted railing. "I didn't know you smoked."

He exhales a stream of smoke, shakes his head. "I used to, years ago; then I quit, but started up again this week. It's disgusting. It'll kill me, I know."

We're silent a moment, and then Josh asks, "So whatever happened with Paul? Didn't you two go out on Friday night?"

"Yeah."

He taps the end of the cigarette, knocking off ash. "That good?"

I nod.

Josh shoots me a narrowed glance. "He can be a bit of a prick."

"Yeah."

His eyes narrow further. "What happened?"

I don't want to talk about it. Don't want to involve Josh. They're friends. No need to complicate things. "Nothing."

"Nothing, as in not good? Nothing as in, didn't go out? Nothing as . . . ?"

"Nothing." I close my eyes, lift my face up to the sun, and suddenly it feels like forever since I was together and on top of the world. I want to be on top of the world again. I want that radiant, joyful, I'm-so-glad-to-be-alive feeling back.

Instead every day feels a decade long, and I know it's because I think so much. Does everyone think this much? Does everyone want as much as I do?

Does anyone else worry that there won't be more? Worry that maybe this is it, maybe this will be all there ever is?

I open my eyes, look down the street at the heavy traffic streaming past the convention center. There has to be more magic still, I think. Somewhere. All the happy endings and good things can't just be at Disneyland. Adults need happy stories, too.

Josh leans over and smashes his cigarette in the sand. "You're not going to see him again, are you?"

"No."

"Good."

I look at Josh. "I thought you were friends."

"I am. But that doesn't mean he's good for you. He's a pain in the ass. So stay clear, okay?"

I wonder how much Josh knows. Probably more than he'll ever say. I nod, grateful Josh is on my side for this one. "Okay."

I stop by the gym on the way home and jog away on the treadmill. I will never be a real runner, but today I'm so restless that I can't seem to stop moving. By the time I'm finished, I've run for nearly thirty-five minutes, a new record for me.

At home I boil water for Cup O' Noodles and try to settle down with a cable movie but can't relax. Cup O' Noodles is not a satisfying dinner. I want chewy and chocolate, like frosted brownies, but have only peanut butter on my shelves, so I spread some of that on crackers.

I need to grocery-shop.

And I need to buy a desktop computer for my apartment. I spread more peanut butter on another cracker, thinking about the computer I used to have in Fresno, an old laptop that Jean-Marc gave me but took back when we parted. That was so cheap, I think, chomping on my cracker. He had a computer at the university, a brand-new laptop in his study at home. He didn't need his old one. He didn't have to take it back.

Jerk.

Another week goes by, and I manage to get into the gym only twice, but walking through my neighborhood one evening I notice that the small flower shop is still open, and I purchase a big bouquet of lilies and gerbera daisies for my apartment.

I keep sniffing the sweet, heady fragrance of the lilies as I walk back to my apartment. I'm feeling really cosmopolitan at the moment. Single city girl doing her shopping, buying fresh sourdough bread at the corner bakery, and flowers on her way home . . .

I hum a little and smile at people as I pass them.

I'm doing okay, I think. I'm actually beginning to like living on my own.

Brian Fadden and I have been talking on the phone for a few minutes every couple of days for the past week, and our sporadic, brief e-mails have gotten more frequent, as well as longer.

Today I get an e-mail from Brian asking if I want to get a beer with him after work.

The e-mail couldn't have come at a better time; after

another weekend alone, I've reached that desperation point. The point where almost anything is better than nothing, where Monday night beer nights are better than Monday night going home after a bad day at work and sitting alone.

I know that in general, Monday night dollar-beer nights are best avoided. Monday nights are not great date nights, but when you're sitting there at your desk at ten thirty on Monday morning and you hate your desk and hate your cubicle and hate the computer and hate that you have to work and that you're going to be sitting here for the next five days, a date for that evening actually sounds good.

Fun.

Why the hell not? I ask myself, staring at the computer screen, studying Brian's e-mail invitation. I don't feel like going to the gym after work. Mondays are already long enough and hard enough, and I don't really want to go home to an empty apartment. And Brian's e-mails are fabulous. Brilliant. The guy has a way with words.

I chew on my thumb, stare at the screen, insides warm and fizzy. I love the warm fizzies. But is it Brian giving me the warm fizzies, or his cleverness? I've always liked dry humor, smart men, but am I physically attracted to him?

It is just drinks at this point. I mean, Brian doesn't have to be "the one," but of course I always wonder when I meet a man, is he possibly Mr. Right?

And Brian does fit the requirements for a Mr. Right (not that I'm looking). He's clever in e-mail, funny over the phone, educated, sophisticated, *and* he knows how to make me laugh.

But what would he be like in bed?

I close my eyes, try to remember what he looks like. Tall—I remember that much—broad-shouldered, relatively lean. Basketball-player build. Athletic. And if he's athletic, he'd probably be quite comfortable with his body. In bed.

That'd be good.

I e-mail back: "Okay. Meet you there at 7."

He replies almost immediately, and we've got plans. I'm thrilled this is just drinks, not dinner. Dinner means serious conversation, requiring a level of sincerity not necessary for drinks.

Dinner means possible romance, while drinks mean light, nonthreatening . . . *fun*.

*D*rinks with Brian are fun.

He isn't exactly as I remembered. He's actually leaner and taller—much taller—but the conversation is light, easy, with lots of banter. On our second beer (we've now spent a total of four dollars), Brian asks me about the ball. "How are the plans coming?"

"So-so. We've picked up a couple of sponsors, and I've got a small piece coming out in the San Mateo paper, but that's it."

Brian looks at me for a moment, his sandy hair flopped down across his forehead, and he looks both wry and serious at the same time. "I've got someone who might be willing to interview your boss, Burkheimer, as part of a look at AIDS, twenty years after. It'd get you a lead into promoting the ball."

It's an amazing offer, but I don't know that David will agree to the interview. "I don't know if David will discuss Tony in an interview like that."

"I don't know, either." Brian leans on the table. "Especially since Tony was Antony Pelloci."

The name's familiar, but I can't figure out why, and I look at Brian blankly.

"He was an actor, very talented, one of those serious actors who does only theater, no film or television."

"Would anyone recognize his name?"

"Lots of people would, at least those that read the pink section." The pink section being the *San Francisco Chronicle's* weekend arts-and-entertainment section, where all the pages are a pale bubble-gum pink for easy identification.

"How do you know so much about Tony?"

He gives me that frank, appraising glance again. "Olivia."

"Olivia?"

"She brought this to me a couple years ago, wanted me to help massage this angle into a story."

"And you wouldn't?"

"Not after the shit she pulled."

But he'd do it for me, I think, and I'm not sure if I'm nervous or excited. It could be a great story, could be a really wonderful human interest piece, but David might not want to do it, and Olivia . . .

Olivia wouldn't be happy if she knew the idea came about because, well, it came from Brian down to me.

But I say none of this. "Let me see what I can do."

Tuesday morning at the office I shoot Tessa an e-mail. "Can we talk?" I write.

I get an e-mail back a little later. "Are you still hiding from the big bad wolf?"

I'm grimly amused and wait for Olivia to head off for lunch before I drop by Tessa's office. I report the details of my conversation with Brian, and Tessa is nodding thoughtfully. "It'd be a great story," she says. "A wonderful human interest piece that would get the focus off the craziness of the ball and back onto the Hospice Foundation."

"Will David do the interview?"

"I don't know. But maybe we don't need David's permission. Maybe we just authorize the story on Tony, kind of a retrospect on the local talent lost since the AIDS epidemic began." Tessa reaches for the phone. "I'll give Brian a call." She smiles at me. "Thanks. This could be good."

Brian gets a staff reporter on the story, but since David can't be interviewed, the story gets bigger, becoming a true feature about the tragedy of AIDS, and a sampling of the great local artists lost in the past twenty years. Staff members at the paper have compiled a list of dancers, designers, painters, writers, actors, models, and more. Stark black-and-white photos will accompany the text.

The story keeps its San Francisco focus, and on the same page where the feature ends, there's a lead-in blurb for the Leather & Lace Ball.

Sunday the story runs, and it's a terrific story, tautly written and yet deeply emotional. Brian and I celebrate by going to a Thai restaurant, and then we're to head to a jazz club to hear some music. But after dinner we stop by Brian's apartment first.

I'm not exactly sure how or why we ended up at his apartment. I think we returned for a coat or tickets, but once inside, I remember little but being shocked by his Spartan apartment. There's no way this man could have been married ten years. He has nothing. Nothing. Ancient milk crates packed with ancient vinyl records. Black-and-white photographs of India and Nepal, matted but not framed, lean against the baseboard. A futon-type mattress on the floor without even the benefit of a cheap futon frame. The one thing he does have is books. Bookcases of them, boxes, stacks.

Books are everywhere, and Brian steps over a stack to head into his minuscule kitchen. "A beer?" he asks.

I keep doing slow circles, checking out his place. "No, thanks." Sounds rude, but I didn't want to stay.

I like Brian, but his apartment feels so empty and sad.

Brian returns from the kitchen, hands me a soda instead. "Sorry about the mess." He nods at the boxes and crates. "I need to get more bookshelves, I think."

You think?

"Have kids?" I ask, and I don't know why. There's just something so lonely about a small apartment without furniture, blinds at the window, without a feeling of home.

"No." He uncaps his beer, takes a drink. "We spent too many years fighting to ever make love."

"I'm sorry." And I am. Brian Fadden just feels so big, so real, so imposing that this little apartment strikes me as wrong. "How long have you been here?"

"Nearly four years." He flashes me his wry smile. "Ever since I returned from Fresno."

"I thought your divorce was only recently finalized."

"It was. I waited a couple years to file. She said she didn't care. She said I could do whatever the hell I wanted. So I took her literally and didn't bother to do anything." He gestures to the brown futon hunched pathetically on the floor. "Have a seat."

I perch on a windowsill instead. "She went down to Fresno with you?"

"For a while." He takes another sip of his beer and grabs a milk carton, drags it forward, and sits down on it, his denim-clad legs looking a mile long. He's wearing loafers—with tassels—but the loafers are so old and scuffed and water-stained, they look fine.

"Do you want kids?" I persist.

"Maybe. Someday. You?"

I circle my soda, the can so cold against my skin. Yeah, I want kids. I want two, three—you know, the usual. "I did. My husband didn't." And it feels so funny even to call Jean-Marc my husband now. I've been in San Francisco only five months, and yet our life together—that brief span of time—seems light-years away.

It probably doesn't help that Jean-Marc never acted like my husband, either.

"Is that why you divorced?"

"That and—" I break off, shocked that I almost blurted, *He didn't want to do me,* as if that's something you can say.

"And?"

I hesitate. "He didn't want to be married to me."

"He's a fool."

I shake my head, bite my lip.

"Maybe he's gay," Brian says.

It'd be convenient to believe, and it's what everyone likes to suggest, but I don't think it's true. I think it's me. I did something to Jean-Marc's libido. I killed whatever attraction . . . desire . . . love existed.

Brian leans forward, grabs my hand, and he's pulling me to my feet, moving me toward him, and I resist only a little. I don't want *him,* but I could use comfort.

Yet do I want comfort from him?

No. Truthfully, I'm not sure what I want from Brian. I like him; I enjoy his company; he's interesting and he makes me laugh. But part of me is still numb and chilly on the inside, as if I were standing one person removed from myself and couldn't quite figure out how to get back inside my own body.

But Brian brings me between his knees. He's sitting on a crate, sitting low, but he's still so tall, we're nearly at eye level. "How old are you, Holly Bishop?"

He's combing his fingers through my hair, and I feel a

little colder. Someday someone will have to touch me. When will that someday be? When will I enjoy skin again? I'm trying not to panic, trying to tell myself to relax, and this is Brian, and you like him, but part of me wants to cry.

"Almost twenty-six."

"I've got at least ten years on you," he says.

And he's still touching me, and I'm still standing here, and everything inside me is quiet. It's as if I had gone to sleep and just handed myself over to him.

He combs through my hair, pushing my long bangs off my face. "You're just a baby." He pulls me down to sit on his lap.

I'm so bare on the inside right now, so much like Brian's apartment, that I let him touch me, let him look at me. It's hard living alone, hard trying to know what to do all the time.

Then he clasps my face between his hands, and kisses me. The kiss starts out tentative and slow and then morphs into something else completely, and yet I'm frozen on the inside, unsure how to respond. The kiss feels so new and different, and I'm not sure what to think, or feel.

Suddenly with a little twist, I pull away from Brian and jump to my feet. "Wow."

Brian stands up. "I didn't scare you, did I?" he asks, and he's suddenly touching the back of my head, a very gentle touch, and it's such a contrast to the intensity of his kiss.

"No." But I blink back tears.

"Because I really like you, Holly. You're a very special woman."

Woman. *Woman?* When did I become a woman? I still feel like a girl.

It's sprinkling outside when I step from his building. The streets are damp and dark, and my hair and skin soon feel equally cool and damp.

Brian waits with me on the curb until we manage to flag down a cab. "I can take you home," he says for the third time in as many minutes.

"I don't want you to lose your parking spot," I reply as the taxi pulls up.

"I'll call you tomorrow," he says, putting me into the back of the cab and bending low to kiss me good-bye, a light peck on the lips.

As the taxi pulls away, I touch my mouth with the back of my hand. I'm not wiping away the kiss, but it feels odd. Brian's the first man I've wanted to kiss since Jean-Marc, but kissing him wasn't what I thought it'd be. When I kissed him, I didn't feel like me. But that's silly. A kiss is just a kiss . . . or is it?

There's so much talk about kissing. Everyone (at least on TV) does it. You see them at the park, lying on the grass even after a rain, kissing as though there were no tomorrow, and it appears easy, kissing. But I have to tell you, kissing baffles me. It's a complete mystery.

A kiss either works for me or it doesn't. There's no in-between, and I can rarely be convinced that a kiss is good if my instincts are telling me otherwise.

The problem is, I didn't feel anything when Brian kissed me, but I did like him. I *do* like him. Maybe I just need more time.

The next day at work, David calls an all-company meeting, one of the first in weeks. He's got the *Chronicle* article up on the wall in the boardroom, and his expression is closed, impossible to read.

Once everyone is seated around the table, he walks to the door, pushes it closed, and turns to face us. "This," he says, pointing to the paper on the wall, "is amazing. This is what we do. This is what we're about. Positive. Supportive. Professional. Relationships."

David glances at Tessa. "You and your team are to be commended. I don't know how you got the paper to run the feature above a write-up about the Leather and Lace Ball, but it's fantastic. The phone has been ringing all morning." He nods at Tessa. "Do you want to share the good news with everyone?"

Tessa is wearing a hot-pink turtleneck that clashes brilliantly with her spiky red hair. She blushes, her freckles dark against the pink of her skin. "The ball has sold out. The event has been completely underwritten."

David smacks his hands together. "Which means the Hospice Foundation should clear at least 2.1 million dollars." He grins. "At least. Amazing work, team."

Everyone in the boardroom claps, and Josh whistles and Tessa smiles, but Olivia is barely clapping. I think her fingers might have touched twice, and she's not smiling. She's looking at me.

Straight at me.

And her eyes are hard, brutally hard, and I inhale swiftly, my blood chilling.

We leave the boardroom, and I think Olivia is going to call a team meeting of her own, but she doesn't. She disappears into her office and closes the door. I grab the phone, dial Brian's number.

"Did you hear the news?" I say. "The ball's sold out— the tickets are gone and we picked up all new corporate sponsorship. The Hospice Foundation will raise more money this year than ever before."

"Fantastic." He's pleased, too, really pleased. "We've got to go celebrate again."

I remember last night's kiss and think I'm not ready for another one of those, but I also want to bask in the glory of the ball's success a little longer. "Okay. When?"

"Tonight."

"Tonight?"

"Is there a problem with tonight?"

"I was going to buy a new computer after work, try to

get it up and running. I haven't had a computer since I moved from Fresno."

"I can help you set it up," Brian offers.

"Really?"

"Sure. I'll bring dinner over and get to work."

I'm a little nervous about him coming over to the apartment, but he's been so awesome, such a great resource as well as supportive that I can't say no. Besides, I could use the help with my computer. Technology baffles me.

"All right. By the time I hit Circuit City and get home, it'll be six thirty or seven."

"Not a problem."

I smile, relax. He is so nice about everything. And it's wonderful getting help. I feel as if I've been battling alone for such a long time. "Thanks again, Brian, for all the help with the ball. The event wouldn't be a success without you."

"My pleasure, Holly. I'd love to see Olivia's face right now. I'm sure she's frothing at the mouth."

"She did *not* look happy in the staff meeting."

"Did she say anything?"

"No. But she gave me a look that could kill."

"She doesn't think you're involved, does she?"

"I hope not. If Olivia knew—" and I suddenly stop because something's wrong, very wrong, and I can feel it all the way through my bones.

I look up. Oh, God. No.

Olivia is standing next to my desk. Her gray-green eyes are fixed on me, and her expression is strange . . . neither warm nor cold, kind nor harsh. It's . . . empty. Vacant.

"Holly?" Brian's speaking to me, but I can't answer. "Holly, are you there?"

"I have to go," I whisper into the phone, and hang up before he can say anything.

Olivia is just standing there, and I know I've royally fucked up. Not a little screw-up, but the kind of screw-up where I can't breathe.

I go numb, the air bottling inside my chest. My skin turns colder and colder until I think I'm just better off dead. "Olivia."

"Who was that?" she asks, her voice quiet. Calm. Perfectly detached.

I can't answer. I just look at her, a horrible spaniellike pleading look saying *I'm sorry, I'm sorry, I'm sorry.* But Olivia ignores me and leans forward, hitting the last number dialed on my phone, and Brian's name and number flash.

"Brian Fadden," she says, straightening.

Shit.

"I'm sorry." Usually my biggest fuckups are private. I don't think I've ever humiliated myself quite this way at work before. My stomach is grinding like a kid who's learning to drive and can't find the right gear.

"For what?" Her tone is glacial, her expression just as frigid and brittle.

I open my mouth to confess but see Josh and Tessa from the corner of my eye, and suddenly I don't know what to say. Because if I confess, I'm probably fired. If I don't, I'm lying. I don't know what's right anymore. I always used to be honest, straightforward, but honesty is beginning to seem a little overrated. I do a sidestep instead. "For taking care of personal matters on company time."

"*Personal* matters?" One of her elegant eyebrows arches higher. "Brian Fadden? My contact at the paper?"

"He and I . . . well, we're sort of . . . dating."

Her head jerks back. You'd think a snake had bitten her between the eyes. "Dating?"

"He's coming over for dinner tonight." I'm so numb and scared and the words are just pouring out of their own accord. "We were finalizing plans."

She looks at me so long that I shrink in my chair.

"You better not have been involved with that article, Holly." Her voice is hard. Ruthless. "Because a mistake is one thing. Betrayal's another."

I can't wait to get home. I hardly leave my desk the rest of the day. Josh shoots me an e-mail: "You okay?"

I answer, "Can't talk about it right now."

Later Tessa sends me an e-mail: "Everything's fine. Take a deep breath. Nothing bad is going to happen."

Maybe not to her.

Even Sara stops by my desk, leaves a big chocolate-chip cookie on the corner. "Thought you could use a little something sweet," she says.

Why do I suddenly feel like a death row prisoner getting her last supper?

I go to Circuit City after work, buy the computer I saw advertised in the Sunday paper, haul it home, shower and change, and am just getting dressed when Brian arrives.

Brian's brought a big pizza and Caesar salads and a bottle of red wine. "She was standing there, wasn't she?" he asks, opening the wine in the kitchen.

I reach into the cupboard for wineglasses. "How did you know?"

"You sounded like Dead Woman Walking."

I still haven't quite gotten over the shock of seeing Olivia standing there behind me, and shudder a little remembering. "I felt that way, too."

I rinse out the Waterford glasses, and Brian pours the wine—the first time I've used the stemware since moving to the city.

"I think I'm doomed," I say, clinking glasses with him, far less celebratory than I was this morning at ten.

"She can't fire you without David's approval, can she?" he asks, leaning against one counter.

"I'd hope not."

"You've been pulling your weight, haven't you?"

"I'm working hard."

"David will see that. From everything I've heard, he's a reasonable man."

I nod and get busy setting the little kitchen table with a red-and-white-checked picnic cloth that now looks Italian and festive, and we sit down and eat and drink and continue talking.

"She'll get over it," Brian says later, as we finish eating.

I wipe my hands on my napkin. I've had two and a half glasses of wine and am mellower but not yet fully recovered. Those bad feelings today were so bad, they're hard to forget. "So what's the story of you and Olivia?" I ask. "Because you both are a little cagey about each other."

Brian eyes me above his wineglass. "Really? What does she say about me?"

"Not a lot. It's what she doesn't say."

He shrugs. "We went out once."

"Just once?"

"Mmm."

"And . . . ?"

Another shrug. "We didn't click."

"She used you." The words just popped out of my mouth, and I don't know why or how, but I look at him, make a face. "Sorry."

"You don't have to feel sorry for me. I used her, too."

I feel my eyebrows climb.

"She does have an incredible body." His look is pointed, and I feel small on the inside, small and insignificant because I can't compete on this level. I will never, ever be the chick with the hot bod.

Brian flashes me a humorous smile. "You asked."

"I wish I hadn't." And it's a struggle to get the rest of my pizza crust down without gagging. I'd give my right arm to have half what Olivia has. Olivia is smart, worldly, sophisticated. She's tough, has attitude, doesn't get stepped on, does the stepping instead.

That's power.

That's something I don't have and don't think I ever will.

We carry our wineglasses to the living room and the little table I've set up in the corner, awaiting my new desktop. "So what kind of computer did you buy?" Brian asks, hunkering down in front of the boxes lying on the floor. He's so big, he makes the table and chair shrink. Even the computer box looks small.

"I'm not sure. But the price was good," I say, stepping around him.

"Women," he mutters, but gently, teasingly, as he tears open the box containing the new hard drive.

For the next fifteen minutes he attaches cords and plugs in things, connecting the various components until he boots the computer, and magic—there's sound and color. Action. Inserting one of the CDs, he does something else, reboots the computer, hits a few keys, registers me, and boom, I'm ready to go. "You're connected, online, free to surf the Net, shop, whatever your heart desires."

Whatever my heart desires. If only I knew what my heart desires.

"Thanks so much," I say, collecting all the plastic bags and bits of Styrofoam and empty cardboard boxes that protected the computer, screen, and keyboard.

"Piece a cake."

"Well, for you, maybe."

"It's easy. But I'm glad I could help." He reaches for me, pulls me down on his lap. "I like helping you."

"You do?"

"I missed you today."

"You did?"

He nods, smooths my hair. "I think about you a lot."

And I think about him, but not like this. I like him, but I'm not sure what I feel. I'm not sure about anything. Brian is everything good and kind and wonderful, but I'm still so numb on the inside, still so scared about everything.

Brian hands me my half-empty wineglass. "Finish," he says.

I take a few halfhearted sips, and his head lowers. I know he's going to kiss me, and I know that I'm not ready to be kissed. Not by him. Not by anyone. His lips touch mine, and I try to relax, try to let the fear and tension go, but I can't. I can't get past the hurt and the hint of panic, can't get past the feeling that I'm Goldilocks trying to find the right porridge, the right bed. Nothing feels comfortable inside me yet. And even Brian Fadden, who is smart and clever, thoughtful and helpful, isn't what I need.

At least not yet.

As his kiss starts to deepen, I put my hand on his chest and gently but firmly push him back. "Brian."

He looks down at me, says nothing.

This is going to hurt him; I know it will, but I can't keep ignoring what I feel. Or what I need. "Brian, I like you. I do." I take a quick breath. "But I'm not ready for this. I need time. Time to sort things out."

He nods, the corner of his mouth curving. "I know you do."

He hesitates, then kisses me in the middle of my forehead before lifting me off his lap and putting me on my feet. He rises, reaches for his coat. "But when you're ready to date, call me."

"Okay."

For a moment he hesitates at my door, and I feel odd—prickly, emotional, sad—but this isn't about him; it's about me. About the things I have to learn and understand and do.

His mouth quirks again, and then he's gone, and the door shuts. I'm alone.

I realize, as Brian's footsteps echo outside, that I'm alone because I want to be.

I'm alone because it's what I need for me.

It's strange when a week goes by without a single e-mail from Brian.

It's what I wanted, but suddenly my life does seem a little lonelier. Brian and I had been e-mailing quite a bit lately, and it was nice getting his quirky notes once or twice a day. He always made me smile, and I looked forward to the interruption, but at the same time I didn't want to be leaning on him like the proverbial crutch.

The whole point is that I have to—as unpleasant as it sometimes seems—stand on my own two feet. I've got to be okay without a man. I think of my mom, and she *says* she is, but is she really?

If you know the story of Snow White and Rose Red, two sisters, daughters of a poor widow, you'll recognize my mom. She's the Snow White sister, the one the story describes as quiet and gentle, who sat at home with her mother and helped her in the household, or read aloud to her when there was no work to do. That's my mother. A woman who keeps her cottage beautifully clean and is unfailingly cheerful. A good, sweet woman deserving of a prince.

But to get princes, Snow White and her sister Rose Red had to be so good. They had to make sure there were always roses in vases on tables. The copper kettle had to shine. The floor had to be immaculate. And the girls had to be gentle, loving, obedient.

Obedient.

I'm sorry, but that sounds awful. Those stories teach that love is reserved for those who sacrifice themselves, rather like the beautiful ballerina from "The Steadfast Tin Soldier," who burns up with her guy at the end, symbolizing true love. I don't think so. One shouldn't have to die—physically or psychologically—for love. Love should be about strength, not weakness. Empowerment, not dependence.

Shouldn't it?

Katie's back in town, and Friday night we go out for happy hour and have such a good time that Katie calls me up Saturday morning, insisting that I go clubbing with her, her buddy Kirk, and a few others. I haven't been to a club, or dancing, in so long I feel like my grandma Bishop, but I'm still basking in the glow of a successful Friday night happy hour so I agree.

I spend a long time Saturday evening trying to figure out what I'm supposed to wear for a club. Most of those places are dark, so I figure anything black will do, and make a huge fashion statement with black jeans, a low-cut black top, and black belt and boots.

Studying myself in the mirror, I know, even without anyone's help, that this is a wrong look for me.

I change out of black jeans and try the top with regular jeans, and it's better. Far from snazzy, but knowing the contents of my closet, I'm forced to accept that "snazzy" isn't part of its vocabulary. "Safe" is. As is "boring." "Predictable." Which is what we'll do tonight.

I make an effort with my hair, try to do something interesting with earrings, and head outside as soon as my phone rings, letting me know Katie's in the drive.

But I'm not fast enough for Katie, and she leans on the car horn once, twice, and as I run out of my apartment, I see Cindy pull back the blinds upstairs and stare out. I can just picture the note I'll get beneath my door later: *Holly, per contract, section 3a of IIb, no cars in driveway and no honking. This is your last and final warning. Next infraction will result in an immediate impounding of family and friends.*

But once we're out, I forget all about Cindy and her rules and just have fun. Kirk, it turns out, is a part-time DJ, part-time journalist (he writes for a popular magazine in the city), and knows everyone, including the bouncer, who lets us scoot past those waiting in line, straight into the club's VIP room.

The club is thumping, the heavy bass vibrating the floor as we take the stairs up to the private lounge.

I've never been in a VIP lounge, and while Kirk offers to buy the first round and goes in search of the cocktail waitress, I sink into one of the low purple velvet couches with scarlet silk throw pillows, thinking that I've finally arrived.

That is, until I look around and see lots of girls with really great tans, bare legs, tiny skirts, and painfully high heels. It's like a Paris Hilton convention, and I'm Paris's chaperone.

(Furious Note to Self: jeans and black top aren't cool club clothes after all.)

Kirk returns with martini-style cocktails: cucumber cosmo—not my favorite drink by a long shot, but he paid for them and I'm not about to look any more fuddy-duddy by turning my nose up at the drink of the hour.

Sipping our cocktails, Kirk and I stand at the window overlooking the dance floor below. Katie's already dancing. She's wearing one of those itty-bitty skirts, and as more people converge on the dance floor, I lose her in the crowd.

"Is Katie going to be okay?" I ask Kirk.

Kirk, who keeps his head shaved and looks remarkably like Andre Agassi, gives me a look. "Katie's in her element. We won't see her until they kick us out."

I'm impressed. "Who is she dancing with?"

"Herself. She meets people on the dance floor." He grins at my expression. "Our Katie's not shy."

Kirk is hailed by a couple across the room who look familiar, but I can't place them. He heads over to talk to them, and I watch him shake hands with the guy and lean forward to kiss the girl's cheek. They talk for a few minutes, and then Kirk returns, joining me on the velvet sofa where I've curled up, feeling quite cozy and content to people-watch.

"You're not going to dance?" Kirk asks.

I don't even recognize the song, but I don't tell him that. "Maybe later. This is just fun being here."

One of Kirk's very dark eyebrows lifts. "You don't get out much, do you?"

I laugh, lean back into the squishy velvet cushions. "Is it that obvious?"

Kirk puts his feet up on the clear Lucite coffee table. "Yes."

I sip from my glass, hoping the cucumber cosmo has grown on me. It hasn't. I do my best not to wrinkle my nose. It's not strongly flavored, but I do feel as if I were out at a Thai restaurant eating a little cucumber salad.

"You're a writer?" I ask him.

"Sort of." He tips his head back against the cushion, and he's got an amazing profile: strong, masculine features, defined Roman nose, square jaw, dense eyelashes. If he had hair, he'd be beautiful. "I write, but I'm not obsessed with it."

"Are you obsessed with being a DJ?" I persist.

One of his dark eyebrows lifts. "Are you obsessed with being an event planner?"

Thank God he doesn't take himself so seriously. "You're not Greek, are you?"

"Do you have a problem with Greeks?"

"No. They're gorgeous. And I love Greek food."

"I agree. But no, I'm not Greek." He drains his martini. "Armenian. My dad's full. My mom's half."

"And your last name is Benneyan?"

"No."

"Shuklian?"

"No."

"Ekezian. Kirkorian. Morsalian—"

"No. No. No. But you do know a lot of Armenians."

"Central California."

"That's where my mom's from. Fresno."

I nod quite seriously. "I used to live there."

Kirk shoots me a side glance. "Should I express my condolences?"

I nearly punch him in the arm, going so far as to make a fist and wave it in the air. "It's not that bad," I protest, but even my protest sounds halfhearted to me. "Why does everyone have to knock Fresno?"

"Because we can." He lifts an arm, biceps rippling as he gestures to the cocktail waitress across the room. "So Katie said you work at City Events."

"Yeah. You've heard of it, then?"

"Olivia's hired me a couple of times to DJ different events."

I groan. "Don't tell me you've dated Olivia, too!"

His eyes crease, and he grins. "No. Olivia's easy to look at, but I prefer men."

My jaw nearly drops just as the cocktail waitress appears to take our drink order.

"Another round?" Kirk asks.

I nod. Then shake my head. "How about a different drink?"

"That was a terrible drink, wasn't it?"

"Awful," I agree, and reach into my purse, extract cash from my wallet. "But I'll buy this round, and let's try something else."

Kirk and I end up dancing later, and Katie finds us on the dance floor, tugs the guys she's dancing with over to join us. For the next hour we're all dancing and shouting over the music and sweating (at least I'm sweating), and by the time we escape the club, it's after one. I don't think I've been out this late in, well . . . in years. At least not since college.

I've only had a couple of drinks. And after several hours on the dance floor, my feet are killing me. I'm dying to rip my clothes off and climb into bed butt naked, but I had fun. *Fun*.

Is that weird, or what?

Monday arrives, and it's work. After work it's the gym, and I'm just glad when Monday's over and Tuesday arrives, because that leaves only four more days in the workweek.

After I escape Olivia's evil eye, I go out to dinner with Josh and Tessa, who act as if they barely tolerate each other, but I'm beginning to think are secretly seeing each other. We go to a little Cuban place in the Mission district, eat great food, drink more mojitos than we should, and then I cab it home.

Tomorrow I'm supposed to be out of the office most of the day on appointments, trying to generate new business, so I dress for success the next morning, spend extra time at home in the bathroom in front of the mirror, polishing my appearance, and the extra effort pays off. As I leave for work, I know I've come together okay. I feel like—and it sounds foolish, but it's true—a million bucks.

Or a cool thousand.

But either way, it's a heck of a lot better than what I've felt like this past year.

In the office I check my e-mail, return a few phone calls, attend a brief team meeting before grabbing a cab for the financial district.

Five minutes later as I walk down the street, portfolio beneath my arm, the San Francisco sun glinting overhead, and reflecting off the shining towers on California Street, from the corner of my eye I see heads turning. I pretend I don't notice, but I do. On the outside I feel good. On the inside I feel . . . great.

Damn. I had to wait a long time to get this feeling. But

it came. Shiny, bouncy hair. Clear skin. A couple of pounds knocked off. It helps that I chose flattering trousers and a fitted blouse that makes me look curvy on top with a nice, small waist. I'm wearing heels, too, which will kill me later, but I'm feeling no pain now, and as I walk, I just let it go.

I reach for the door of One California Street, and suddenly an arm stretches out above my head, opens the door for me, and I try not to smile too broadly as I glance up and nod my thanks. I'm not a particularly polished princess, and I think that deep down, men don't really want princesses that are too sophisticated, too demanding. They want someone like me. Attractive but not plastic, smart and yet fundamentally kind. I can't believe men really want the hard, beautiful bitchy royals out there. They want real, don't they? They'll want me, won't they?

I press the elevator Up button, enter the elevator when the doors open, press 21 and step back.

Three men have entered with me, and they, too, press their floors and step back, and we're all standing there, staring ahead. In the reflection I see one man looking at me. Watching me.

Glancing up, I see a shimmer of my face in the reflective stainless steel of the elevator ceiling, and for a moment I understand what this man sees—good hair, good face, good look—but instinctively I know that what he wants isn't me.

He has his own idea of me. His own wish for me. I'd be the woman he needs, not the woman I probably am, and it crosses my mind that all the hair and clothes and makeup we women wear just add to the deception. Our exterior covers more than it reveals.

I'm not always so impeccably groomed, and I don't want to be Barbie. And yet to get the attention, many of us put our best face forward, the carefully plucked, arched eyebrow, the flawless foundation, the smooth matte lip liner with the smoother tawny lipstick. It's the illusion of a perfect face, but for me it's not my real face. My real face is like me. Crooked. Flawed. Likable if you get to know it. But most men don't get to know it. They get to know the shiny Holly, the Holly who cleans up well, the one who can talk sports and make pleasant conversation, and for most men, it's enough.

For most men, that's what they want. Well, that and nice tits and a hopefully cellulite-light ass. Oh, and also hot in bed, and a mouth that's big enough to give a great blow job. And the desire, too, to give frequent head. Have I forgotten anything?

I don't think so.

The elevator opens at the sixteenth floor, again at the nineteenth, and for a moment it's just the guy who looked at me, and then the elevator stops at the twenty-first floor, and as I get off, the guy suddenly speaks.

"Have a good one," he says.

And I turn, look at him. He's tall, broad-shouldered in his dark suit, and he has a strong face with a hint of a cleft in his chin. I smile gratefully. "Thanks. You, too."

The doors close.

I stand there for a moment, feeling a wave of regret. The bittersweet sense that I lost something somewhere. What was it? Opportunity? Hope? A dream?

Then I reach for the door of Bloomberg, Bloomberg and Silverman and exhale hard, fiercely, growing my thicker skin. It's going to be okay. Everything will be just fine. And now it's time to sell. Not just City Events, but myself. Because after all, that's what clients are buying.

The clients bought. City Events, with me coordinating, will plan their holiday office party, a dignified supper party at a dignified restaurant, and yet with style and flare, because Bloomberg, Bloomberg and Silverman is a law firm for today's generation, and today's generation wants more than sound legal advice—they want sensitive sophistication and compassion.

Leaving the law firm, I'm just about to hail a cab when my cell phone rings. I answer without checking the number.

It's Brian. "Where are you?" he asks.

"Financial district." It's easy to inject warmth into my voice. I'm glad to hear from him. I had this horrible feeling he was just going to cut me out of his life. "Just about to cab it back to the office."

"Cab it to Market instead. Meet me for a late lunch."

I glance at my watch, knowing that Olivia will be pacing, waiting for an update on my meeting with the law firm. "I don't think I've time."

"Of course you do. You haven't taken a lunch today, and you deserve a lunch if you're out pounding the pavement."

He's right, and yet I hesitate.

Brian sighs. "Olivia takes lunch every day."

"She's my boss. She can do what she wants."

He makes a rough sound. "Ain't that the truth."

I laugh. I can't help it, and I give in. "Okay. Where?"

He names the restaurant, and I tell him I'll need a few minutes. I get there in less time than I think, and yet he's got a table at the window, and I see him as I enter the restaurant. His long legs define the space; his big upper body takes up even more room. Jean-Marc was fairly tall, but not like this. Not big and broad like this.

We order lunch. I want the chicken salad, and Brian does the soup-and-salad combo. We both reach for the sourdough rolls between us. I tear mine open, and Brian slathers his with butter. I'd like to slather my dry bits of bread with butter, too, but I'm supposed to be focusing on my goals. You know, the weight and attitude goals, where I put myself first, and take care of me, but giving up butter is a serious sacrifice.

I grew up close to Hanford and Tulare, capitals of California's dairy industry. Remembering the dairies reminds me that it's been ages since I was last home. I miss the valley. I miss the orchards and the fields and the farmers visiting town wearing their green John Deere baseball caps and their snug Wranglers and their weathered boots.

My favorite farmer of all was my friend Paige's father,

Paul. Paul was the kindest man you could hope to meet, and he had the bluest eyes. When he looked at his wife and daughters, you knew he loved them, knew he'd do anything for them. And he did. He was rock solid, rooted to the soil, and if I could have been his daughter, I would have.

"So how's it going?" Brian says, leaning forward, expression frankly curious.

"Good."

"Really?"

I do a quick inner scan, and I'm warm inside. Relaxed. "Really."

"I'm glad," he answers, and I believe him.

Returning to the office, I spot Olivia in the conference room talking to the man I hung out with in the VIP lounge Saturday night. Kirk, Katie's friend, the DJ/journalist guy.

I hesitate in the lobby, uncertain whether I should go to my desk or stick my head into the conference room and say hello. Would Olivia be pissed that I've interrupted her meeting? Would it be rude of me not to say hello? But before I can make a decision, Kirk is rising from the board-room table and heading my way.

"Holly," he says, leaning forward to kiss me on the cheek. "I hope you don't mind me dropping by."

"You came to see me?"

He pulls out a driver's license and hands it to me. "Yours, I believe."

It is mine. "How . . . ?"

"You must have dropped it when they carded you. The bouncer called me. He remembered you'd come with me, and I thought you'd miss it sooner or later."

I would have, too, and glancing at my driver's license, I see the address printed on the front, and it's my old address in Fresno, the one in Old Fig, where I used to live with Jean-Marc. "Thanks."

I can see Olivia hovering in the background. I don't know if she's waiting to speak with Kirk again or waiting to talk to me, but I'm suddenly in no hurry to get rid of Kirk. I'm tired of feeling as if I have to jump every time Olivia opens her mouth, tired of feeling half-rate, second-best, tired of the pins and needles, the worry, the guilt. I've done a good job here. I work hard; I help others; I'm a team player.

"Thirsty?" I ask Kirk. "Would you like coffee, soda? Bottle of water?"

"Water would be great."

"Follow me." I lead him out of the lobby, away from Olivia, toward our minuscule break room.

Kirk takes the water I give him, twists off the cap. "Olivia was telling me about the Leather and Lace Ball. Apparently it's going to be bigger and better than ever this year."

Olivia said all that? My eyebrows lift. Interesting. But it's also one more reason for me not to trust Olivia.

But Kirk wants to know more about the Leather & Lace Ball because he used to attend a number of years ago, so I fill him in as much as I can, talking about changes, new things happening, and how at this year's event there are the usual fun things but also an increased effort at public education the night of the ball.

I glance up as a shadow passes in the hall, and I think it's Olivia, but it's not. It's David. I haven't seen David in two weeks. He's been off on another trip—something to do with the new office he's planning on opening in Los Angeles next summer—and I put my water down as he enters the break room.

"David," I say, and gesture to Kirk. "This is my friend Kirk—"

"Yahnian," David finishes for me, extending his hand to Kirk. "You write for the *Guardian*. I love your column."

Kirk registers surprise as well as pleasure. He shakes David's hand. "Thanks. It's nice to hear."

"What did you think of the article the *Chronicle* ran?" David asks.

"A great piece, especially coming from the mainstream media." Kirk leans back against the break-room counter, arms crossed over his chest. "I've just written a column in response to the *Chronicle* story. It'll be in Sunday's edition."

"I'll look for it."

My cell phone rings, and I reach into my bag. "Excuse me," I murmur, and leave the conference room to take the call.

It's Josh. "Well?" he demands. "Just who is that guy anyway?"

"Why? Are you interested in him, too?"

"Interested in a guy?" Josh pauses, hugely offended. "Holly, I'm not gay."

"I didn't say you were—"

"So why would I be interested in a guy?"

"I don't know."

He swears. And I've never heard Josh swear. "I'm sorry, Josh," I say. "I didn't mean anything by that."

"It's fine." But he's disgruntled and defensive. "And not that it's any of your business," he adds, even more prickly than before, "but I'm crazy about Tessa." And he hangs up on me.

His cubicle is just a couple of feet away, so I walk over and stand next to his desk. "Josh."

"Gay." He's fuming.

"Josh, I didn't think you were—"

"Do you think Tessa believes I'm gay?"

"No." And I don't. I actually think Tessa's interested in him, too. "Have you asked her out?"

"No."

"Why not?"

"Because I don't believe in office romances. It just muddies the water."

He has a point. I glance toward the break room, where David and Kirk are still talking, and I can't see them but I can hear their voices. "Maybe you'll meet someone else," I say.

Josh scowls at me. "I don't want to meet anyone else." He falls silent, shakes his head, expression brooding.

"Maybe you should work in a different office."

Josh glares at me, more peevish than I've ever seen him. "Thanks, Holly. You're a big help." He clicks on his computer, opens a new window. "I think I'll get back to work now," he says pointedly, and I return to my cubicle.

Kirk and David talk for nearly an hour, and when Kirk leaves, David walks him to the elevator.

I wonder how it went between them, but I can't ask David and I won't call Kirk, and I put their meeting out of mind. But the next day at work, a bouquet of red roses arrives. The card reads, "Thanks. I owe you. Kirk."

I guess the intro went well.

15

It's Wednesday, the last week of October, and the Leather & Lace Ball is Saturday, two days before Halloween. Returning from lunch on Wednesday, David stops by my cubicle and asks if I'd like to join him as a guest at his table Saturday night. "I can only offer you one ticket," David adds, "but you'll know Kirk—"

"He's going?"

"We're seeing each other."

"Sounds serious," I tease.

"Could be."

I'm surprised by David's candor but don't dwell on it. Kirk and David's relationship is still relatively new. "Is anyone from the office going to be at the ball?"

"Tessa will, because she's working the event, and I think Josh is going along with a couple folks from Tessa's team, to lend a hand if need be."

Josh is going. Sneaky bastard. "I'd love to go."

"Great. Just give your name Saturday night at the door. You'll be on my guest list." He starts to turn away but remembers one last thing. "And don't even think about attending without a costume. This is the Leather and Lace Ball. It's got to be exotic, or erotic."

Exotic. Or erotic. Hmmm. This requires a shopping expedition to the Castro district, and I'm not going to Castro without some girl power. I call Katie, tell her what I need.

"We're going to sex shops," she says, getting the picture quickly.

"Pretty much."

We agree to meet on Castro Street after work. I drive from Market to Mission, and then Mission to Noe Valley and up Castro. After I park, I look at the sky, and it's the twilight I love, the sharp clear light of autumn, the colors all pewter and gold.

The leaves are turning yellow and red, and the wind gusts, and leaves blow in rolling circles, little dervishes of crackling red and brown. This is what it would have been like to star in a Cary Grant movie. Beautiful. Elegant. Poignant.

Katie's on the corner where we agreed to meet. She suggests we fortify ourselves with a quick cocktail before we start shopping, and I agree. We duck into a bar, and even though we're the only women there, we order cocktails and drink our lemon-drop martinis as if they were just good old-fashioned lemonades.

I haven't bought new clothes in ages, having pretty much blown my paychecks on rent (nice) and the new computer and printer, which hardly get used, because I live at the office lately instead of my home. When Katie thrusts a pair of leather pants at me in my size, I discover they're too big when I try them on. I am thinner, I note in the dressing room mirror, and I actually don't look half bad in black leather, but the guy working in the store pushes aside the red velvet curtain and shakes his head at me as I try to cover up my bra.

"No, no," he says. "That's not what you want. You want in-your-face," he adds, turning away, his own spiked Mohawk black with white tips. He riffles through his rack of clothes and pulls out a black leather bustier and a pair of little matching leather panties. "Something like this."

I eye the leather bustier and try not to look at Katie, who is about to burst out laughing. "Okay, but what do I wear on the bottom?"

"On the bottom?" Mr. Mohawk frowns. "What do you mean on the bottom? You wear these bottoms on your bottom." And he shakes the little leather panties.

"That's underwear."

"It's a G-string," he corrects.

"Right."

"And you wear these."

I look at Katie, who is grinning like a fool. I turn away.

I can't handle her mirth now. "My butt will be hanging out," I say as carefully and kindly as I can.

Mr. Mohawk sighs with exasperation. "You're going to the Leather and Lace Ball."

"Yes. But I'm sitting at my boss's table, and I can't very well parade around in front of my boss with my big white . . ." I nearly say ass, but I substitute ". . . *behind* . . . sticking out."

"Wear fishnet stockings, then."

"That's an idea," Katie pipes in.

I grind my teeth together. "That's not an outfit."

"Well, we're not finished yet, darling." Mr. Mohawk spins away and digs through a drawer of accessories, pulling out a couple of different black leather belts. Only they're *small* leather belts. And they're not belts but dog collars.

One is studded.

One is spiked.

And one has a leash attached.

"Katie, maybe we should go," I whisper because there's no way I'm going to wear one of the collars around my neck. I have fantasies like every other girl. I've imagined being tied up, a pair of fur-lined handcuffs, but dog collars? Leashes? In public? Uh-uh. No way.

"Can't go. This is important." Katie's eyes are watering and she's grinning and she's about the happiest I've ever seen her. "We're shopping, girl."

Of course we're shopping. But she's not the one covering her personal assets with scraps of leather and studded dog collars. "I can't wear this stuff."

"Yes, you can. It's time you took some risks. Lived a little. Now, try your outfit on."

It's four o'clock on Saturday afternoon before the long-anticipated Leather & Lace Ball. Katie has come over to my apartment to make sure I dress properly, i.e., wear the Elvira-meets-Dr. Frank N. Furter costume our local Castro sex shop has so thoughtfully assembled.

But good Katie Robinson hasn't come empty-handed. She's brought tequila and some orange juice and assorted bottles of mixers and juice.

"Take me to your blender," she says, heading directly for the kitchen. She's a confident girl, our Katie. "We're having margaritas."

Katie has a reason for her confidence. She's a whiz at the blender. She doesn't measure anything, pouring with a liberal hand great gulps of tequila; throws in a handful of ice, glugs of orange juice, a squeeze of lime, and floats of Grand Marnier and pushes "Liquefy." Seconds later we've got slushy-smooth margaritas, and I—crystal-savvy girl that I am—have the right glasses for the occasion. Katie takes the glasses, dips the rims in water and then the salt she's remembered to bring.

You know, if Katie were a man, we'd be formidable together. One of those power couples. We know each other, get each other. Why the hell don't guys get girls?

Why are guys *guys*?

But that's a moot point, and Katie and I clink glasses and drink. Awesome. The best margarita I've ever had. And it's damn strong. "You're going to get me wasted," I say, but it's a compliment, not a protest, because I'm going to need to be a little loopy to wear fishnet stockings, black boots, a leather G-string, and a bustier that presses my breasts up toward my chin.

"Good." Katie knocks a little salt from her glass. "Hopefully you'll have fun."

"I'm going to be sitting with my boss. In what amounts to leather underwear."

"Could be awkward, but I think you'll handle the challenge beautifully."

"*Hmph.*" I glower at her and then at the gray light coming through the kitchen window. The shorter days have arrived, and setting the clocks back an hour last Sunday didn't help.

"Kirk will be there," she reminds me. "You said you like him."

"Yeah, I do like Kirk, but I still wish you were coming." It's going to be an incredible party. Katie would love it. She's so much wilder than I am, and I've heard all the stories, how people parade around the decorated convention center like something from a twisted play—drag queens and divas, dominatrixes and sexual playthings. There are whips. Chains. Boots. Heels. Masks. And that's just the beginning.

"Maybe next year." Katie tops off our drinks, draining

the blender. "You'll just have to tell me the stories tomorrow when we meet for brunch."

I nod. "You still want to go to the movies afterwards?"

"If you're not too hung over."

"I won't be."

She makes a *hmph*ing sound, and I shrug.

"Okay, I might be a little buzzed, but I'll be fine. Especially since we're going to see Orlando Bloom's new movie. I loved him in *Troy*."

"I liked him in *Pirates of the Caribbean* better. He seems more innocent."

"You like innocent?" I ask Katie as I lick my finger, sticky from the margarita.

"It's sexy," Katie answers.

"I like wicked." I lick the other side of my finger. "I would have loved to be a pirate."

"A *pirate*?"

"You didn't ever want to be a pirate?"

"*No*."

"How about *do* a pirate?"

Katie groans. "You're really buzzed."

"I'm serious." I lick the other side of my finger. "I'd love to be a pirate. Be a bad girl. Break all the rules. Fly in the face of convention." I nod, thinking about it, picturing myself on a big ship flying over white-tipped waves, sails snapping, wood creaking and groaning. I'd be free. So free, and no one, *no one*, could tell me what to do. How to act. How to speak. "It'd be great."

"You're not a pirate kind of girl."

"I could be."

"You like nice things."

"True," I say, and yet I know I'd look damn good in long, tattered skirts and my leather bustier, big gold hoop earrings, and a knife tucked inside my boot. Maybe I'd even wear an eye patch. Have a parrot on my shoulder. I'd swagger, swear, spit. Sit with my legs far apart, and sip straight rum from a split coconut. "I could still have nice things. I'd buy nice things with my share of plunder."

"Your plunder." Katie's trying hard not to laugh in my face.

"It's possible," I answer primly, and maybe it's not, but it should be. We shouldn't have to be good girls. Sugar-sweet girls who follow all the rules. There's no reason good girls can't still be good girls even if they're bad. Who gets to define what's good and bad anyway?

"So how are you going to wear your hair tonight?" Katie asks, and I'm back to the party and off my Johnny Depp–Orlando Bloom–inspired fantasy.

"I don't know. What do you think?"

"Go severe," Katie suggests. "Pull it back, gel it smooth."

"That *is* severe."

"And go crazy with your makeup. I'll do it for you. Super-pale face. Heavy black eyeliner. Dark red lips." Katie's carrying her drink and heading for my bedroom, where all the purchases are waiting. "Did you buy the fake eyelashes?"

I follow her into my room. I do feel a little bit unsteady on my feet and reluctantly set my glass down. I definitely don't need anything more to drink right now. "They're in the smallest bag."

Katie dumps everything out on my bed, sorts through the clothes, the stockings, the boots. She nods approvingly. "Let's get to it."

Thank God for my nice black wool coat, I think as I climb into the back of a yellow cab an hour later, black fishnet stockings peeping from beneath the coat hem.

Even fortified with great tequila, there's no way I could go out in public without my coat.

The cab drops me off in front of the convention center as the setting sun turns the sky a dark blood red. People are streaming in, and it's like a circus atmosphere. The energy's up; everyone's talking and laughing animatedly, eager to be there.

I give my name at the door, they assign me my dinner table number, and I check my plain wool coat once I'm permitted in. I feel naked, but I'm also distracted by the red chiffon draped everywhere. The entire convention center is a sea of red. And the dinner tables are all swathed in black. Music's playing, the first of three different live bands, and somewhere a photographer is taking pictures, little white flashes popping in my peripheral vision.

I wander between tables, keeping my eye out for Tessa

and City Events staff, but all I see are caterers and wait-persons rushing around. But then someone's shoving a glass of red something at me, and I look at a masked face, the glimpse of light brown hair, and then the pale bare chest with the pierced nipple. I don't take the drink. I can't stop looking at the pierced nipple above tight black leather pants.

"It's Josh," the voice says.

I kind of thought it was. But the nipple ring? "Is that fake?" I ask, gingerly pointing to the silver ring protruding from his nipple.

"No."

I can't believe Josh—quiet, corduroy-wearing Josh from the Beckett School—has a pierced nipple. It's just too bizarre, too out of character. "Did you do it for the party?"

"No. I've had it for years."

I want to be a pirate, and Josh has body piercings. What is the world coming to?

Josh thrusts the red drink into my hand. "I'm not the nice gay boy you thought I was, am I?" Still smirking, he walks away, fading into the crowd.

I watch him go, and I think, *fuck 'em.*

Fuck polite society. What did polite society ever do for me? Nothing.

And with that, I sip my red drink—a cosmo, thank God—and decide that no matter what happens tonight, I'm going to have a good time.

Dinner's a relatively straight affair, considering I'm one of only two women sitting at David Burkheimer's table. I'm introduced around the table, shake hands with a couple of the men, getting a blur of names and faces, before David suggests I take the empty seat next to Kirk, who looks as if he'd just returned from a Hell's Angels road trip: black leather motorcycle pants, white T-shirt pulled tight over bulging biceps, black vest, black boots, and a faded bandanna tied around his shaved head.

But Kirk the hell-raiser is still a gentleman, and he rises, holds my chair for me while I sit. "Nice dog collar," he says, leaning forward to kiss my cheek.

"Katie liked it, too."

He grins, sits, muscular forearm resting on the table. "Did she also want to put a leash on you, take you for a walk?"

I shoot him a dark glance from beneath my lashes. "I don't do leashes."

"You might like it."

"Shut up."

He laughs, reaches for the bottle of red wine in the center of the red-and-black table, and fills David's glass and then mine. Candlelight flickers, shadows dancing across everyone's faces. I glance at David, who is talking to the man seated to his right. In the candlelight David looks relaxed. Young. I smile faintly, a little wistfully. Life's good, I think. Hard, but good.

Later, as the dinner plates are being cleared, the band starts playing again, and it's a great song, one by Wild Cherry. *Play that funky music, white boy . . .*

I can't sit still. I'm tapping my foot, drumming with my hand, dancing in my seat. David looks at me, black eyebrow arched, and I toss my head and just keep dancing. It's been so long since I felt this good, so long since I had fun like this. The costumes, the colors, the mood, the music, make me feel as if anything is possible, and maybe anything *is* possible.

Kirk rises, grabs my hand, and drags me out onto the dance floor. "What about David?" I protest, but follow him anyway, eager to be free of my chair and out on the dance floor, where the party has moved.

"He doesn't dance, and I'm doing him a favor. You're darling in that outfit, but your breasts were jiggling quite a bit back there."

Before I can punch him, Kirk takes my hand again, pulls me against him in a provocative bump-and-grind that's meant to shock, and hip to hip, knees between knees, Kirk and I do some very dirty dancing.

We dance for nearly an hour straight, the dance floor jam-packed, outrageous costumes everywhere, shocking amounts of skin exposed. It's hot on the dance floor, but Kirk and I keep dancing and sweating, and we don't stop until the band takes a break.

As the band clears the stage, we thread our way back to the table, breathless and laughing. Kirk's T-shirt is plastered to his chest. I reach up to catch the perspiration running down the side of my face, and my fingers come away inky black.

"What's happening to my face?" I ask as we reach our table, showing him my hand smeared with black color.

"You're melting," he answers in a wicked-witch voice, "and it's very scary."

At the table, Kirk drops into his seat, and I reach under the table for my purse and head for the ladies' restroom.

In the bathroom mirror I inspect my face, and it's even worse than I thought. One false eyelash has lifted up and off, as if about to fly away, and the heavy mascara and black eyeliner form circles and smudges that make me look like something from *The Rocky Horror Picture Show*, when Frank and gang have all been swimming and are dancing wet on stage.

I do my best to wipe away the excess eyeliner and blot the rest of the face, apply a little powder over the still damp skin, and redo my lips. As I snap my purse closed, I realize I'm having an absolutely amazing time.

This is craziness—me in leather and fishnet stockings and a wide dog collar—but it's the kind of craziness I needed. This is freedom. Freedom and fun.

Leaving the ladies' room, I go in search of Tessa and Josh, but before I make it very far, someone grabs my hand.

I look up, a long way up, straight into a mask.

He's tall, and he's wearing a loose white shirt and strange-looking pants and he's carrying a . . . whip.

My mouth opens, closes, as he snaps the whip and it makes a sharp cracking, hissing sound.

"That's . . . impressive," I say.

The masked man laughs and uses his whip to push up his mask onto his forehead. Brian Fadden smiles down at me. "You think so?"

I make a face. "So what are you?"

"A eunuch."

"A *eunuch?*"

"I'm in charge of the sultan's harem," he answers quite seriously. "It's an honor."

"Yeah, after you're castrated."

"It *was* quite painful."

"I'm sorry."

He smiles. "If I'm allowed to compliment you, you look . . ." He shakes his head and exhales. "Hot."

"I am hot. I'm sweating like a pig."

"That's not exactly what I meant," he says delicately.

Brian has always been able to make me laugh, and I laugh now. His humor is such a relief. It's wonderful to feel light, easy. "So what are you doing here? I didn't think this was your kind of thing."

"It's a good cause."

"So people say."

"And I'd hoped I'd see you," he admits.

I blush, suddenly shy. "It's a lot of money if you just wanted to see me."

"The ticket was donated."

"Well, there you go. I'm a cheap thrill."

"You're a thrill, but cheap . . . no. This outfit cost a fortune."

"Never mind the castration."

Brian's blue eyes glint. "Maybe we shouldn't talk about that."

"Sensitive subject?"

"Very."

"Pointed comments getting to you?"

"You're a funny girl, Holly Bishop."

"I try."

He takes my hand, fingers wrapping around mine. "Come on. Let's dance."

And we do.

Brian and I spend the rest of the night dancing, and it's close to two thirty when he finally puts me into the back of a cab. We don't make any plans to see each other again, but somehow I know we will. I just don't know when.

16

Halloween is anticlimactic after the outrageousness of the Leather & Lace Ball. I stay home Halloween night in case I have trick-or-treaters, and there are just a handful, which leaves me alone with a big bowlful of miniature Butterfingers, Milky Ways, and Baby Ruths.

November third I throw out what's left of the candy, which isn't as much as it should be.

At City Events it's always intense and frazzled, and even though the Leather & Lace Ball is over, Olivia is tougher than nails on me and even less forgiving of errors.

I hit the gym frequently, not just for my hips (well, those chocolates have made an appearance on my butt and thighs) but also for my sanity. Nothing seems to make Olivia happy anymore, and I'm constantly biting down, holding back, hoping that eventually she will lighten up.

The Beckett School's seventy-fifth anniversary celebrations are organized. The details for Bloomberg, Bloomberg and Silverman's holiday party are set. Oracle's big shindig, scheduled for January, is nearly complete, and I'm spending one day every week meeting prospective clients, showing the City Events portfolio, telling them how we can help and what we do.

The weather has been mild in San Francisco—the fall is always one of the city's nicest times of the year—and before I know it, it's Thanksgiving week, and I've just two more days of work before I head home for turkey and cranberries and stuffing.

Tessa shoots me an e-mail Tuesday: "What are you doing this weekend?"

I answer without thinking, "Going to Mom's."

And the second my finger hits "Send," I remember she's from the East Coast and doesn't have family here. Immediately I type another e-mail. "Do you want to come home with me for turkey?"

She sends an answer. "Josh has invited me to his house."

"Great," I type. "That should be fun."

"No, it won't," she replies. "You know how he said his parents are stiffs? He was right."

"All parents are stiff," I type back, thinking we might as well be instant-messaging, or talking to each other face-to-face. It'd be much more efficient timewise.

I get a new e-mail from Tessa. "Your mom isn't."

My mom would be flattered.

Driving home Wednesday afternoon, fog shrouds the fields lining the highway, and massive, gnarled oak trees look like lone soldiers in the sea of gray, their dark green leaves soupy with clouds.

I've heard others say this drive through the Central Valley is lonely and boring, the winter fog depressing, but it's a melancholy beautiful to me. The fog is symbolic somehow of what we see and don't, what we imagine versus what we know.

We're always wanted at home for the holidays, and usually its just Ashlee and me who make the trip home.

I don't know why Jamie can't fly in from Phoenix. It's not as if he couldn't afford the airfare. He's got a good job in sales, and a serious live-in girlfriend who enjoys the house and lifestyle he provides.

But even though Jamie's not coming home for Thanksgiving, Mom's still excited and has been baking all week. She's a great cook. Her pies are the best I've ever had: perfect flaky crust, fillings that are light, flavored just right.

Jean-Marc used to say he fell in love with me after eating one of Mom's banana-cream pies.

Mom loved it when he said that. She'd blush and shake her head, get that little-girl shine in her eyes, that little-girl smile.

I hated that she'd get so excited over a compliment

about pie, but I understand it now. It's wonderful when someone can make you feel good. Important. Valuable. God, I used to take that for granted. No more. I swear, I will never look a gift horse in the mouth again.

Ashlee arrives home late Wendesday night, and within a half hour of kissing Mom and downing a Diet Coke, she's out the door to hook up with friends she hasn't seen since her last time home.

Mom's face falls as Ashlee blithely sails out the door in a cloud of Bliss beauty products and Estée Lauder Happy perfume. "Are you going out, too?" Mom asks.

I think of the friends I could call, people I know who are sure to come home from Los Angeles, San Diego, Sacramento. It'd be great to get drinks with my old high school crowd, compare notes, but most of them don't know about the divorce, and I'm not sure I'm ready to explain. "Nope. I'm here for the night."

Mom's pleased. "We can make the pies together, then."

In the kitchen, Mom tackles the pie crust and I start the filling. The radio's on, and we're chatting about Christmas and we're doing great until she asks, "So what's Jean-Marc doing this weekend?"

I nearly drop the nutmeg. "Why would I know?"

"You were married."

"For about three weeks."

"It was a year."

I grind my teeth together, dump the nutmeg in the

bowl, and focus on the cinnamon, hoping Mom will take a hint.

She doesn't. "You are still friends, aren't you?"

I sigh exasperatedly. *"No."*

"Why not? There's no reason you can't be friends." She's rolling out the first pie crust, and I don't understand how her touch with the dough and rolling pin can be so deft, so light, while her conversational sensitivity is next to nonexistent.

"You're not friends with Ted," I say, dumping the cinnamon on top of the nutmeg.

She frowns as she lifts the crust, turns it. "You shouldn't call him Ted."

"Okay. Bastard Ted."

"Holly."

"He *is* a bastard. He left you, left us—"

"He didn't leave you kids—"

"Bullshit." I attack the pumpkin mixture with the wooden spoon. "He did. He left us, all of us—you, Jamie, me, Ashlee. He's a rat bastard, and Jean-Marc is a rat bastard, and I won't forgive either of them."

Mom looks at me reproachfully. "That's not very nice."

"Maybe I'm not nice." I set the bowl down, but I set it down hard, and little globlets of pureed pumpkin splash up and out. "Maybe I've never been nice."

Mom's lips purse. "That's not like you, Holly."

"Why isn't it like me? Why do I have to be nice? You never cared if Jamie was nice—"

"He's your brother."

"A man, right," I say in disgust. "And it's okay for men to be competitive, territorial, insensitive, but women have to be good. Sweet. *Nurturers*."

"Holly, I don't want to fight."

"And I don't want to be stepped on." I take a quick breath. "Being nice is overrated. Being nice gets you ignored. Forgotten. Being nice means you wait and wait and never get a turn."

She looks at me for a long moment, her flour-dusted hand resting on the yellow Formica counter, and I see she's had her nails done for Thanksgiving. Burgundy polish with squared tips. "Are you mad at me?"

"No." I reach for the pumpkin puree bowl. "I don't know. I just wish you hadn't read me all those fairy tales growing up."

"You loved fairy tales."

"They're not true."

"That's right. They're stories."

Stories. Good guys. Bad guys. Towers. Dungeons. Heroic men and imperiled women. "They all ended happily." I give the pumpkin a halfhearted stir. "But life's not like that."

"You don't know that. You're still young."

"And what about you? Are you still young?"

Mom pulls back as if I've struck her. "Yes. Well." Her voice is soft, bruised, and she's reaching for a dish towel, briskly wiping the flour off her hands. "I'm not complaining."

"Maybe you should."

She just shakes her head and swiftly, expertly crimps the edges of the crust and doesn't look at me.

"Maybe we could go slay dragons together, Mom." I'm trying to make a joke, get her to smile. "We could be the first mother-daughter dragon-slayer team out there."

"Sure, Holly. If that would make you happy." But she's dismissive, and it's gentler than Olivia's dismissals but it's still a dismissal, and our mother-daughter time is over for the night.

Saturday night I vow never to eat turkey again in my life, since I've now had it in all its glorious forms: hot turkey, cold turkey sandwiches, turkey tetrazzini, turkey stew, turkey soup.

Bleck.

I pack my bag after the dinner dishes are done, since I plan on leaving early in the morning. Once my bag is packed, I head out, climbing into my car for a drive downtown.

I've got to escape the house. Have to escape the TV and the worn, faded chintz sofa and the framed school photos on the wall. I feel trapped here sometimes. Scared.

I go to the Starbucks on Main Street, and it's a proper Main Street. I love this town. You could go all over the valley—Hanford, Tulare, Sanger, Porterville, Exeter, Kingsburg—and each one has its Main Street with its turn-of-the-century brick buildings and the one big high school stadium and the trees.

It's not really foggy yet, but it's cold, and only a few people are walking around, heading either to or from one of the theaters or restaurants that have sprung up downtown.

But at Starbucks I find a crowd, and I wait in line with everyone else before carrying my coffee outside, where I sit on a chilly green metal chair and clutch my warm paper cup.

My breath comes out in little clouds, and as I sit there, the red-and-white candy cane swags that have been strung up and down Main Street for tomorrow night's Candy Cane Parade turn on. Red and white lights glow everywhere, and it's both gaudy and wonderful.

I watched the Candy Cane Parade every year growing up. I used to love Christmas—the stockings, the carols, the pretty wrapping paper—but after Bastard Ted left, it was never the same.

Mom tried. God knows she did. But it wasn't the same.

I bite my lower lip and stare up at the red and white lights, the colors glowing through the fog. I'm not going to cry. It's silly to cry. And yet my chest aches for the girl I was and the woman I am.

Who am I? What am I? And when is my skin going to fit?

When do I get porridge that will taste just right?

Standing up, I toss away my now empty cup and head back toward my car.

It was relatively easy moving to the city, I think, but it's been damn near impossible taking the small town out of me.

The paperwork arrives in the mail two weeks later, on December 7.

Standing on the front steps of Cindy's butter-cream Victorian, I open the envelope, look at the piece of paper for a moment, not understanding what it is. I read the legalese, see the various stamps and dates, and then it hits me. My divorce is final.

It's over, I think, feeling nothing. No sadness, no pain, not even relief. I read the wording again and again before slipping the folded paper back into the envelope.

The marriage should never have happened, and now it's as if Jean-Marc and I never were.

In my bedroom I file the paper away before taking out a notepad. Time to concentrate on Christmas shopping.

Christmas comes and goes, leaving me with all kinds of new credit card debt.

I spend New Year's with Katie and a couple of her crowd up at Lake Tahoe. I'm not a great skier, but I rent equipment and give it a go, spending much of each afternoon sliding down slippery mountain slopes on my butt. But I tried, and that's what counts, I tell myself.

In January I work hard, bringing in lots of new business, and in the first February all-staff meeting David gives me a gift certificate in front of everyone as an award and a thank-you for bringing in the most new business in the new year.

I'd hoped that by my working hard Olivia would see I was a team player and would relent in her hard-ass attitude toward me, but the award from David, as well as the gift certificate to Neiman Marcus, makes her even snarlier than usual.

Valentine's Day approaches, and the Schlessenger wedding demands hours of Olivia's and Sara's time because this wedding, with the black-tie reception for five hundred at the Palace Hotel, seems cursed. Everything that could go wrong does, and what should have been a slam dunk threatens to unravel even up to the last minute.

I'm just glad the wedding's not my problem, and I spend Valentine's night at home alone, watching old movies and eating microwave popcorn kettle-corn style.

I shouldn't be eating kettle-corn popcorn, though. If I were smart I'd lose another five to ten pounds and get really expensive highlights and learn something about fashion and attitude.

Instead of lying on my couch in mismatched sweats, I should be working harder to make myself look like a million bucks so I can go after a man who has a million bucks.

If I were smart, I'd just give up on love and the whole idealistic, romantic thing and become a realist.

I'd know that love and passion never last, that infatuation is based on a mixture of pheromones, novelty, and projection. Which reminds me, there's a great book published called *Why We Love*, packed with research. The author did all these MRIs of the brain, studying romantic couples, people hopelessly besotted, and in every case the brain chemistry was markedly different. You see, love *changed* the brain. But the research also revealed—tragically—that even with those hopelessly besotted who've become addicted to love (yes, romantic love leads to obsession, making one crave the beloved just as a junkie craves his drug of choice), love goes.

Love goes.

Despite my pessimism, only a week later I'm accepting my first date in nearly five months.

He's a man I met last October at the Leather & Lace Ball, a friend of David's. Ed Hill's his name, and he sat at our table and apparently has had a soft spot for me ever since.

I'm a bit worried that this man, Ed Hill, fell for me when I was wearing a bustier, a leather G-string, and fishnet stockings, because I don't usually wear leather, G-strings, or fishnet stockings. But David has assured me that Ed knows it was a costume and not a personal fetish, so I accept the date when Ed calls.

Dating is still not all that appealing, but at Katie's urging, I'm determined to approach relationships differently. I'm not going to wear rose-colored glasses anymore. I'm going to be practical, unemotional, and logical.

And being practical, I check out Ed Hill's company's Web site and discover he doesn't just work for Arrow Software—he's the founder. And the CEO. I surf around the Web site, discovering that Arrow has offices all over the world, including Australia, the UK, Germany, and Japan. I'm impressed and read whatever I can, including posted press releases (company profits are up; new growth opportunities abound) and a bio about top management execs, including Ed.

And continuing to be practical, I study Ed's head shot on the Web site, trying to remember him from the ball, and I do but I don't. Ed was quiet, I think, and not a particularly big man—medium height and slender, definitely not flashy and not dressed in anything outrageous.

I'm nervous about the date, but David has assured me that Ed is a really nice, genuine man, and he'll treat me very well, and isn't that the first step on the road to recovery? Stop dreaming about unavailable men and date those who are available?

I dress for my Saturday date with care.

Ed's offered to pick me up, but I tell him I'm happy to meet him at the restaurant, and I do.

I sit outside in my parked car, just across the street from the restaurant, and watch people arrive. I spot Ed as he steps from his sports car. It's a nice car, and he's pleasant enough looking—not handsome, rather nondescript—but as he locks his car and heads toward the restaurant door, adjusting his sport coat, I think he has a kind face.

I get out of my car, smooth my long skirt over my knee-high boots, and pat my sweater flat and tell myself to relax, try to keep an open mind, and have fun.

And Ed is nice, surprisingly unflashy for being a CEO of a multimillion- (billion?) dollar company. During dinner he asks intelligent questions and then seems perfectly content to let me talk while he listens.

But finally I turn the table and ask questions, and Ed answers simply.

Ed's from Marin, he's thirty-eight, the middle of three sons, and his parents are still alive and together. He golfs a little bit, but his passion is tennis, and he does his best to follow the Bay Area professional teams.

"Your parents must be really proud of you," I say as he lapses into silence.

Ed shakes his head, expression rueful. "My dad's a little disappointed. Dad always wanted me to be a doctor."

"But you've been so successful."

"Everyone has their own definition of success."

I look at him a long moment, trying to see who thin, balding megamillionaire Ed Hill really is. "And what's your definition?"

He nudges his water glass with his finger. He doesn't drink, abstains from alcohol. "Happiness."

"Happiness?" That sounds too simplistic.

"Liking yourself when you open your eyes every morning. Gratitude that you've got another day."

Gratitude that you've got another day. Liking yourself in the morning. I repeat his words as I drive home later that evening. It's still simplistic, but it does work for me.

Ed calls me on Monday and thanks me for a lovely evening, and follows up by asking if I'd like to go to the Lakers-Warriors game with him on Thursday. It's a huge rivalry, Bay Area versus L.A., and both teams are strong contenders this year.

"Okay," I say, after checking my appointment book to make sure I have nothing going on.

"It's going to be rush hour," he says. "What if I pick you up so you don't have to hassle with traffic?"

"Oh—"

"I can pick you up at work if you prefer. Won't go near your house."

I blush, and he can't see my blush over the phone, but I feel bad anyway. "It's not that—"

"You don't have to apologize. I understand perfectly. Women are always trying to follow me home."

"They are?" And then I clap my hand to my head. Of course they are. He may not be handsome, but he's megarich.

He laughs faintly. "I'm joking."

"I'm sure they are," I say, just digging my hole bigger.

"What time should I pick you up from City Events?"

"You tell me." I'm eager to make amends.

"Five thirty?"

"Sounds great."

I hang up and look at the phone and think, I don't feel any sexual sparks here, but he is nice, and nice is what's important. Nice is what you can base a relationship on. I just have to keep giving nice a chance.

Thursday arrives, and I've brought a change of clothes to work, and at five I sign off my computer, disappear into the bathroom to change and touch up my face and hair.

I'm not wearing anything fancy tonight, just jeans, boots, and a bright red blouse that ties at the waist. I drag my hands through my hair to give it a suitably casual but sexy date-night hair look. With gold hoops in my ears and a funky necklace, I'm done.

I look myself over one last time. It'll have to do. This is who I am. What I am.

Josh walks me downstairs at five thirty, and as we emerge from the building, a black limousine is waiting at the curb.

"Nice car," Josh deadpans.

"Yeah. That's the life."

And then the back door opens, and Ed Hill climbs out. "Ready?" he says to me.

I look at Ed, and then Josh, and then the car, and back to Josh. Josh leans forward, hugs me, whispering, "It's just as easy to fall in love with a rich man as a—"

"Ssssh," I silence him, cutting him short, and leaving Josh, I head toward Ed, who is standing by the limousine, waiting for me.

That night at the game in the Oakland Coliseum we have courtside seats, two amazing seats just down from the Warriors bench. It isn't until I'm sitting next to Ed and the television cameras keep panning over the front rows, lingering on the rich and famous, including Ed and me, that I understand the seduction of money.

Limos and courtside seats. Chauffeurs, chefs, valets, and personal trainers. Houses in Pacific Heights, Carmel, Jackson Hole, and Maui.

If I were Mrs. Edward Hill, I could buy anything I wanted. Travel anywhere I felt like. Get immediate attention by entering a room. Respect by pulling out my credit card.

I wish I could say I fell in love with Ed Hill and that my life finally turned into a fairy tale. But Ed, despite his kindness and his goodness and his luxurious life, doesn't make me . . . happy.

I don't open my eyes in the morning and think, I can't wait to see him.

I don't go to bed dreaming about him.

I don't want to rush through work so we can be together at the end of the day.

Ed is hoping he'll grow on me, and he is doing his best to spoil me, but it's not going to work. I'll never love him the way he wants me to love him. He's a friend. Nothing more.

In late March I finally tell Ed what he doesn't want to hear: that although I like him very much, my feelings are platonic.

Ed listens quietly and then asks one question. "Is there someone else?"

"No."

"You're just not interested in me?"

"Not the way you want me to be."

And Ed Hill stops calling.

It isn't until I've broken things off with Ed that I notice Olivia has actually relented, pulled back, no longer focuses on me with so much savage fury.

What changed?

Looking back, I realize she started easing up around the very same time I started dating Ed, and the closer I got to Ed, the nicer she became to me.

Coincidence? Or not?

·17·

$\mathcal{T}$he weeks pass, and April's here.

I'm in the middle of hammering out the final details for Kid Fest, an annual event for disadvantaged kids and teens taking place later this month, when I'm summoned to the front by the City Events receptionist.

The only thing on my mind as I leave my desk is getting publicity for our Kid Fest sponsors. People who donate time, money, or material for charity events want their good deeds known. Not necessarily the most altruistic form of giving, but a fact of corporate American life. And I'm puzzling over how to get the media out for yet another nonprofit event when I round the corner and freeze.

No. Way.

Jean-Marc.

I very nearly turn around and run, but my legs won't move and my chest feels tight and I just stare at him where he stands in the lobby, chatting away with our young receptionist.

I say nothing, but the smiling and blushing reception-ist spots me and breaks off midsentence. Jean-Marc turns, looks toward me. I just look back.

He looks the same: tall, lean, sexy in that intense way European men have. He's wearing old jeans that hug his narrow waist, and a dark gray cashmere V-neck sweater that hugs the hard planes of his chest, showing off taut pecs and chiseled abs, even as the deep V-neck plays up his arresting Gallic features.

He is and always has been disgustingly handsome. His hair, his pride and joy, is still a thick dark brown with that wave at the front that continues over the ears, and he has light brown eyes that in sunlight look almost golden.

I swear, the man used to stand in sunlight all the time.

"*Cherie*," he says, moving toward me and clasping my shoulders and kissing me on each cheek. "Surprise!"

Yes, it is. And I can think of nothing to say.

"I was in the city to see friends and thought I'd stop by and say hello," he continues, speaking in that deep voice that makes vowels and consonants sound sexy. Wicked. The French are so unfair.

"Hello," I say shortly even as I find myself wondering when it was I last saw him, and realize it's been close to a year. He was already bunking down at a friend's the week-end I moved out.

Glancing past his shoulder, I see the office receptionist,

a young intern from one of the local universities, craning her head, trying to listen.

"This is where you work?" he says, gesturing to the huge colorful event posters lining the enormous brick wall.

"Yes."

"Interesting."

"Mmmm." I just don't see any point in continuing this conversation. I mean, what are we supposed to say? Months ago I needed him, missed him . . . loved him. But now I feel only weariness and bits of regret. Not for him, but for the girl I used to be.

It's been such a long, hard year. Make that a long, hard couple of years.

I'm ready for easier. I'm ready for simpler. I'm ready to get back to my desk and get my work done.

"Do you have time for a coffee?" Jean-Marc asks, breaking the silence. "I saw a Starbucks down the road. I know how much you like that place."

He's being conciliatory, and he knows this and I know this, because Starbucks was always a bone of contention between us. Jean-Marc likes small European-style coffee-houses, and my love for Starbucks (and my Starbucks Visa card) irritated him beyond belief.

"I've got a lot of work to do."

"Just a half hour, Holly."

"Why?"

He looks puzzled, and for a moment I feel almost sorry

for him. He went out of his way to come by the office today, and he's suggested Starbucks, and clearly something's on his mind. But what?

Yet he shrugs, one of his famous Gallic shrugs. "It just seems like a nice thing to do."

Is that what this is about, then? Being *nice*?

I nearly spit in disgust. He broke my heart—crushed me just weeks after marrying me—and he wants to be nice now?

Maybe I don't want to be nice. Maybe I want to be rude, hurtful, *cruel*. But nothing particularly rude, hurtful, or cruel comes to mind.

I get my purse and coat, and we take the elevator down in silence until we step out onto the street. Parked a half block down is his slate gray Citröen. I used to love that car. We pass his car, head for the Starbucks. We could have gone to Mr. J's, but I see no point. That's a cool, funky place, and it's where I met Brian. I won't ruin the memory by getting coffee with Jean-Marc there.

At the counter inside, Jean-Marc orders an espresso, and I get a white-chocolate mocha. With whipped cream. I look at Jean-Marc, daring him to remind me about the calorie content as he used to, but he doesn't.

He takes our cups to a table, and we sit in the corner overlooking the sidewalk and parking lot. Just weeks ago the trees outside were nearly all bare, but little green tufts have begun to protrude from the branches, bright bits of spring green in tender shoots and tiny leaves.

"So what brings you here?" I ask after we've lapsed

into silence for a second time. "You're not getting married again, are you?"

He looks at me, surprised. "How did you know?"

He's getting married.

I stare at him, jaw dropping, absolutely dumbfounded. Jean-Marc is getting married already?

"You didn't know," he says now, reading my shock.

I slowly shake my head, throat working, but no sound comes out.

He grimaces. "I know our divorce was final only a couple of months ago, but I met someone last summer, and she's great. A really nice girl."

There's that "nice" again, and I'm so sick of it I could scream. But I don't. Because I am nice, too. Even if I don't want to be, even if I resent and resist everything the word represents.

"And she's pregnant," he adds, looking up at me.

"But you didn't want kids," I whisper, feeling strange, feeling torn. I don't love him now, but I did. I wouldn't marry him knowing what I know now, but two years ago I thought he was wonderful.

"I know." He makes another face. "It wasn't planned. Wasn't what I wanted. Believe me."

I do. Jean-Marc and I had some serious battles near the end, and the issue of children came up again and again. And sitting there with my white-chocolate mocha, I exhale, a short, hard breath that leaves my chest feeling hollow. Empty.

"So why marry her?" I ask carefully. "Why do what you obviously don't want to do?"

He runs a hand through his thick hair, features tightening. "She needs me."

And I didn't?

"She can't afford to raise a baby on her own, and she really wants the baby, wants a family."

So did I.

He sighs. "I can't hurt her, Holly. She's fragile. Delicate. I have to protect her."

I bite my lip and look away. He couldn't, wouldn't, protect me, but he'll ride in on his white stallion and rescue someone else.

"I just wanted you to know, to hear it from me," he concludes awkwardly. "I wanted you to understand."

Understand? He wants me to understand?

Is he insensitive or what?

I lean forward, hands wrapping tightly around my cup. "Once you loved me, Jean-Marc. You had to have loved me. What happened?"

"It's complicated—"

"Explain it to me, then. I need to know. Where did the love go? What was it that I did?"

He lifts his head, looks up, his expression sympathetic. "It wasn't ever you, *cherie*—"

"It was, because one day you loved me, and the next"—I snap my fingers—"we were over. The love was gone."

He leans back in his chair, groans beneath his breath,

shifting in his chair. "It was . . ."—and he looks at me and then away before plowing on—"your mother."

My *mother?*

My *mother*, I silently repeat, staring at him, a dull pain in my middle, more of a memory of hurt than real hurt, since I don't understand what he means, but I'm afraid anyway.

"What about my mother?" I force myself to ask, trying to sound natural, normal, despite the terrible tenderness filling me.

My mother has not had an easy life. My mother has battled alone.

I look at Jean-Marc and try to contain the rush of anger. He has no right attacking Mom, or any business criticizing her. What's happened in my mother's life should happen to no one, let alone a woman.

Women are just grown-up little girls, and little girls may appear delicate and fragile, but they also dream of Jedis and samurais, pirates and kings. They want adventure and excitement. They want life. But mostly, they crave happily-ever-afters.

My mother did not get a happily-ever-after.

And I see my mom in an old black-and-white portrait when she was five, and she has a big bow in her hair and dark spiral curls à la Shirley Temple and a stiff little dress on, pudgy knees, ankle socks, and black patent Mary Janes. My mother is smiling into the camera nervously, hopefully, as she waits for her big moment to come.

Her big moment.

I feel a massive lump inside my chest, huge and hot and tender.

Her big moment never came.

"She scared me." Jean-Marc laughs a little, as if he's making a joke.

I feel my lips stretch, and I don't know what it looks like on the outside, but on the inside I feel as if I were twelve again, on one of those nights when Mom had a rare date and she invited her date home for Sunday night dinner, and her roast is tasty, her mashed potatoes light as air, and the table is set with an ecru lace cloth and two white taper candles and a plastic floral centerpiece that looks dusty even to me. But her date is stiff, and he can't seem to get comfortable with the three little Bishop kids sitting around the table, staring at him. And Mom is trying so hard to make conversation, trying so hard to have a nice evening, trying so hard to be a woman and a mom, and that's maybe the thing I remember most. She's just trying so hard, and it's too hard, and everyone knows it but her, and I want to go upstairs to my room. I want to go far away from the good person she is and from the mistakes she unwittingly makes.

"I know this is unfair, but I thought"—and here Jean-Marc breaks off, rubs his forehead, and smiles his charming, rueful smile—"I thought you were going to turn out like her. Become her."

I stare at him, appalled.

Mom liked you, I want to say. *She thought you were wonderful. She thought you were just what I needed. Prince Charming from a glorious French chateau.*

I get to my feet, a jerky motion, and stare down at him.

Toad, I think—a big, green, horrid wart-covered toad.

I kissed him, and there was no prince in disguise, no Mr. Wonderful waiting to be freed from a witch's evil spell.

Just a toad that will always be a toad. So much for the Frog Prince.

I grip my cup so hard, I crush the top half. "I'd love to be like my mom." My voice trembles with fury. "Because she thinks the best about people, not the worst."

And I walk out, quickly, not even bothering to slow down to throw my cup away.

I'm on the street, heading back to the office, when Jean-Marc races after me, catches up with me, but I don't stop walking. I just keep going, heading for City Events and my desk and peace.

"I'm sorry," Jean-Marc says, taking my arm, dragging me to a stop. "I'm sorry."

"*Sorry?*" He's attacked my mother, the one person who was always on his side, and he's *sorry*?

"I hope you'll accept my apology."

Thank God this is over. Thank God this empty sham of a relationship ended when it did. I can only imagine the misery if we'd been stupid enough to have a baby together.

There are small blessings, I think, as I look him in the eye. As toads go, he's still good-looking, still handsome and charming to those who don't know him. But I do. And he's not charming anymore. He's not what I want or need. And he never was supposed to be my future.

"Sure, Jean-Marc." I drag my purse strap higher on my shoulder. "Go back to your lily pad and don't give it a second thought."

"My lily what?" he asks, not understanding.

"Never mind." And I set off again, and I'm walking fast, but my step is longer, lighter, and I feel as if an enormous weight had toppled from my head.

I don't need to kiss any more frogs. I'm done with hunting for Prince Charming. Because I don't need a man, or a relationship, to fix me. I may not be perfect, but I'm me, and I like myself just fine.

Two weeks pass, and it's Palm Sunday, and Katie, ever my good Catholic friend, goes to mass and then meets me for brunch after.

I get to the restaurant first and watch Katie enter, carrying her little bit of palm that's been folded into a cross. We like having breakfast together because we both indulge—waffles, pancakes, eggs, whatever we want—and there's no one here to remind us to watch our weight or waists.

"Are you going home to Visalia for Easter?" Katie asks, diving into her beautifully pan-fried country-style potatoes.

"No. I'm staying in town. What about you?"

"In town, too."

"Then let's do something," I suggest. "Like Easter brunch at my place. I'll make something, and we can dye our own Easter eggs. What do you think?"

Katie spears a golden-brown potato. "You want to dye eggs?"

"Yeah. I love decorating Easter eggs. Don't you?"

"Haven't done it in years."

"Exactly why we should do it, then. We'll make it a party. You and me." I grin. "Girl power."

Katie's forehead wrinkles. "Do you think you might be taking this single-girl thing too far? Perhaps it's time you started dating again."

"I've thought about it."

"And . . . ?"

"I might if Gorgeous Guy asked me out. Or Brian Fadden. I like them both."

"So?"

"They haven't asked me out."

"Why don't you ask them?"

"Nah. Don't need the hassle."

"Holly, there are girls in this world, and there are guys."

"I know, but guys are seriously overrated."

Katie is still giving me a sharp look. "You're not . . . going to start liking girls now, are you?"

"Be a lesbian, you mean?"

"This *is* San Francisco."

I just crack up. "You wouldn't want to have sex with me?"

"No."

"Why not? I'm cute, I'm smart, I'm funny—"

"Yeah, and you have breasts."

"Thank you."

Katie just rolls her eyes. "And hips and a big butt . . ."

I frown at her. "Now, that's kind of harsh."

"Perhaps. But you have girl parts," she concludes, waving her fork around, "and girl parts don't do it for me."

"So that's why we have men."

Katie grins, leans forward on the table. "What else did you think they were for?"

"I don't know."

"They were never meant to be nurturers, Hol. They're cavemen. They live for food, sleep, and sex, not necessarily in that order. But face it, men are driven to procreate. That's what they do."

"And what do we do?" I ask, knowing I've gone years without sex, years without love.

Katie pops a grape from her little fruit plate into her mouth. "That's a very good question. That's the part I haven't figured out. What do we do?"

I don't know, and as I leave brunch to walk back to my apartment, I still haven't a clue.

We're raised on fairy tales and baby dolls, Barbie dolls and *Modern Bride*. We read Oprah books and cozy mysteries, romances, *Cosmo,* and *People* magazine. We watch soaps and dramas, romantic comedies and action thrillers with our guys. And what's the one thing all these have in common?

Others.

We read, dream, watch, and fantasize about *others.* Loving others. Giving to others. Helping others. And one day being loved by others.

But do we ever learn to love ourselves?

Do we ever get to the point where we're fine on our own? Happy, without others?

I can only hope so.

Katie and I do our own little Easter thing, and it's not quite the celebration I'd planned, but it suffices. Next year I'll do better, invite more people over, but it was a start.

Monday I'm back at work, and Kid Fest is coming up. Just six days away. It's my project, and I'm beginning to feel the heat. It's a high-profile event—lots of media folks cosponsor this one—and Olivia keeps asking if I'm sure I have everything handled. And I think I'm sure, until she asks yet again, implying failure. But I don't fail; I'm not a failure. And as I leaf through my paperwork again, make last-minute calls, I know I couldn't be any more organized than I am.

Sunday, Birch Museum at the Presidio, ten A.M. to two P.M.

Carnival theme replete with clowns, face painters, balloon artists, magicians, a game alley, and fun food (corn dogs, hot dogs, cheeseburgers, popcorn, cotton candy, snow cones, and more).

There'll be music. Free T-shirts and treat bags for all the kids to take home, plus the requisite photographers and minor San Francisco celebrities. It's an event. A proper event, and I'm a little stressed but mostly satisfied.

I'm still tidying up my desk when Josh stops by and invites me to join him and Tessa and a couple other people from the office for happy hour. I'm definitely in, and quickly finish putting away the Kid Fest files and shutting down my computer.

Tessa has a craving for sushi, so we head to her favorite place in the Marina called Mas Sake. Mas Sake is on Fillmore and Lombard Streets, Lombard dividing Cow Hollow from the Marina. Tonight Josh drives, and we circle the block several times with everyone shouting in his ear, giving parking pointers, before he secures a spot several blocks over.

We're all in a good mood. It's late April, and spring has definitely sprung; it's staying light later, and the sky has that lovely hazy violet-blue color with tinges of pink on the horizon.

Mas Sake on weekends is a zoo, and when Josh pushes open the glass door, revealing the yellow interior with dark red beams, it's loud. Very loud. All music, clinking glasses, and shouting voices.

The bar is packed for Mas Sake's famous happy hour, featuring dollar wine, beer, and sake, and all-you-can-eat sushi for twenty dollars, which is what brought Tessa here tonight.

I'd like to wait for one of the booths lining the side of the narrow restaurant, but Tessa, the intrepid New Yorker, elbows through the crowd and plunks herself down at the long table running the length of the middle of the restaurant and starts commandeering spare chairs, squeezing them in next to her to create room for the rest of us.

"There," she says, "sit." And we do.

We order drinks next: wine, beer, and Mas Sake's own cocktail, the sake-rita. Tessa wants sushi, but I study the appetizer menu, skirting the traditional and nontraditional sushi choices, for chicken satay. What can I say? I'm a Valley girl, landlocked, aggie based. I like meat: steak, chicken—absurdly nonthreatening, but that's me.

We're on our second round of drinks when my cell phone rings. I peek into my purse, look at the number. It's Olivia. I frown, wondering if I have to answer it. It's Friday, after six o'clock, and the workweek has officially ended. She may be my immediate supervisor, but she doesn't own me. I snap my purse shut without answering. Olivia can leave a message. I'll call her back later.

We hang out at Mas Sake for another hour, and then, when the other girls go and Josh and Tessa talk about heading next door to La Barca because Josh is now hungry and craving Mexican food, it's my cue to leave. I say good night and go home and spend the rest of the evening quite comfortable in front of my TV.

But as I climb into bed, I remember that Olivia phoned, and I retrieve my cell phone from my purse, but there's no message. Good. I didn't want to talk to her anyway. Yawning, I stretch, snuggle contentedly into my covers, and drift off to sleep.

I'm up early on Sunday for Kid Fest, go for a quick run and an even quicker shower before changing into dark charcoal slacks, a tailored periwinkle blue blouse, and low-heeled but still stylish shoes. I'm going to be on my feet all day, and I'm going to need to be comfortable.

That's when the good day ends and the bad day begins.

To put it bluntly, Kid Fest is a disaster.

Sunday, 10:45 A.M., the sun's up, the morning fog has burned off, and I stand in the Birch Museum's parking lot, watching hostile social workers and foster parents reloading even more hostile kids into cars.

I arrived at the Birch at nine, an hour before the event was to start, only to discover the science and technology museum dark and locked up tight, the parking lot empty except for my lone car. I couldn't even find a security guard around.

I immediately got on the phone, but who would I even call regarding the museum? And never mind the dark museum—where was everyone else?

My caterers? My balloon artists? My clowns and magicians?

Where was my party?

And even as I was struggling to get answers, the first bus pulled up, jam-packed with kids and staff from the South San Francisco Boys and Girls Club. The guests had begun to arrive, and soon vans and cars were filling the parking lot, emptying out parents, sponsors, and kids, and there we gathered in the parking lot in the April morning sunshine.

Before I knew it, I was under siege. A crowd gathered around me. Children started crying. Adult voices were raised.

"What the hell is going on?"

"How did this happen?"

"Where is your boss?"

"I demand an explanation."

"I want to speak with the person in charge immediately . . ."

It only got worse from there. I was alone with the parents, social workers, and angry at-risk children, without even one face painter or popcorn maker to back me up, lend support, or offer assistance.

It was truly as if the event, Kid Fest, never existed. No clowns, no caterers, no carnival booths, no inflatable bounce house.

No anything.

Just the kids. Crying.

I hired a dozen different companies to be here today,

and there's no one at the Birch. No one I've worked with in the past. No one I paid money to, signed contracts with. *Nothing.*

I'm beyond baffled. I'm freaked. Panicked. Sweating away in my periwinkle blouse.

I do fruitless, desperate mental calculations. This is the 26th of April. Sunday. Kid Fest Day. This is what I've been working so hard on for the past few weeks. Nailing down the details, double- and triple-checking the entertainment for the kids, making sure they had more than enough to do. Arts, crafts, games, sweets, treats, goodie bags. But the phone calls, the packet of confirmations, the letters and contracts in my briefcase, might as well be nonexistent. The entire event is gone. Vanished.

Now I'm on my cell phone, running from one cluster of adults to another, pleading with them to wait a minute, let me just get someone on the phone, that there's been a mistake and I can get this fixed, even as I begin dialing my contact list all over again, calling one vendor and then another. No one answers, but then, this is Sunday. The Lord's day. The day of rest.

Hell and damnation.

Maybe I should have gone to church more after all.

White noise fills my head. My heart's pounding so hard, I think it's going to jump through my chest. I suppress the panic with everything I can.

Please, someone, have a cell phone, or call-forwarding, or something.

Something.

Cars are pulling away; one fifteen-passenger van leaves fast, the driver leaning heavily on the horn, and the bus packed with kids from South San Francisco Boys and Girls Club is now exiting from the parking lot.

Sick, I watch the departing stream of buses and cars, all the while my fingers punching in phone number after phone number. Someone has to know something. Someone has to know—

"Hello?"

Thank God! It's Barb from Balloon Wizardry. She works from home, and she picks up the phone. "Barb, it's Holly from City Events."

"Hi, Holly—"

"Barb, where are you?"

There's the faintest pause. "What do you mean?"

"Kid Fest. Today. Where are you?"

"Kid Fest was canceled."

I go cold all over. *"No."*

"Yes."

"Barb, it can't be canceled, because the kids are all here with me, and we're standing outside the Birch Museum, wondering where everyone else is."

"But you called—"

"I didn't call."

"Your assistant called."

"I don't *have* an assistant."

"Maybe she wasn't your assistant. I actually don't

remember her name, just that she said due to a low turnout the event had been canceled."

"When was this?"

"Friday."

"Friday?"

"Day before yesterday, late afternoon, early evening, something like that." Barb cleared her throat. "And I reminded her about our cancellation policy. There's no refund within forty-eight hours."

And it was obviously within forty-eight hours.

Barb adds apologetically, "Most of the balloon statues were already made. They hold air for weeks, and the storybook figurines were completed."

I do not know what to say.

Barb doesn't either. She hesitates. Silence stretches, and I watch another car leave the parking lot, and children pile into a minivan. Soon everyone will be gone.

This has to stop. This is wrong. Kid Fest was never canceled. Kid Fest was for kids in need, and it's a big deal to the kids, and it's supposed to happen today.

Right now.

"I better go," I say.

"Okay," Barb answers uncertainly. "But call me if there's anything I can do."

I hang up and race toward the vans and the adults trying to corral kids who've begun to go berserk. Some of the adults are ballistic.

Do I have any idea what this has done to the kids? Do I know how this looks? How it feels? These are children already unloved, unwanted . . . these are children isolated, alienated— and to treat them this way, it's just a slap. A slap, and I should be ashamed . . .

I *am* ashamed. I've no idea what happened, although there's a sick knot in my stomach that says I kind of do know, but there's got to be a way to salvage something today.

I stare at my phone, wanting it to speak to me, to give advice, to tell me who to call.

I punch in Olivia's number. She's on speed dial, number 1—ironic, isn't it?—and get her voice mail. I try again three more times and finally leave a slightly hysterical message, begging her to call me.

I try Josh. Nothing, just voice mail, and I leave another, more hysterical message.

Tessa next. Her phone is off.

My God. I'm alone in this, completely, horribly alone, and the disaster is complete when I see a reporter and a photographer from the *Chronicle* step out of a car across the street and head toward me.

The event's canceled, but the press still comes? Irony number 2.

I get home. Let the door swing shut. Allow my coat and keys to fall onto the couch while I slide down in my dark charcoal pants, onto the carpet next to the couch, until my head leans against the cushions.

I'm boneless, nerveless, *gone*.

How did this happen? Correction: I know how this happened; I feel it in my gut, hard and heavy as a rock—but how? *How*, as in, how can anyone be so malicious? So selfish? So frightened? So insecure? So cruel?

I want to cry; it'd be such a relief, but I can't. The sick feeling in me is so strong, too strong, and it threatens to swallow me whole.

How could I have screwed up anything this bad? How could something good—an event for kids, *troubled* kids—be the right vehicle for getting back at me?

Why should the kids be hurt in all this?

How could whoever did this—Olivia, or Sara, or both of them—think anything has been achieved?

And will David believe me when I tell him this fiasco isn't my fault? Will he listen when I point a finger in someone else's direction?

I doubt it. I'm low man on the totem pole. Olivia represents power, success, clout. I'm . . . nothing.

I roll off the couch, grab my cell phone from my purse, and call Josh again. He answers this time.

"I was just about to call you," he says. "What happened?"

I tell him in as few words as possible, and he's silent a moment before exhaling in a low *whoosh*, "This is bad."

"I know."

"This is Kid Fest."

"I know."

"Let's go to the office," he says. "Check out your computer and files—"

"I don't have access."

"I do. I'll come by and pick you up in thirty minutes."

Inside the dark, cavernous loft of City Events, my cubicle looks very small, and Josh and I stand over my desk with just its individual desk light on, poring over my file fat with notes, contracts, and event details.

I rummage through the papers, and everything in the first contract looks fine—right date, right numbers, right event description—until I check the location for delivery. It's been changed.

I look up at Josh, hand the paper to him. He takes it, scans it, hands it back to me, but I'm already on to another contract, and this one is altered, too, but the event date is different, postponed to June.

Another contract reads. "Canceled."

Another one, for the caterer, is simply missing.

"Josh . . ." I open my mouth, close it. I don't know what to say, and I glance down at the contract in my hand, read through the changes again. "I'm screwed."

He's silent a moment before he clicks off the light on my desk. "Just hope those photos the *Chronicle* took this morning don't land on the front page."

I don't sleep at all that night, tossing and turning, praying and then fearing my cell phone will ring. If Olivia should call me back . . .

But she doesn't call, even though I leave both phones on the nightstand next to my bed, and finally at four thirty I give up on sleep and climb out of bed, go for a very early morning run, and on the way back to my apartment I buy the Monday *San Francisco Chronicle*, leafing through the pages as I enter my front door.

And there it is. A photo and an article: "Kid Fest Travesty." The story and picture isn't on the front page. But it does land on page three.

I'm in the office at ten after six, and Olivia is the first person I see. She's tall, slim, still and watchful, and I'm reminded of a cobra before it strikes.

She's going to strike. And it's going to hurt. Worse than it's already hurt.

I approach her. I have to force the issue; I can't wait anymore.

She watches me walk toward her, her gray-green eyes intense, speculative, dangerous.

But she preempts me by speaking first. "I wondered if you'd come today, Holly. After your fiasco yesterday."

God, she's good.

"I've had about fifty calls already," she continues in the same brutal tone, words clipped, disgust dripping in the silences between. "You've screwed up bad, girl. I don't think there's any way I can save your skin this time."

I burn on the inside, angry, so angry. I'm outraged that people like Olivia can behave the way they do. "Of course you can't save my skin if you're too busy hacking it off."

Her chin lifts. "What does that mean?"

"You know what it means. You've been out to get me ever since you discovered that I worked on the ball behind your back."

"You admit it."

"I admit it. And I don't regret it, either." I look her hard in the eye, unflinching now that it's come to this. "I'd do it again if I could."

"You sabotaged your own success. You could have been good—"

"No, I *am* good. Maybe in your eyes I may never be great, but I'll leave greatness to those who need their egos stroked."

"This isn't about ego—"

"It's *only* about ego." I take a quick breath. "I just wish I'd understood this earlier. Might have saved us both a lot of wasted energy and time."

"I did my part."

"To destroy me."

"You worked for me, Holly."

"Wrong. I worked for City Events—"

"I hired you."

"David owns the company, Olivia. Not you."

"Then I guess it's going to be David who fires you, isn't it?"

David doesn't arrive at the office until nine, and the mood at the office is deadly, the tension thick. Mondays are never cheerful days, but today is especially grim.

For nearly three hours I sit in my cubicle, ignoring the e-mails pouring into my in-box, e-mails from Josh, Tessa, other City Events staff. I can't talk to anyone. I have to see David. I have to explain, and yet I know it's going to be bad.

I close my Outlook Express and focus on gathering

whatever evidence I can. I put all the Kid Fest contracts and documents into a folder, then remember my e-mails in my Sent box in Outlook that would prove I'd spoken with vendors, including my Friday noon e-mail from the Birch, which confirmed the Sunday morning details. I open Outlook again, click on my Sent folder, but it's virtually empty. There are some e-mails in the folder, but nothing about Kid Fest.

I check my trash folder. Nothing there, either.

Olivia was damn thorough.

David finally arrives, and Olivia disappears straightaway into his office. I see her go in, watch his door close, and the moment the door is closed, Tessa marches from her office, storming toward me.

"I will kill her," Tessa explodes, slapping her palm on my desk. Tessa's tiny, but she's wound tight, reminding me of a bomb about to detonate. "I'll *kill* her."

My eyes burn. "You don't want to go to prison. You're so cute. You'd be *everybody's* girlfriend."

Tessa, punk in hideous puke green and black, scowls at me. "She fucked you over, Holly."

I glance up, see Sara standing not far from us. She looks like a hunted rabbit, all fear and trembling in her wide blue eyes.

And I know then that whatever happened here with my Kid Fest account, Sara was part of it.

Maybe Sara was my "assistant," the one who made the calls.

My throat squeezes; my head's throbbing. I turn my back on her. I've no proof, no facts, just a hunch. A suspicion.

I'm in trouble.

But I don't tell Tessa that. Tessa's too much of a hothead. "It's going to be okay," I say to Tessa instead. "Everything will be okay."

"You swear?"

"I swear."

Tessa returns to her desk.

Moments later David calls me into his office. Olivia's still in there, too.

My stomach does a free fall as I enter David's office. He gestures for me to close the door. I do. And then he asks me to sit, and I take the chair opposite Olivia's, but I don't look at her.

"You saw this," he says, sliding the newspaper across his desk toward me. It's today's paper, open to page three and the big color photo of the crying little girl staring out.

"I did," I say.

"Can you tell me what happened?" he asks—the same question everyone's been asking, but in his voice there is weariness and resignation.

I hear rather than see Olivia shift. She's waiting to

attack, I think, waiting for me to show a chink in my armor and she'll go in for the kill.

But there's no point in blaming her. I've no hard proof that Olivia was behind this, and I'm not about to turn this office into some kind of turf war, even though I know Tessa would love to make this bigger, something personal, even political. It's tempting, but it's also emotional and irresponsible, and I can't do that.

As Olivia said months ago, City Events isn't a sorority. It's a business. And I'm a professional, and professional enough to know that City Events' success is built on Olivia's talent and back. David may like me, but he needs Olivia.

"There was miscommunication," I say at last.

"One hundred disadvantaged children were disappointed," he answers.

"I'm sorry."

"This landed on page three."

I nod.

"We can't get the media out for anything we do right, and the second there's a fuckup, its front-page news."

Yeah. With a nice big color photo, too.

"Holly, tell me how this could have happened."

He's pleading with me now, and I've never liked David Burkheimer more. He's a good man—kind, fair, and his heart is in the right place. I like the fact that he loved his Tony so much, and yet I'm glad he's got someone new. And I feel bad for David because I like him, and I know he liked me, and this whole thing is just shit.

"What did Olivia tell you?" I ask stiffly, shooting her a cold, hard glance.

"She said you were disorganized. That your files were missing contracts and many of your contracts were incomplete."

What a piece of work she is, I think. "It's not true," I say.

"She made copies of your files." David lifts a stack of papers. "They're here. I've seen them, Holly."

"I've seen them, too, and they weren't like that when I left here Friday with Josh and Tessa."

"Then how did this happen?"

"I don't know."

"Serious mistakes were made," he adds.

"I know. But they weren't mine."

"Then whose are they?"

I can practically feel Olivia's smile. She's sitting with one leg crossed above the other, an arm casually flung over the back of her chair. She's an Egyptian queen, and I'm just some palace flunky.

I count to five, trying to keep my cool. "I don't know."

"It was your event."

"Yes."

"Our donors and sponsors lost thousands and thousands of dollars."

I nod.

"They want answers."

I nod again.

"I have to take action," he concludes.

I knew we'd get to this part, but it hurts anyway. I hold my breath, waiting a moment for the stab of regret to fade.

I shouldn't be surprised that I'm going and Olivia remains, sitting pretty. I've worked hard here in the past year, but I did cross party lines. It wasn't as if I hadn't been warned, either. Plenty of people cautioned me—Sara, Josh, Tessa, Brian, and Olivia herself all told me to be careful, to be smart, to think things through. Why didn't I listen?

Because I wasn't afraid.

Because I believe in doing what is fair, even if it isn't always "right."

"I have to take action," David repeats, and his dark gaze holds mine. "Olivia and I've discussed this."

He stops talking, and it's now quiet in his office, and the three of us sit there, but I look only at David. And David's expression has grown increasingly grave.

I know what's coming. He's going to fire me. And I'm angry, but I also understand. He's doing what he has to do. I'm just one of seventeen employees. He has the whole company to think about. City Events' reputation. The staff salaries. The company morale.

David clears his voice, and when he speaks again, his voice is gruff. "Holly, I regret that I must terminate your employment with City Events. Due to the nature of your termination, I must ask you to clear out your desk and hand over your accounts and files to Olivia today."

The stiff formality of his words belies the sympathy in his eyes.

For a moment I do nothing but nod my head, and then, as silence stretches, I force myself to my feet, everything in slow, awkward motion, and I extend my hand.

He takes it, fingers closing around mine. "Good luck, Holly."

I can't speak for a moment. My chest is hot. It burns. I blink. "Thank you, David."

I look at no one as I pack up my desk. It doesn't take long, since I've very few personal things at work. Olivia never permitted personal clutter, and it's really just a matter of taking the Certs and keys, change and odd business cards I've collected, and stuffing them into my purse.

I refuse to make eye contact with Josh as I walk out. I nod to the receptionist, take the elevator down, and head toward Market.

This morning I took a cab to work, but I take a bus home. There's no reason to hurry now. Nothing to do.

It's the middle of the morning, not yet ten thirty, and the bus isn't even a quarter full. The bus stops, and no one gets on or off, and I watch the city pass by, beautiful in the crisp yellow morning light, the sky overhead an endless French blue.

The snorts and squeals of the bus are a strange melody as I head toward my part of town, the little city within the city that's become home.

I'm going to miss City Events. I really liked working there, and even though there were games and stresses, I learned a lot. I made new, true friends. I discovered I can handle pressure and juggle multiple accounts. I realized that Jean-Marc wasn't the be-all and end-all, that life continues even after heartbreak and failure, and it'll continue now. I might feel horrible (and I do; I'm about as low as I could imagine being . . . rejected and cast out), but I'm not alone or lonely.

I forget who said it to me, but all things end. Yet endings are also beginnings, and someday I'll look back and see this as the beginning of something new. Something good.

I don't feel good, and as I climb off the bus, I feel as if a thousand pounds rested on my chest. I breathe in little gasps, because if I breathe too deep, it hurts far worse.

Don't think about feelings, I tell myself, turning the corner to my street. Think about goals, action, plans. Think about what needs to be accomplished, not what's happened. The past is the past. I can only go forward.

Again.

Change is inevitable. Change is essential. Change—

"What are you doing home, Holly?"

Cindy.

She's in the driveway, loading some kind of athletic gear into her trunk, and even in her cropped khakis and fitted white Gap T-shirt and her baby blue Skechers she looks taut, polished, honed. Maybe it's her smooth, glossy hair, her pale olive complexion, or the snapping glints in her eyes, but she's always on the money. Tough. Incisive.

And I know I will never be this way. Ever. It's not bad. It's just not me.

I know this. I will always give others the benefit of the doubt. Approach with high hopes and expectations. Trust because trust is better than mistrust. And maybe it's naive, but I learned to be open and kind and friendly in my small town in Central California, where the Marshes and the Parkers and the Bothofs treated everyone well. Visalia was where you could buy seventy-five-cent hot dogs and twenty-five-cent strawberry sodas at Taylor's Hot Dog Stand, and your bearded pediatrician, Dr. Castiglione, made you feel as though you were the only patient in the world.

I will always be grateful for the lessons learned in places that are small and friendly, kind and unpretentious. I may have missed out on the glamour lessons, the sophisticated shops, and the distinctions between designer shoes, but I got other things, like how to distinguish orchards, drive in the tule fog, and enjoy the sweetest smell in the world: the scent of orange blossoms on a hot, dry summer night.

No one in a city can know that smell.

No one from a city can know the dust and boots, the jocks and the rebels, and the hundreds of kids with big-city dreams.

"I got fired," I say calmly.

"Are you going to be able to pay your rent?"

"Hopefully." And with a nod, I jog up the stairs to the apartment I never really could afford anyway.

I've been home barely twenty minutes when the phone rings. It's Tessa. "What the hell did you do?" She's swearing, cursing, a gibberish of angry words. "You are such a dumb-ass," she rages. "Jesus, Holly. Jesus, Mary, and Joseph. Why cut your own throat? Why be a freaking martyr?"

"I'm not—"

"You damn well are." She takes a short breath, a swift intake that sounds almost like a sniffle. "Don't be a dumb-ass anymore."

Is Tessa *crying?* "I'm okay, Tessa—"

"The fuck you are." She sniffs, pauses, then clears her throat. "Jesus." She takes another breath. "Didn't your mother teach you anything? When things are hard, you don't quit—"

"Right."

"And when things get bad, you don't lay down and die."

"I know. But, Tessa, I don't have any proof, and I don't even know for sure what happened."

"Bull. You know, I know—everyone knows: Olivia shafted you."

And I do know. But I also know that David needs Olivia in the San Francisco office. She brings in big business, high-profile clients, and represents a significant amount of the company's revenue.

"Tell David the truth." Tessa isn't done, hasn't given up. "Tell him you helped with the ball, got the article

336

written. Tell him how this feud between you and Olivia started—"

"I can't. But I'm not done yet, Tessa. I'm going to fix this Kid Fest thing. I've got to."

She exhales softly. "Let me know how I can help."

. 19

For the next several hours I can't think of anything anyone can do for me, Tessa included. I lie in a semicomatose state on my couch with a stack of magazines I haven't yet read: *Cosmo, Vogue, In Style, Glamour, People, Us, Condé Nast Traveler.*

Surrounded by stacks of magazines, I read and read. I study pictures of pretty party dresses, tips on fresh make-up, how to get that summer glow with the latest in creams and bronzers and spray-on tans, the new cocktails, the cool "in" places to go.

I look at fashion.

I read bios and profiles.

I compare each of the different magazines' horoscopes, reading mine and glancing briefly at Jean-Marc's in *Cosmo,* hoping he'll have a bad month, which is petty, but I'll stoop to pettiness if it keeps me from thinking about me.

About my day, my career.

My abruptly terminated career.

And there the pain, the shock, the rage sneaks in, crawling between my ribs to sink deeply within. My chest hurts. Every breath aches.

Fired.

Fired.

I close my eyes to keep the tears from forming, but they do anyway.

And because it hurts, and because even if I'm a tough strong girl, I still need a friend right now, not one connected to City Events or my disastrous Kid Fest, I call Katie. Unfortunately her cell phone is off, which means she must be in a meeting or on an airplane and I hang up without leaving a message, not trusting myself to leave a coherent one anyway.

I'm embarrassed.

And angry.

If I were someone else, someone lighter, funnier, more clever, I'd laugh this off, say fate or karma will take care of Olivia—but I'm not particularly light or clever. I want fairness. Justice.

Footsteps sound on the stairs overhead. Cindy. I wait for her to pass by my apartment, on her way to her car or the garage, where her bike is, but her footsteps stop outside my door instead.

Tensing, I wait for the doorbell to ring. It does.

But I don't move. I can't. I'm in no condition to talk

to Cindy now. She rings the doorbell again, harder, longer this time.

The fact that she can't—won't—take a hint, the fact that she's such a hard-ass and unrelentingly cold and formal with me, the fact that today, when I need peace, she won't give me any, makes me grab a pillow from the couch and squish it against me, mashing it into a little ball of down and cotton.

Finally the footsteps go away, echoing back up the stairs, and I exhale slowly, but there's no sense of reprieve. She'll be back.

Wearily I climb off the couch and go to the door. I open it, take a step out, and nearly step on the bouquet of flowers lying on my doorstep.

It's a large bouquet, filled with expensive flowers wrapped in pretty pink and green paisley paper, tied with raffia, bought from my favorite florist down the street.

I pick up the flowers, see the card tucked inside the paper between the fragrant pink lilies. Glancing upstairs, I pull the envelope out of the lilies and open it. The card reads simply, "I'm sorry. C."

I'm sorry.

Two little words, and those two little words undo me. The tears I fought earlier fall, and I scrub them away without much success, because new tears keep falling.

I'm sorry. C.

I glance up the stairs once more, uncertain if I should go up there and thank her or if anything needs to be said right now. I actually don't think she needs my thanks right now.

Suddenly I want to go home. I don't know why; I don't know what I think home will accomplish, but it's the one place I most want to be.

I throw clothes into my bag, pen a quick note of thanks for Cindy, and slide the note beneath her door before I head to my car.

Home. Visalia. Mom.

It's not a short drive home; the trip takes a good four and a half hours without traffic if I'm lucky, and today I'm lucky. I leave my apartment around noon and reach Visalia around four thirty.

I pull in front of the house. It's a small house, not architecturally interesting, but there are flowers everywhere—Mom's famous late spring tulips (pinks and purples of course), along with pansies in the front and irises in the back.

Mom's car is gone, but the front door's open, and I enter the house.

I'm home. Home. There's the chintz sofa in the living room, and the acorn-colored framed school photos on the hallway wall. I can see the edge of the kitchen counter as I look down the hall toward the back of the house, the part of the house where we always lived.

Picking up my suitcase, I take it to my former bedroom, the one I shared with Ashlee growing up. Her cheerleader stuff is still up all over her half of the room, along with her homecoming tiara and the Miss Congeniality sash she won in the Miss Tulare County Pageant.

My side is sparser. There are books and a silk creeping Charley plant. One old doll still perches next to the table lamp. Photos of high school friends and some of the girls I roomed with at UC Irvine jostle for prominence while dusty *Seventeen* magazines fight for space with rows of Kathleen Woodiwiss and Danielle Steel paperbacks.

I sit on my twin bed with the white chenille bedspread and see the little girl who grew up here and lay on this bed for hours reading, and who sat for even more hours on the phone in high school, talking to girlfriends. Then there was her diary, the one where she recorded every detail about every teenage crush she ever had.

I wonder if the red diary is still squished between the mattresses of my bed, and I get up, reach between the top mattress and the box springs, and slide my arm around. My fingers bump something rigid and close around a corner.

It's there.

I pull it out but don't flip it open. I don't need to read the entries to remember how I used to pour my heart into it. All those teenage loves and problems, the worries, the hopes, the wishes, the hurts.

I put the diary back. It's hard being home. It makes no sense; I shouldn't feel this way all these years later, but Ted should still live here. Bastard Ted should still be our father.

In the bathroom I wash my face, put on some fresh makeup, before leaving a note for Mom in the kitchen. I ask her to call me as soon as she gets home.

It's after six, and I'm at the Sequoia Mall, getting ready to head to Borders, when Mom calls.

"You're in town?" she says first thing. "When did you get here? Why didn't you let me know?"

"It was spur-of-the-moment," I say, not about to tell her I'm newly unemployed over the phone. "Have you had dinner?"

"I was just going to open a can of soup."

I shudder. "Meet me for dinner."

"I can heat some soup for you, too. It's really good. Progresso split pea—"

"Mom." I have to stop this, get control of the conversation now. "I'll take you to dinner. My treat."

"Oh."

"Come on, Mom. You love eating out. We'll go to Estrada's—"

"They closed, Holly. Years ago."

That's right. Why can't I ever remember that? Estrada's made the best hot tostada *compuestas* in the world. It wasn't a fancy restaurant; in fact, it was rather dark and plain inside, but the waitresses were so friendly, and they knew Mom, and they knew us kids, and they welcomed us every time with open arms.

Isn't that just like a small town?

"How about the VP, then?" I suggest, knowing it's Mom's favorite restaurant and usually out of her price range.

"Oh, Holly—"

"Just say yes, Mom." My voice cracks, nearly breaks. "All you have to do is say yes."

"Okay. Yes."

"I'll meet you there."

"I'm on my way."

I'm standing on the curb in front of the Vintage Press when I spot a familiar face, a face so known to me, I feel a pang.

It's like seeing me approach, but it's not me. It's Mom. Which in some ways is the same thing, because isn't she the first person I knew? The one I identified with before I knew myself?

No wonder mother-daughter relationships are so impossible. We're two women forever tied to each other. I am indebted to her for life, for *my* life, and I wouldn't be here, foolish, foolhardy, sentimental, and foolishly brave, if it weren't for her. I wouldn't know how to dream or feel or be . . .

She sees me. "Holly!" She hugs me, then steps back to look at me and push my hair around, rearranging my bangs on my face. "What are you doing home?"

I take a step back now, away from her interfering fingers. "I needed to come home."

Mom is still looking at me, and there's that now familiar bewilderment in her eyes, as if she doesn't quite know what to do with me, and I suddenly have to know what she's thinking. What she sees when she looks at me.

"Why do you always look at me like that?" I ask her.

"Like what?" She sounds immediately defensive.

"Like that," I say, nodding at her. "You get that expression on your face—"

"What expression?"

"That one." And I'm frustrated. I'm frustrated with all the secrets and silence in my life, the things that have gone wrong, the things that I believed that weren't true. "When you look at me, Mom, what do you see?"

Mom, poor Mom, gets quiet, and her smile quivers. "Love," she whispers. "I look at you and think, 'Wow, look at her. There's my baby.'"

Christ. Can it get worse? Can I feel any worse? "Mom—" I break off as my voice fails me.

How can people love each other but still not feel loved?

How can we say the right words and still feel wrong?

Because Mom is saying all the things I want to hear, Mom is saying everything I've needed to hear, but somehow it doesn't ease the last twenty-something years, when I needed more . . .

She must feel my tension, must see the struggle in my

face, but she can't cope with it. "Shall we go inside?" she suggests briskly. "Get a table?"

We enter the restaurant beneath the pretty arched awning, through the mahogany-and-glass doors, and we're seated immediately.

"You don't come home very often," Mom says as the busboy fills our glasses with ice water.

"It feels funny coming home." I wait for the busboy to leave. "None of my high school friends have been married. Not even engaged. While I've been married and divorced and—" I exhale. "It feels strange. They're all Catholic, too, and you know it doesn't help. Catholics can't divorce—"

"They do it all the time."

"But it's frowned upon."

My mom laughs. Bless her heart. She does have a sense of humor after all. "It's *always* frowned upon. You don't know how many times I've felt frowned upon for losing your dad—"

"You didn't lose him, Mom. He walked out."

She looks tortured as she shifts her purse from one arm to the other. "Doesn't matter how or why he left. A good woman is supposed to be able to keep her man."

And I understand her perfectly, perhaps for the first time ever. We have both spent our entire lives trying hard, so very hard, and it's still not enough. And despite wanting to be good, we have been found wanting.

If we were different people, or this were a Hallmark after-school special, this is where I'd hug her. There'd be a swell of music—lots of strings—but this isn't a movie. This is my mom and me.

So we sit there at our corner table in the Vintage Press and smile awkwardly with that intense history of love and loss between us. Probably no one but us will ever understand how brutal it was for Dad to leave and for us to be left behind. No one else will understand in quite the same way, not even my brother and sister, because they're not emotionally built the same.

My mom . . .

My mom . . .

. . . is so much like me.

Maybe that's why I've pushed her away all these years. It's hard enough living all your own struggles, hard enough to try and fail, without seeing your pain mirrored in someone else.

"Did something happen at work, Holly?" my mom asks hesitantly, and yet with a measure of parental possession.

My eyes burn, a gritty, hot sting, and I swallow hard. "Yes." And I'm just about to tell her when the waitress approaches. Mom knows the waitress, and they chat, and then Mom introduces me proudly as her daughter, the one who lives in San Francisco, the PR daughter, the one who does event planning.

Mom is proud of me, I think. She loved visiting me in San Francisco, going to my office and seeing where I worked. And now I've got to tell her I don't work there anymore. That I've been fired.

By the time the waitress leaves, I know I can't tell Mom now, at least not here, not before dinner. She's so happy at the moment, so excited to be out having dinner with me.

"Don't you ever get lonely, Mom?" I ask an hour later, as our dessert dishes are cleared. I had crème brûlée and she had cheesecake, and we're both stuffed, but it was so worth it.

"No. I've learned to stay busy."

"Doing what?"

"Puttering in the garden. Scrapbooking. Volunteer work."

"That's good." But is it? Because, God help me, I don't want to end up like this. I don't. I want so much more out of life. And I don't want to be her age, living alone, trying to find ways to fill my time so I don't know that everybody has up and gone and left me behind.

That *life* has left me behind.

I don't want to miss out on anything. I'm struggling with the dreams, all those dreams I still have and can't let go of, when Mom and I gather our purses and head out.

It's nearly the first of May, and it's a beautiful night. It's warm outside, and the sky is clear, and the stars spread out above my head everywhere.

As we walk toward our cars, I take a deep breath, thinking that coming home always undoes me. Here in Visalia I remember everything. I remember Bastard Ted leaving, and I remember my mother valiantly coping, and

I remember how Christmas was never the same. I remember the ugly clothes I used to wear when we couldn't afford better, and that big purchase, the first pair of high heels. I remember falling in them, and I remember people laughing, and I remember always wanting more.

Next to Mom's car, I suddenly blurt out, "I lost my job."

Mom's just starting to sit in the driver's seat, and she grabs the steering wheel. "You were laid off?"

"Fired."

"Fired," she echoes. "Why? What did you do?"

"Nothing."

"But you had to do something if you were fired."

I love how she always takes my side. I shake my head, angry. "I'll see you at home," I say, and I walk quickly to my car.

I don't mean to cry, don't want to cry, but the tears fall as I enter the house. I shouldn't have come home. This was the wrong place to go.

Mom's hovering in the kitchen anxiously. "Holly?"

"I'm tired, Mom. I'm going to bed."

"You don't want any tea?"

I stand in the shadows near my room, dashing away tears. "No. I just need sleep. I'm tired. It's been a long weekend."

"But tea will help you relax better."

I want her to stop talking. I can't bear it right now. I can't think, can't feel, can't. Can't.

Can't.

But she won't leave me alone. She turns on the hall light, comes toward me. "You're crying."

"I'm not." And I step back, and I dash away more tears because I am crying. I can't stop.

She reaches for me, and I snap, *"Don't."*

Mom freezes, and I shake my head, angry, so angry, and I don't want to be angry with her, God knows I don't, but when she starts talking, when she has that expression on her face, the one that says she's trying so hard to please me, I just want to get away.

I want her to go away.

I want to run away.

I've needed her my whole life, and I still don't know how to have her, the mother I want. I don't know how to let her comfort me or talk to me. I don't know anything anymore.

"Holly, I hate seeing you so sad."

I look up, fiercely wiping away tears. "Well, Mom, I hate seeing you so sad, too."

"I'm not sad."

"You are. You live in this horrible little house all alone. You don't travel or do things. You just wait for us to come home."

"Because I love it when you come home."

"I know, but we're adults. We've got lives of our own, and I know you want me here, and I know you need me here, and I can't be here—" I break off, cover my mouth, and I don't know if other people feel this way about their moms. Does anyone else worry and struggle and feel guilty for growing up and going away? "*Mom.*"

"What, Holly?"

I shake my head. I don't know. I don't know how to explain anything, and I don't understand what I'm feeling or what I want from her. I go sit down at the round oak table in the kitchen, and Mom sits down, too.

"You'll get another job," Mom says.

I know she's trying, and I give her credit for that, but she's not saying what I need to hear.

What I need to hear is that she knows she's hurt me, and that she's sorry.

That she's sorry she didn't see me as I wanted to be seen instead of as the daughter she was so sure she knew. Yes, she knew me as one thing. But I wanted to be the other thing.

I wanted to be magical and special, strong, tender, invincible. I wanted to be like all the daring heroines in fairy tales. Not the ones who were waiting to be rescued, but the ones rescuing, the ones saving. Not the sleeping princess needing to be awakened, but the warrior woman like Belle, who'd rescue her father from the monster's dungeon, a brave woman who'd fight a powerful curse.

That's the me who has always been here, but maybe she was buried so deep inside that no one—not even me—knew how real she was.

She is real. And she wants more.

So much more. She wants the big adventure she's never had; she wants the victories; she wants to be the confident, daring hero, not the damsel in distress.

No more waiting like Rapunzel locked up in the ivory tower. No more Sleeping Beauty dozing in a high palace chamber. No more Snow White laid out on ice beneath glass.

"Mom, I'm different from you," I say, "and you should be glad I'm different. You should be glad I want to be me."

My mother looks at me, and she isn't crying, but her eyes aren't completely dry. "Of course I am."

There's the "of course" again.

"All I ever wanted was for you to be happy," she adds, and I think for a minute, think about what's happened and what will happen, about the things I know and the things I don't, and I'm not afraid of the future anymore, or the things that could go wrong . . . because things will also go right.

I can get things right.

I *do* get things right. And slowly I'm figuring out life. Figuring out me.

Mom's still sitting here, looking confused and a little lonely. I know that face because that's how I've felt most of my life. That's the way I thought I was supposed to feel: not knowing we can choose other paths, other thoughts, other directions, other selves, and not looking back but going forward.

And going forward means doing something for Mom,

who has tried so hard all these years to do for me, and because I love her (and fear her), because I need her (and fear that), I've made it difficult.

I've pushed her away, worried she'd cut my wings and trap me, worried that in this fight called life she'd always be higher than me on the hierarchy totem pole. But it shouldn't be a fight anymore, at least not a fight between us. We really should be on the same team.

If I can't protect her back, then who will?

If I can't defend her against the world, then what good is it being strong and the hero in the fairy tale? If I can't let my mother know she has succeeded and done well, then how will I ever encourage my own daughter?

But, God, the words are hard. I still don't have the words. I've never known quite what to say.

Awkwardly I reach toward her and take her hand on the table and hold it in mine. Mom looks at me, and the tears are there again, the tears that let me know she hurts far more than she should ever have been hurt, that life hasn't been easy and maybe all she ever wanted was what she said—for me to have an easier path than hers. For me to be . . . happy.

"I love you," I tell her. I don't know what else to say, don't know how to make up for all the lost years when we were two strangers trying to find their way home again.

Mom reaches up to wipe away a tear. I must have been one hell of a tyrant daughter if I can make my own mother— a nonweepy woman—cry. "I know you do, Holly."

"If . . ." I pause, knowing I can't say, "If we could do

things over," "If we had another chance," because life isn't about going back. It's not a series of reruns and instant replays. There are no second chances, not the way we'd like. Sometimes we biff it and have to suck it up, living with the consequences. And even if I didn't always get what I needed from Mom, I realize she didn't get what she needed from me, and that maybe we'll never be that close, maybe we'll never be best friends or bosom buddies—but I am what I am because of her.

I am a hero.

A fighter.

A warrior woman.

I wouldn't have known how to face challenges and my own fear if I hadn't been raised by her. And really, does it matter that I learned by distancing myself from her?

Does it matter that I've taken the hard-knocks approach to life?

I don't think so. Not if the outcome is good, and the outcome is good because I'm determined to learn this time, determined to keep putting one foot in front of the other, making corrections where I have to, apologizing when I can. And you know, I won't change the world, but I'm taking it a step at a time by changing the things that don't work in—and for—me.

I'm still holding her hand, which is not entirely natural or comfortable for me, the girl with intimacy issues, so I squeeze her hand and let it go. But there is something else I can say. Something else I should say. "Thanks."

My face feels funny, tight, crooked. I don't know if it's embarrassment or a sense of helplessness, but there are so many chaotic emotions inside me, so much that doesn't feel smart or strong or rock solid. Just mushy, chaotic emotions and the sense that time passes fast. Too fast. No one should have to go through life wondering if they've done a good job or if they're adequate.

I certainly don't want to go through life feeling like a half-baked citizen of planet Earth.

"You know, Mom, you should come up to the city again. We'll go see some shows, have dinner, maybe do Fisherman's Wharf."

"That would be nice."

And I know this now: every princess needs goals. A plan, a map, a compass. She has to know where she wants to go or she'll never get there, spending too long in dungeons, stone towers, and dangerous woods.

I also know this: I'm not the kind of princess who's going to wait around. I never was.

"It would be nice," I say, and I mean it.

*D*riving back to San Francisco Wednesday morning, I know I can't—won't—let my year at City Events end so ingloriously.

I refuse to let Kid Fest be the conclusion, because there's no resolution. Only failure. And shame. But I'm not ashamed of me, or my efforts, and this isn't even about me anymore. It's about the kids. The kids who got caught in the middle of something they shouldn't have been involved in.

The kids deserved better. And I like to think that good conquers evil and that in the end the just are rewarded, but I'm not so sure that's true.

But even if the just *aren't* rewarded, I know that until the kids from the Boys and Girls Club get their event, I'm not through.

Kid Fest may be over, and I may not be able to salvage the carnival at the museum, but I can give them something else. A different reward.

Back in my apartment, I spend the night brainstorming a new Kid Fest. I curl up on my bed, thinking back to when I was a kid: the things I loved and the things that were pleasurable, exciting, an escape.

I think about the things kids want to do, need to do, and the things kids are curious about, and I make lists, and in each of these lists a word appears again and again: *movies*.

What if I give the kids a day at the movies? But not just as a passive audience, but as budding filmmakers, too?

What if they get to learn how movies are made, and have the chance to write stories of their own and maybe even get some hands-on experience shooting film?

Find a cool theater . . . order tons of pizzas . . . serve popcorn . . . give the kids not just fun but information that might actually inspire? Encourage their own dreams? No passive princes and princesses here, please. Everybody's got to be a warrior, little boy and girl alike. Kids need to be taught to go after life, seize opportunity, not wait for something good to fall into their laps.

I scribble more ideas down, take tons of notes. There have got to be local filmmakers I can contact, people who'd be willing to donate their time, help me put together something creative and meaningful for the kids in San Francisco.

Thursday morning I get on my computer, shoot out e-mails to Josh and Tessa, telling them what I plan to do.

They're both enthusiastic and offer to help, and that night they come over after work, bringing me files from the office with all the Kid Fest contacts.

Josh knows someone who owns an old art deco movie theater in the Mission district, and offers to contact the owner, see if he'd loan out the theater to us for a Sunday afternoon. Tessa said the guy at Pop's Pizza, just south of Market, owes her a favor big-time and can probably come through with food and drink.

I go to the kitchen and pull out a bottle of champagne that Ed Hill brought me once back in late February when we were dating. Sitting on the floor of the living room, I open the bottle and fill three Waterford flutes, make a toast: "To good times and good friends."

Josh and Tessa clink glasses with me, and we drink our champagne and lounge on pillows on the floor. I realize I've never liked my apartment as much as I do tonight.

This is why people need big apartments with bay windows and glossy white trim—not for cozy couples on the couch, but so you'll have lots of room to sprawl out with your friends.

During the next week I make dozens of calls and talk to more people than I've ever talked to before. I explain what's happened to the kids and what needs to happen, and why putting cameras into children's hands would challenge them and encourage them and validate their experiences.

Josh gets the theater for me on a Sunday two weeks from now.

I get cameras donated, and videotape, and secure a promise from several film students from the local university to come and speak to the kids.

I contact a screenwriter who wants to talk about her work, and then there's the big-name comic actor who's lived in Cow Hollow most of his life and wants to do something good, too.

Tessa gets pizzas and sodas from Pop's, and then Pop from Pop's takes it a step further, promising sheet cakes for dessert.

I go with Josh to check out the old movie theater built during the art deco period, and it's beautiful. The owner has refurbished the place, the gold stars on the blue ceiling are freshly stenciled, and the columns lining the auditorium are in gorgeous, vivid color.

The theater's big, too, and the owner has some old sci-fi films he'll show in the morning before the kids start work on their own films, if I'm interested. And I'm interested.

Back home I send e-mails to the student filmmakers and the screenwriter and give them the place, date, and time we're meeting, as well as mention the classic sci-fi films the theater owner has offered to show.

I pore over my to-do list.

Location, firm. Time and date, set. Entertainment and speakers, secured. Food, covered. Drinks, covered.

Now it's time to invite the guests, and this is the hard part.

No one at South San Francisco Boys and Girls Club wants to talk to me. No one from the city organizations cares to take my call, either, so I show up in person, hand-deliver big invites in even bigger gold envelopes with purple, gold, and black balloons attached.

"I know it's short notice," I tell staff members, receptionists, directors, "but it's going to be a wonderful day, and the kids are going to learn something, too."

It's a hard, hard sale. The only thing that seems to spark any real interest is when I mention the famous comedian who has agreed to come and perform some funny stand-up routines appropriate for kids during their pizza lunch.

I call Barb from Balloon Wizardry and ask if she could send a crew the morning of the event and do something special to the art deco movie theater. "I want glamour," I say, "and fun. Something almost Oscar night–like."

"What's this for?" she asks.

"Kid Fest Two."

"So I bill the company?"

"No." I hesitate, suddenly nervous. "I don't work for City Events anymore."

"You don't?"

"No, but I do need your help, and you'll just bill me."

"You're not paying for this, are you?"

"Yes. I can give you my credit card number now."

She sighs, a worried sigh. "I don't understand any of this. What happened?"

I wish I could say I don't know, but I do know. It was Olivia, getting even. Olivia, sticking a big, fat butcher knife in me. But maybe I did have it coming. I certainly pulled rank in my own little-minion way. "I made someone mad," I say at last.

"Troublemaker." And then Barb laughs. Real laughter that makes some of the horrible sick feeling that's been in my stomach the past two weeks go away. "Shoot, girl, who did you take on? Olivia Dempsey?"

I nearly choke on my own tongue. "How'd you guess?"

"Long story. But I'll tell you someday." Barb makes a clucking sound. "Well, well, well. Let's see what we can do to help you out, and no, I'm not going to take your money. This is my gift—"

"No—"

"For the kids," and she rides right over my protest as if it had never been said. "I'll make a few phone calls, too— see if we can't put together something fun for the kids to take home. You know, a goodie bag, something like that. What do you think?"

A lump fills my throat. "I think that's very generous."

"And I think you're going to end up on top, girl. You just stay strong."

I am.

May 16, the morning of Kid Fest 2, arrives, and I'm up early, practically at the crack of dawn. I'm nervous.

What if no one comes and it's just a huge waste of time?

What if all the kids show up and they hate what I've planned?

Or what if Olivia has found out about Kid Fest 2 and she's already sabotaged the day?

I'm chomping on Rolaids as I arrive at the theater two hours before the event is scheduled to start, panicked we're going to have another lockout, but as I approach, the marquee out front reads, "Welcome Kid Fest!"

That's a good start.

Inside the lobby, Barb's balloon crew has just about finished transforming the old art deco theater into a kiddie paradise.

But Barb hasn't just sent her crew; she's there, too, and she spots me by the concession stand and comes over and gives me a huge hug. "How are you doing?"

I pull the package of Rolaids out of my pocket and show her. "Good."

She chuckles. "It's going to be fine. The kids will have a ball. I love *The Blob*—"

"That's what we're seeing?" I interrupt, vaguely remembering the black-and-white horror film from the '50s, a story about a flesh-eating blob from outer space that gets bigger with each kill, and nothing about it strikes me as appropriate for children.

"It's a classic."

"The blob kills people."

"No kid today will be frightened by it. Even in the sixties people thought it was corny."

I'm not so sure, and I reach for another Rolaids.

"What are you eating?" a male voice asks, and I know that voice. I turn around to find Brian Fadden standing in the theater lobby.

He's still tall and rather rumpled, but he's got the makings of a tan, and he looks so at ease in his jeans and denim shirt. "Rolaids. Want one?"

He lifts a hand. "I'll pass."

I pop another one into my mouth. "I don't remember sending you an invite to Kid Fest."

"Tessa did. She thought you could use the moral support."

"I thought she was coming."

"She was. But at the last minute Josh invited her on a weekend getaway. So they got away."

"And here you are."

"You're disappointed."

"I'm not." Barb moves away, and I walk toward Brian, and it's like walking toward a great friend. It's really wonderful to see him. He's disgustingly tall and very smart, as well as funny and creative and kind to me. "I'm glad to see you. It's been a long time."

"Six months."

"Wow."

"So do you have a new boyfriend?"

"No." I grimace. "I think I scare most guys away."

He laughs, and the sound is deep and husky and makes me smile. "Let me take you to dinner after Kid Fest ends."

I hesitate.

"Come on," he says, his smile slipping a little.

"Okay. But on one condition."

"What's that?"

"I get to pay."

His wry grin is back. "Deal."

Kid Fest 2 is a success. The event, "A Day at the Movies," works. It's not what it was before, but in some ways it's better.

I wasn't sure the kids would get *The Blob,* and even less sure the chaperones would approve of the film, but there were no complaints as the kids and adults settled into their seats with drinks and tubs of buttered popcorn.

After the film, Chaz, one of the graduate film students, a tough-looking twenty-something-year-old who dresses like a gangster rapper, got up in the front of the theater with the microphone and began to speak.

Chaz told the kids he grew up on Potrero Hill, spent most of his life in and out of bad situations and foster care, but was now a graduate student on a full film scholarship at University of California in San Francisco. He made movies because he had something to say. The kids all leaned forward, listening hard. Movies give you a voice, Chaz said. It's about being heard, making your thoughts known, standing up and being counted in life.

The next filmmaker, a slim, pretty, and very intense Latina, talked to the kids about how many independent films were made today, demonstrating how she and Chaz used nothing fancier than a video camera to shoot their films, and then explained how they edited and did special effects on a computer at the campus, though lots of filmmakers edited at home. Today's technology and software, she told them, allows everyone to be filmmakers.

Then Chaz asked the kids how many of them would like to make movies, and nearly every kid in the audience raised his or her hand. When Chaz suggested the kids break up into groups and brainstorm story ideas for their movies, the kids were wildly, hugely enthusiastic. They broke into groups, sitting on stairs and the carpet in the balcony, and began to chatter, outlining their ideas and dreaming big.

I stand at the side near one of the velvet curtains, and I can see Brian. He's crouching next to one of the small groups, listening to the kids talk.

This is good, I think, crossing my arms, holding the happiness in. This is good, what we did today. All we have to do is open the door to possibility, and incredible, hopeful things can take place.

Kid Fest 2 ends, and the kids leave, filling their buses and vans, and I've shaken hands and hugged little people, and even hugged some of the big people who were so angry with me three weeks ago.

I've drained my savings to make today happen, but it's okay. I'm glad. I needed to do this, needed to try to put things right.

Brian's still waiting for me as the theater goes dark and the last of the kids have gone.

"What now?" he asks as we head outside into the late afternoon sunshine. We both have cars, and we stand on the pavement facing each other.

"Meet me for dinner later," I suggest.

His brow furrows. "Tonight?"

"Tonight."

"Where?"

I think of special places, places with good menus, great cocktails, cool ambience. "Balboa Café."

"That's pretty spendy."

I feel as if I'd swallowed a big soap bubble. I feel intensely happy. "Yeah. I know." I pull my car keys from my purse. "But maybe you're worth it."

The corner of his mouth slowly tilts, a crooked smile, very dry, very cute. His eyes are a pale blue, like the color of faded denim. "Maybe?"

"Maybe." I turn, head for my car, but glance back at him over my shoulder. I'm smiling big. "Seven o'clock?"

"I'll be there," he says.

"I'll be waiting."

On my way home I call Balboa Café, make reservations for two at seven. The hostess tells me I'm extremely lucky, that they've only just had a cancellation for that evening; otherwise she wouldn't have been able to squeeze us in.

I feel lucky, too, and I drive home with my window down, singing far more loudly in my car than I should.

In Cow Hollow I find a parking spot just steps from my doorway—I *am* lucky!—and climbing the stairs to my apartment, I try to figure out what I'll wear to dinner. I wish I had something new to wear, something pretty and fun, but it's been ages since I went shopping, and now that I've wiped out my savings account to put on Kid Fest 2, I won't be doing any shopping anytime soon.

I'm standing in front of my closet when the phone rings. "Hello?" I answer, still staring at my pathetic wardrobe.

"Holly? Alex."

Alex? Alex who? Then it hits me. *Gorgeous Guy!* "Hi."

"I don't know what your schedule's like—"

And somehow, most unluckily, I drop the phone. I'm on the floor, scrambling for the phone when it rings again. "Hello?" I pant.

"Holly Bishop, please." It's not Gorgeous Guy.

I suffer serious disappointment. "This is Holly."

"David Burkheimer."

Not as disappointed. "David!"

"How are you, Holly?"

"Good. Thank you." I sink down on the foot of my bed, wrap my arm around my knees.

"I've had calls about your 'Day at the Movies.'"

My stomach rises up, and I suddenly think I could use another Rolaids. "I had to do something, David. I couldn't let Kid Fest end the way it did—"

"Thank you."

I fall silent.

"I'm sorry how things ended a couple of weeks ago," he adds. "I know now your event was sabotaged. Sara came to me, told me all about it the end of last week."

I don't know what to say.

"Olivia's moved down south to be with her boyfriend," he continues. "And we're looking to fill her job."

"Oh, David—"

"Don't say no yet. Just think about it."

I fall back on my bed, stare at the ceiling dappled with late afternoon sunlight, all shades of dark rose and deep gold. I see the outline of tree limbs and shapely new leaves before closing my eyes.

"You're good, Holly."

I smile despite myself because, bless him, he said "good," not a "good girl," and he's right, I am good. I'm really good, but it has nothing to do with being nice.

I'm smart and fun and clever, and I've great friends and great hope and all kinds of opportunity.

"I'll think about it," I say after a moment, and I'm grinning up at nothing, grinning just because it feels so damn good to be alive.

David's still talking. "How about we meet for lunch on Friday and we can discuss the salary and benefits in person."

"Um . . ."

"It's a significant pay raise."

"I don't know . . ."

"Everybody here likes you."

Yet I still hesitate, and I'm not sure why, because I'd love to be back at City Events with Tessa and Josh, but at the same time, I'm not ready to commit to anything. I kind of think I should check out my options, see what else is out there.

"I'll think about it," I say finally.

"Let's still have lunch on Friday."

"I don't know, David."

"We want you, Holly."

We want you, Holly. Now, there's something every girl wants to hear.

I stretch, cradle the phone against my ear. "I'm not promising you anything, David. It's just lunch."

"Just lunch," he echoes. "At Boulevard."

Boulevard, tucked into the historic Audiffred Building on the waterfront, happens to be the coolest, swankiest, hottest restaurant in the city. I've always wanted to go there. *Always*.

"That's kind of a nice place," I say.

"Well, I intend to make you a nice offer."

I feel my stomach somersault, but it's with happiness this time, not fear. "How nice?"

He pauses. "One you can't refuse."

"Oh. I like the sound of that."

He laughs. "You really are a princess, aren't you?"

"Yep," I agree, feeling that soap bubble of happiness return. It's rising inside me, full and glossy, shimmering with possibility. "I'll see you Friday."

As I hang up, I jump off my bed and do a crazy war dance around my bedroom. I'm meeting Brian for dinner at seven tonight, my former boss on Friday for lunch, and—oh! Gorgeous Guy! I've got to call him. I'll apologize for dropping the phone, smoothly segue into asking him out for a drink. . . .

Things are definitely looking good.

Getting married and divorced in a year was pretty damn awful, but I have to say, kissing that toad two years ago probably saved my life. I wouldn't be where I am today if I hadn't discovered that all the magic I ever wanted is right inside me.

I *am* a princess. I'm the Frog Princess.

For a reading group guide to *The Frog Prince*,

please check out our Web site:

www.twbookmark.com